Clementina

a Leathan Wilkey novel

Simon Cann

Coombe
Hill
Publishing

Published by Coombe Hill Publishing
33 Melrose Gardens
New Malden
Surrey KT3 3HQ
United Kingdom
coombehillpublishing.com

ISBN: 978-1-910398-12-8 (paperback)
ISBN: 978-1-910398-13-5 (ePub)

A big thank you to Cathleen Small for her editorial input.

3 June 2016

one

Clementina was clearly offended.

Offended by my apparently uncouth utterance. Offended that I was not paying due reverence. Offended that I was thinking money, when I should be appreciating the art. Offended in the way that only a seventeen-year-old can be offended.

She was able simultaneously to be both a child and a world-weary adult. Neither of whom was accepting of my situation; both of whom were deeply saddened by my obvious circumstances.

She was saddened that I could live in a world like this.

Some people are saddened about famine in Africa. Some are saddened about wars or religious fundamentalists imposing their unyielding doctrines on populations, killing and mutilating children and innocent adults. Clementina was saddened and offended—on my behalf—that the world of jewelry and the exquisite pleasure of fine gems set in delicate pieces of lovingly shaped precious metal had been withheld from me.

She knew—as only one who had been indoctrinated into the secret society knew—that if I had been exposed to the world of bijouterie, then I would appreciate the treat that was waiting for me.

What she didn't know was that I hated being patronized by seventeen-year-olds. Even if their father was paying me. Not that her father and I had actually done anything as tedious as agreeing a fee.

Or meeting.

Or talking. Even on the phone.

Instead, a few hours earlier—before I had been introduced to Clementina—Reece, our chauffeur, had met me at the designated location at the top corner of Place de la Concorde. During the revolution, it was called Place de la Révolution and was the location where many nobles were guillotined, including Louis XVI and Marie Antoinette. After the revolution, it was renamed as a gesture of reconciliation.

I had arrived on the Eurostar from Brussels an hour before that, having received a call the previous evening. Once I was in Paris, the largest public square in the city seemed like a convenient place to meet. It wasn't as if I had any luggage to lug—I had what I wore and as I waited, I pulled my leather jacket against the biting chill as the weather turned from late autumn into early winter.

As the Maybach—in truth, a Mercedes with a posh frock—pulled in, I hoped my newfound temporary employment with the current aristocracy—that heady mix of money and business—wouldn't see me lose my head.

I approached the driver—the man who I now knew as Reece—and introduced myself. He seemed delighted to meet me. He was like a kid who had been made to play on his own for months but who had now been given a friend. A friend who couldn't run away.

While Reece drove me back to what he called the apartment, but which was more of a mansion set several floors above street level and which just happened to have other people living below, I grew to understand the driver's priorities.

His first priority was food. Apparently, the cook was sick at the moment. This greatly disappointed Reece—although his disappointment was nowhere near the level of disappointment that Clementina encountered when I muttered that if you need to ask the price, you can't afford it. With the cook being sick, food preparation duties had fallen to the housekeeper. The housekeeper, according to Reece, was a good cook, but nowhere near as good as the cook, hence, this morning's breakfast had not been up to Reece's usual expectations.

"But they can make coffee?" I asked.

"The coffee is good," said Reece before telling me about his second priority: his quarters. The apartment where the family lived came with two service apartments—he took one and the housekeeper, and current purveyor of disappointing food, took the other. Cook lived out; she was a local. Reece's apartment was small—which he liked—and comfortable. He declared himself delighted with his accommodations and thrilled that it took less than 90 seconds to reach the family's apartment.

Having two parking spaces under the block was also a boon for Reece, although my guess was that this was a requirement by the family and wasn't a choice to ease the life of their chauffeur. He continued: "Two storerooms." I wasn't sure what the advantage of two storerooms was—wouldn't one big room be better, I wondered silently. Still, Reece thought it was good.

Reaching the apartment, I met Angeline Bautista, a pleasant Filipino woman who was working as the housekeeper for the apartment and currently performing cooking duties, much to Reece's disappointment. She had taken the other service apartment, but unlike Reece, who accompanied the family from the UK, she came with the apartment—or at least had been provided by the agency handling the apartment as part of the deal.

Reece guided me to one of the barstools along the counter demarcating the edge of the kitchen area. From the side, it looked like a small kitchen with a big counter. Viewed from the other angle, it was a huge kitchen with a comparatively small counter that was wide enough for four or five seats.

I sat without viewing the apartment further, without being introduced to anyone apart from Angeline, but was aware that behind me there was an aircraft hangar's worth of space that was sparsely furnished. And somewhere beyond the leather-covered floor that stretched in all directions, I was sure there were other rooms—bedrooms, bathrooms, dressing rooms—hidden from view.

Angeline Bautista's English and French were both labored and heavily accented. My Filipino was limited to three or four words, so we conversed in French. Not that there was much to talk about— she asked me if I wanted a coffee, and after that Reece took the opportunity to talk to me, his new best friend forever. And it felt like forever—I had no escape.

"Is the boss around?" I asked. Angeline and Reece looked at me blankly, as if I was describing an incomprehensible new idea.

Reece looked as if to ask: "Why?"

"I thought I was going to chat with him," I said weakly.

The driver frowned. "Is something unclear?"

"I thought he was going to explain what I'm meant to be doing." My tone was apologetic.

"Keep the paparazzi away from Clementina," said Reece. Angeline nodded her affirmation. "They'll explain later."

"Later?"

"The lawyer and the media relations guy," said Reece. "I guess they'll explain."

"So we wait for them?" I asked.

Reece shook his head, the disenchantment evident. "If only."

Somewhere in a passageway leading to an area I couldn't see, there was the sound of movement. Footsteps. Lazy footsteps. Soft shoes being dragged over the leather floor covering. To the right, a figure appeared.

Female. Slim. Five eight. Long blond hair, styled with a just-got-out-of-bed look, which may have been due to her just getting out of bed. Her age could be anything between early teens and late twenties. She was wearing fluffy white slippers, which she was dragging across the floor without picking up her feet; light, but slightly elasticated cotton pants, cream with brown patterns; and a sweatshirt emblazoned with intricate embroidery and diamanté swirls. Her clothes were not so much as clean, but rather they looked brand new.

Reece placed a hand on my arm and gently shook his head. He released my arm and lifted a finger to his lips.

The female continued into the kitchen and opened the fridge, which was taller than her. She stepped toward the appliance and was hidden behind the door, apart from her fluffy feet, which remained visible below the stainless steel door. After a few moments she appeared again with a one-liter smoothie bottle from which she poured herself a glass before returning the bottle.

She picked up the glass, then shuffled in the direction she had come before stopping. She turned to Angeline. "Have you seen my... with the...?" She pointed absentmindedly to her chest as if outlining a pattern. The housekeeper nodded and half walked, half ran out of the kitchen.

"I'll just..." she said to Reece. "Five minutes."

"I'll be ready," said the driver. "This is Leathan, by the way."

"Hi." She turned to face me and confidently made eye contact, a broad smile spreading across her face, which had the makeup-free perfection that is granted only to teenagers, and then only the lucky few teenagers.

"Hi," I said. She broke the gaze and shuffled off.

As she left the room, Reece said: "And now you've met Clementina. She's in quite a chatty mood this morning." He paused, then continued. "Do you want another coffee?"

"I thought she said five minutes."

"She did," said Reece. "But you don't start counting those five minutes until she's actually in the car and ready to go. It usually takes less than five minutes for whatever she's forgotten to be retrieved. It'll be another forty-five minutes before she's ready."

Fifty minutes later she was back with us. The hair no longer had that just-got-out-of-bed look, mutating to some sort of perfect straightness, and her face was now hidden behind a mask of makeup. It took another fifteen minutes until she was ready and then gave her instruction: "Rue de la Paix."

I knew Rue de la Paix. Or rather, I knew of the street and had been there many years ago. But it's not what you would call my thing. The guidebooks will tell you why. Two words are prevalent in any description: fashionable and jewelry.

And as we sat in the car—Reece driving, Clementina and me in the back; she had pulled me in with her before realizing that I was staff—I made my comment. I said the only thing I knew about jewelry in Rue de la Paix: There are no price tags. European legislation mandates that every item for sale has a visible price tag showing the full price, including any sales tax, but jewelry in Rue de la Paix has a special dispensation.

"Of course!" said Clementina, "It's art! You can't put a price on such beauty."

"And yet somehow the stores manage to find a price to charge you," I muttered, sparking Clementina's offense. She was offended by my comment and by my obvious ignorance. She then decided she was offended that she was sitting with staff. Then she was offended that they—whoever they were—had deemed that she needed a babysitter.

The offense lasted until we drew near, when the childlike excitement about sparkly things took over. As the Maybach slipped into Place Vendôme, the square that meets Rue de la Paix, she was barely able to contain her excitement and was happy to forget her offense if I could somehow be persuaded to acknowledge the beauty of what we were about to see.

As we walked into the store, superficially she and I were dressed the same: We were both wearing jeans and a leather jacket.

But there was no way you would say we were dressed the same. My jeans had an American brand. Hers were a high-fashion label—at least, I assumed that was high fashion. My definition of high fashion was anything I hadn't heard of and looked expensive. When compared to mine, the leather of her jacket was a different grade—it had a fine grain and looked to be softer than a baby's skin.

Under her jacket she seemed to be wearing a white T-shirt where I was wearing a light blue Oxford shirt. I was sure her T-shirt cost more than my jeans, jacket, and shirt together.

And whatever that unspoken difference between us was, the shop assistants could smell the difference. As far as they were concerned, I was a piece of glass to be looked through. Clementina was their target, and they all cooed around her like pigeons fighting over a lump of bread.

The trays were out. Necklaces were draped around her. Bangles and bracelets laid over her arms. Earrings—some small, some with gems, and some dangling monstrosities—were all held up to her earlobes. And any number of brooches and other attachable sparkly adornments were laid out in front of Clementina.

There was silver, gold, platinum, and metal of different shades that I would have thought was cheap rubbish, except the lack of price tags told me otherwise. The stones were all colors of the spectrum and more. Greens, reds, blues, in various hues, shades, and darknesses—set on their own and in clusters with other gems, their colors setting off one another.

Politely, and in rudimentary but passable French, Clementina had cleared away all of the staff with the exception of one fastidious and highly attentive man, and had sent away most of the jewels. She was now busy painstakingly assessing each piece, checking her look in the mirror as she held up an earring or laid a necklace. She slipped off her baby-soft jacket, placed it on the carpet next to her bag, and continued trying the jewels. When she saw something she thought she liked, her phone would appear and she would snap a selfie.

Within five minutes, her phone was pinging with alerts. She tapped out a few swift messages, took more selfies, and sent the attentive little man to find more for her to try and to photograph. There was another peal of pings, and she returned her attention to her phone, checking for the responses.

"What do you think of this?" she asked, holding up a very delicate necklace. To me it looked silver, but I guessed it was platinum.

"Looks good," I said, not knowing what to say. As I've said, jewelry isn't my thing.

"Say more than that," said Clementina, clearly disappointed in my response.

I shrugged.

She exaggerated a shrug back.

I held out my hands, letting her see both sides. Then I pushed back my sleeves to show there was nothing around my wrists before I indicated my earlobes, each lacking any adornment. Finally, I tugged down my collar to show I wasn't wearing a necklace. "Do you see something missing? Something I don't display?"

She paused, letting the expression on her face fall before talking. "Oh God, I'm sorry!" she said, throwing her hands over her mouth. "Leathan, I am so, so, *sooo* sorry. Now you mention it, it's obvious: You're missing any sense of style. Oh, you poor thing. I am so, so sorry."

I should have been upset, but she managed to carry off the put-down with a certain aplomb.

I was about to say something when a camera flash lit the window, then another, and a third. The staff moved quickly and adjusted something in the windows. The room became fractionally darker, and the flashes diminished.

My phone rang. "It's Reece. This is only the first course; the second wave is just pulling up on their bikes now. They know you're in there, and they seem ready to sit it out."

I cursed under my breath. "Have they twigged you're with us?"

"Nah," said the chauffeur.

"Good," I said. "Then drive around the corner before they do. I'll figure a way out and give you a call."

"Right," he said, and hung up.

"Is there a back exit?" I asked the woman behind the counter.

"No," said the assistant, barely able to force herself to acknowledge that I—an obvious nothing—had fallen through the door to her exalted store.

"What do you do if there's a fire?" I asked.

She shrugged and looked behind her.

two

"What's the hurry?" asked Clementina, trying some dangling platinum earrings, which she had paired with the platinum necklace she was considering. "The blinds are closed—they're not getting any more pictures."

"There are more coming," I said. "More people, more risk, more trouble."

She ignored my concern and snapped another selfie with her phone. "I need to know what Piedad thinks about these before we go anywhere."

"Piedad?" I knew it was the wrong response as the name fell out of my mouth. Clementina ignored me, turning her gaze to seek out the fastidious and highly attentive man who had been fluttering around her. She found him and sent him scurrying on another errand, shortly to return.

She looked at his offering and firmly shook her head. He disappeared again, forcing a smile before he left.

There was an electronic trill, and Clementina reached for her phone while keeping another dangly piece of metal held to hear earlobe. "Has Piedad given her approval?" I asked.

Clementina seemed to ignore me, but then lowered the jewelry and looked to her phone. "She has."

"Good," I said. "Can we go? We'll come back at some other time when there are no paparazzi around."

"Paparazzi?" she asked. I had her attention—apparently there was a life lesson I needed to learn. "Paps, Leathan. We call them paps."

I tried not to sigh as she turned away. "We'll come back at some other time when there are no paps around. Can we go now?"

"I'm getting this." She waved something—it might have been the necklace—and then proceeded to dive into the large bag she had dragged with her. When she didn't find what she was searching for, she started emptying the bag on the counter—makeup; purses and pouches; tissues, both fresh and crumpled; receipts and other pieces of paper; three handkerchiefs, one white, one cream, and one black with a lace border, all scattered across the glass surface.

The attentive little man returned with another tray. She ignored his offering and passed him the necklace. "I'll take this." He took the necklace and picked up its box, which was lost under the flow of waste from Clementina's bag, and with his tray in the other hand momentarily disappeared from view.

She found her credit card and proceeded to reload her bag, with a single arm movement scooping the mess spread over the counter back into the large leather piece of high fashion, and then moved farther along the counter, handing her chief servant the plastic.

He said something. I didn't hear clearly, but I was sure he said, "Fifteen thousand euros." She made a small squeak of agreement and within a few moments was handed a glossy bag far larger than seemed necessary for a necklace.

"Ready?" she asked, turning to me. "What are we waiting for?" It was a combination of self-awareness and cheek that only a seventeen-year-old could pull off with such equanimity.

"Shall I take your jacket?" I replied, picking the soft leather from the carpet before taking my first steps behind the counter without asking for permission. When Clementina began to follow, I looked to the highly attentive man, who was probably still busy calculating his commission on the sale. "Show us how to get out the back."

Some primitive reaction seemed to be kicking in. He knew that a disappointed customer was bad for business. He just couldn't figure whether she would be more disappointed if he broke the illusion and showed us what happened on the other side of the counter or more disappointed if he refused.

The sparkle, the glitter, and the cleanliness on the shop floor disappeared at the second doorway as he led us through a labyrinth of narrow corridors coming to a fire door. He laid his hands on the horizontal push bar and paused—unwilling to let us through, but seemingly unwilling to disappoint his customer.

I pushed the bar and let the door swing open to reveal a small yard. It might have been concreted over fifty years ago; now, it just seemed dirty with the grubby rear elevations of the surrounding buildings penning us in.

Clementina had been a few steps behind and hadn't seen the hesitation. She followed the two of us into the small space. Instinctively, she smiled as she came from the darkness to the light, but the smile rapidly faded as she saw the tawdriness surrounding her. "Oh," she said, still looking up.

Not only were we penned into a space that seemed to be used only for smoking and dumping rubbish, but the square formed by the rear elevations had been cut in half by a wall. I stared up at the six-foot pile of brick held together by cement, then turned to the fastidious man. "I'm sorry, I didn't catch your name."

"Vianney," he said.

"Vianney. Is this the only way out?"

He nodded, a precise tilt of his head like a movement fashioned by a watchmaker.

"Do you know who is over the back?" I pointed over the wall.

A shake of his head, equally precise. I pulled out my phone. Vianney shook his head again—three small twists. "No signal." He pointed back inside. "Seven paces."

I took seven paces and got two bars. "We're going out the back," I said when Reece answered. "I'm not sure what's there, but come and find us there." Back outside, Clementina was still staring up at the sky. "Ready?" I asked.

She seemed perplexed.

"We're going to meet the neighbors," I said, taking her shiny bag and handing it to Vianney. "You're going first."

"What are you talking about?" she asked.

"We're going over the wall—you're going first. Give your bag to Vianney to hold." I pointed to the large lump of leather still hanging from her shoulder. "And put this back on." I handed her the leather jacket I was carrying. I was sure it wasn't designed for rough and tumble, but I preferred it be scraped rather than her.

"Why...?" she began.

"Because it's the only way out, and you're going first because if I go first there's no one to help you over the wall," I said, predicting her range of questions. "What else did you want to do today?"

"I wanted..." she began, slipping on her jacket. "That was rhetorical, wasn't it?"

I leaned my back against the wall and linked my hands together, lowering them so she could step onto my lift. "Put your foot there."

"You're serious?"

"Yeah."

"What do I do?"

"Put your foot there." I indicated my linked hands. "I lift; you scramble onto the wall."

"And then?"

"Then Vianney gives you back your stuff, and I..." I sighed. "Just do it. It's much easier to do it rather than explain." She shrugged and lifted her right foot into my hands. "Now stand," I said.

She placed her hands on my shoulders and stood, locking her knee as I lifted my hands. "Whoa."

"Onto the wall," I said, using the momentum to keep lifting my hands. "You can stand on my shoulders."

It was inelegant as she scrambled, but I felt her weight lifted away, leaving me with linked fingers holding nothing. As I turned, Clementina was sitting on the wall, grinning broadly, her legs dangling down as if her feet were being cooled in a stream on a summer's day.

"What's over there?" I asked.

"Pretty much the same shit that's over here," she said. "But there's a window."

I scrambled up onto the wall and sat next to her. "Nice view," I said.

"How do we get down?"

"Jump."

Clementina looked horrified at my suggestion.

"Pass up the bags," I said to Vianney. He passed the two bags, which I gave to Clementina. "Thank you for your help—hopefully we won't be needing you again today."

He looked at me quizzically, then looked to his customer, hoping she could explain. As they pondered, I twisted, moving my legs to the other side of the wall, then jumped off. As Clementina had said, this side of the wall was pretty much the same as the other side. The key difference was that there was a window and no door.

"Give me the bags," I said to Clementina. She still seemed confused, but offered me the two without argument. I placed them against the wall under the window. "Now you need to get down."

"How?" she said, slowly understanding that I was serious about leaving this way.

"First, turn. Legs on this side." Cautiously she shifted, keeping her weight balanced on the wall. As her legs dropped onto my side, I stood in front of her and put my arms around her legs. "Lift yourself off."

She lifted and gently let her weight fall onto me. I carried her across to the window, softly bringing her down next to her bags. "What now?" she asked after reuniting herself with her bags—checking that the contents of her new shiny bag hadn't been disturbed.

"We ask nicely," I said, picking up a small stone and beginning to tap on the glass.

The window was a plain sash window. It was dirty and poorly maintained—I suspected it hadn't been painted since de Gaulle was president. But the wood in the runners had been rubbed clean, suggesting it was opened frequently. The thin carpet of cigarette butts in a semicircle under the window affirmed my theory that humanity did use the window.

On the other side of the window was a narrow passageway. After minute or so of constant tapping, the light in the passage changed. Maybe a door had opened or the sun had managed to find another crack to push through.

I kept tapping.

A woman in her fifties appeared at the window. It didn't seem odd that there were two strangers outside her window.

"Bonjour," I said as she lifted the lower sash.

"Bonjour madame," offered Clementina cautiously, flashing a natural smile.

There was a realization by the woman who had opened the window that she didn't recognize us, and a further thought that maybe it was unusual for two people to simply appear in what appeared to be a closed cell.

"Paparazzi," I said, pointing loosely in the direction from which we had come. "Can we come through, please?"

She offered no words, but instead leaned forward and craned her neck up as if she suspected we had fallen from the sky or climbed down from one of the windows above. Seeing nothing, she stepped back and shrugged.

"Through you go," I said to Clementina.

"What?"

"Through the window," I said. She frowned. "Look around—do you see any other way to get out of here?"

I took her bags and offered a hand to steady herself as she climbed through, then followed, lowering the sash behind me. "How do we get through to the street?" I asked the woman who had yet to utter a word. "We want to get as far away from Rue de la Paix as we can."

She tilted her head and walked away from us, turning through a door at the end of the corridor. Clementina and I followed through another maze of dark passages usually hidden from the public until we spilled out onto a cobbled courtyard.

Our escort stopped and pointed across the courtyard. It was a sight familiar across Paris—a courtyard that could be viewed from the six floors of apartments surrounding us, and on the other side, an archway with large double wooden doors big enough to get a van into the courtyard.

"Merci, madame," I said and offered a few more words of thanks, then pulled out my phone. "We're about to come onto the street behind," I said as Reece answered.

"I'm already waiting for you," he said and hung up.

Clementina was frowning. Not a bad frown—more a quizzical look. "Your French is very good," she said, almost disbelieving what she was saying.

"My French mother would have been pleased to hear that," I said.

"But you don't have a French accent."

"Scottish father," I said, answering her question but giving nothing further.

A smaller door was inset into the left of the large double doors. I opened it. "Courtesy dictates you go first," I said to Clementina. "However, caution says I'm going to have a look before."

I stepped through the door and onto the backstreet. The street was directly behind Rue de la Paix, but it felt about a million miles away. Where Rue de la Paix was busy and bustling with tourists, shoppers, paparazzi, and cars going in each direction across six lanes, I now stood in a road that could accommodate a row of parked cars and a single lane for traffic. It was little more than a firebreak between the buildings that towered over either side.

Where on the other side there were glittery shops begging people to enter and elegant hotels quietly shielding their guests while still offering them a view onto the outside world, on this side the sandstone building lacked adornment and the windows at street level all had heavy iron bars.

I scanned. No paparazzi. No camera flashes. Not even any tourists. But a few yards up the street was a Maybach with Reece sitting on the hood. He mock saluted as he stood, returning to the cabin before driving the vehicle level to the door.

"We're safe," I said to Clementina, leaning through the door to hold it open before leading her to the Maybach.

"That was fun!" she said as I closed the car door behind us. Her smile was irrepressible.

"Go past the front," I said to Reece. "Let's see how many are there."

Reece drifted the car along the narrow side street and turned. The road he turned onto was broader and had a mixture of cafés and jewelers who couldn't afford the rent on Rue de la Paix. Despite the bustle, the crowd of photographers around the jeweler was obvious as we pulled onto Rue de la Paix.

"Duck down," I whispered to Clementina as we drew level with the crowd.

"Seen enough?" asked Reece.

"Yeah," I said and immediately felt the car pick up speed.

"How did they find us, Reece?" I asked. "How did they know where we were and get there so quickly?"

Reece muttered something without conviction.

"You were watching; did they try anywhere else first?"

"No," said the driver, his eyes still fixed on the road. "They went straight to you."

"How did they know?" I articulated each word of my question individually.

"I don't know," said Reece without any real conviction. "They weren't following us and they came from a different direction to the route we traveled."

"Any ideas?" I asked Clementina.

"No." She was shocked, offended that I would even ask. "You were there with me. Did I send out any messages?"

I held her surly teenage gaze. "Quite a few, actually. To Piedad, for instance."

She tutted and sighed. "Did I send any messages to the paps saying 'Here I am, come and photograph me'?" She tutted and exhaled huffily, then turned—moving her whole body so her back pointed directly at me—and faced her head to look straight out the window.

"What about the people in the shop?"

"Now you're being stupid," she said and fell silent for the remainder of the journey. Reece and I—the paid help—didn't break the quiet.

As the driver pulled into the parking space in the underground parking lot, Clementina let herself out of the car and disappeared toward the elevator before either Reece or I was out of the car.

"It's not my place," said Reece, locking the vehicle.

I smiled broadly, "And yet."

"And yet," agreed Reece. He looked around furtively, then whispered, "I'll just say this: social media, selfies with GPS data." He sniffed and picked up his pace.

three

Reece led me from the service elevator to the front door of the apartment and rapped softly. "I'll be in my apartment," he said. "They'll call me if they need me."

"You're not..." I indicated inside.

Reece shook his head, his movement expressing the sadness of the outsider.

"What about Clementina? Do I need to worry about her?"

"She'll calm down," said the driver. "This isn't the first tantrum a teenage girl has thrown...and it was her fault, even if she won't admit it."

Angeline Bautista opened the door. "They're waiting for you," she said in her stilted English and indicated for me to come in. The cavernous hallway was a contrast to the narrow passageways that Clementina and I had followed while we made our escape, but the additional size offered no additional function.

Reaching the main space with its leather-covered floor, which was sure to become a must-have for rap stars, there were two men in the lounge area, each on a sofa.

But these weren't regular sofas. These weren't the kind of seats you'd find in a Swedish furniture store or in an out-of-town shopping outlet. These were the kind of sofas that had the word luxury attached to them, and like Clementina's wisp of platinum, their price was disproportionately high. If you needed to ask, you really couldn't afford.

The seats were long—at a guess, you could probably sit eight people on each in comfort. Their leather had the softness of Clementina's jacket, and like those hides, these showed no visible flaws.

The two sofas were arranged to curl around two large tables—each topped with maybe gold, maybe marble. Stone or metal—I couldn't figure. It was either gold-hued marble or gold with a marbling effect. All I could be certain about was that each man had laid his briefcase on a table, and one had taken out a laptop, which was resting on the taller table, although clearly the table was too far from the sofa to function as a table while he worked.

The two stood as I approached. "Leathan," said the taller. It was a question but posed as a statement. He held out a hand before I could confirm. "Good to meet you, I'm Johnson McElroy, and this is Orville Mallet." The shorter man mumbled something, offering his hand. "Coffee or maybe something stronger?"

Both handed me their business cards without waiting for me to consider the offer of refreshment.

The taller man, who was dressed in a dark blue suit with a patterned red tie, was Johnson McElroy, a lawyer—the company's lawyer. The shorter man—Orville Mallet, or as his business card stated, Orville Michael Mallet—was the company's media relations adviser. He was, to my way of thinking, less well dressed and less well groomed than McElroy, with an unmatched jacket and trousers and no tie. In practice, he had probably spent just as much on his clothes and his haircut, but he was clearly after a look that fitted with the role he saw for himself as being more of a creative type.

The business addresses for both men were the same—the company's headquarters in the west end of London. The same address that I presumed would be shown on Zackary Norden's business card.

And yet.

And yet both men seemed to be behaving like members of a medieval king's court. While they might have had status bestowed upon them, they were still following their master on his progress through the lands, and in this instance, they had followed their king by Eurostar when he summoned them from London. I suspected their position could be withdrawn at their master's sole discretion. And likely would be should he have a capricious temper that they might prickle.

They only had power and status while they had their master's favor, and they only had their master's favor while they succeeded in keeping him satisfied.

As I understood, Zackary Norden was a financier. That was a term applied to any number of activities with varying scales of morality and competence. Neither of these two men was a financier or anything vaguely financial—in other words, neither of these men made money in the way that their master made money. They were flunkies there to serve. Like me, but more expensively dressed and with employment rights.

"Shall we get started?" asked Orville Michael Mallet.

"Aren't we going to wait for Mister Norden?" I asked.

Mallet looked vaguely affronted. Not angry, more the look of a call-center worker hearing for the fifteenth time that day a request to speak with his supervisor. "We handle these things."

"I thought he had to decide whether I'm hired," I said, surprised by my lack of assurance.

"You're very much hired," said Johnson McElroy, the lawyer with two surnames and no sensible forename, taking over from the media relations man.

"No interview?"

The lawyer smiled a condescending smile. The condescension that only comes when someone is trying to make a point. "There's no interview—we took out references from people we trust. They say good things."

"References?"

"Alexander Boniface, Sam Cartwright, and Gideon Latymer," said the lawyer, listing three men who may loosely have been regarded as three of my recent employers, but who also—to a varying extent—were men I called friend. "They were all more than satisfied with your work and will stand by your character." He paused. "Zack was quite impressed to get a member of parliament to give such an unambiguous answer."

There was something that rankled. Something in the references—the comments about me, behind my back, sought without my knowledge—that niggled the lawyer. Maybe it was that Norden seemingly took the references directly, maybe it was that Norden and not these men had decided to hire me, or maybe it was that I seemed competent, and therefore these men who owed their position to the man who was now the master to all of us had competition for his favor. And competition from someone who had skills that they couldn't offer when their master was in need.

"Doesn't Mister Norden want to be here to explain his expectations to me...for this job?"

"That's why you've got the two of us," said Mallet, the media relations man. I could deal with a lawyer with a crazy name, but a media relations man with a stupid name just upset me. Surely if you're going to go into media relations, you do something about your initial perception.

"Clementina?" I asked, throwing out my final question. "Should she be here?"

"Oh no," muttered both men.

"She," began the lawyer, "is the problem. She is the reason you've been hired."

He was insisting that I'd been hired, but I was sure that as a lawyer he should know that a contract requires an offer and acceptance, and I hadn't accepted. Or rather, I wasn't aware that I had formally accepted, but seemingly my presence said otherwise. I had only the loosest idea of the task I was being hired to perform, and no salary had been discussed. Or maybe they agreed the figure with my three friends when Zackary Norden took up references.

"What do you know of Zackary Norden and his business?" asked the media relations man.

"Finance," I said.

Mallet flinched, like a man hamming it up when he is told how much it will cost to fix his car. "Would that it were so simple."

He looked across to the lawyer. Between them they shared a private moment, each agreeing that what they were involved with was so much more important and wide-ranging than mere finance. Clearly, it was the sort of thing that required people of caliber, breeding, and intelligence.

Not that the two had much of any of those qualities from what I had seen so far.

"On one level, yes, it is finance," said the media relations man. "But Zack doesn't simply deal with other people's money—he arranges deals. He finds businesses to buy and structures deals with his money and investors' money."

It sounded pretty much the dictionary definition of what I understood when someone said finance.

"If people find Zack is interested in a business, then its price will go up, or the price of the sector will change, or the deal will become harder." The lawyer was talking. "So confidentiality is important."

"If people know that Zack is in Paris, then they may figure the business he is chasing—especially as he's here for a while." The media relations man indicated the apartment. "He always takes an apartment to ensure confidentiality. Hotels have too many people, and it's easier to set up a base in an apartment."

He sat back with a self-satisfied glow. I got it—this was the base and he was there. He was on the inside, not the outside. If I had got a piece of paper and drawn a gold star, he would have felt proud.

"So what do you want from me?" I asked.

"Keep Clementina out of the press." The lawyer had taken over. "If people know she's spending the school holiday here—without her mother, who's back in London—then they'll make the link to her father. And then they'll start looking for his deal."

"But she's just a kid," I said.

Mallet responded. "She is—but she's the daughter of a wealthy man and she attracts a lot of media attention. Especially since that incident last year when..." The media relations man trailed off as if I knew about the incident he was referring to. He shrugged, half apologetically. "Rich kids, social media, tabloid fodder."

The lawyer started speaking again. "Listen, Leathan. You have a background of working for and with the press. You understand how they work. We want you on the other side—our side—using your knowledge to keep Clementina out of the press while she's in Paris. And for that, you will be paid."

"How do I keep her out of the press?" I asked, trying not to imply that they had just asked me to make water run uphill.

"That's why we're hiring you," said the lawyer. "If we could answer that question, we wouldn't need you."

I guess he could have been more condescending, but he would have had to try much harder.

I waited. I counted to ten. "We had an incident today."

Both men fixed on me.

"Paparazzi."

"Where? When?" asked the lawyer.

"Out buying jewelry," I said. "A whole pack of photographers seemed to turn up out of nowhere."

The two men both started asking questions at the same time. I waited for them to stop.

"I don't know how they found us. I suspect they didn't get a good picture—we left by a rear exit."

The lawyer looked to the media relations man. "I can handle it," said Mallet. "I'll put out a story that she came over for lunch and picked up a few trinkets while she was here. Train over this morning, train back this afternoon, nothing to see here."

four

Johnson McElroy and Orville Michael Mallet seemed pleased to have fixed a problem. A problem where I was having trouble understanding what really made it a problem.

The two men—one groomed to look like a logical and rational arguing machine; the other determined to display his individual creativity, which looked exactly the same as everyone else's individual creativity—shook my hand at the door.

"You know the way out," I said, as if I had a clue. I only knew how to enter and leave if I was driven by Reece.

The two headed for the elevator and doubtless their next fearsome task, which they would perform with equal bravery for our master. I shut the door and made my way through the cavernous entrance hall back to the open living space and the kitchen area. The kitchen area, which had more floor space than most apartments I had lived in.

"I should have a word with Clementina," I said to Angeline Bautista, the housekeeper who had remained invisible while the two company men had been present.

"She's gone out," said the housekeeper.

"When?"

"While you talked."

"Where?"

She shrugged.

"What did Reece say?"

She looked confused.

"Reece—the driver. What did he say?"

The confusion remained. "Nothing."

"But he must have said something when he came up."

"He didn't come up," she said.

"She went to him?" I could feel the hesitation in my speech as my brain tried to catch up with the situation and make sure my language was unambiguous for the non-native English speaker.

"No. She went out on her own," said Angeline.

"When?"

"While you talked," she said with greater emphasis.

"How long ago?"

She tilted her head from side to side. "Ten minutes?" she said. More a question than a statement.

I pulled out my phone and called Reece. "Does Clementina go out on her own?"

"Nope," said Reece. "Daddy says no."

"Well, she has."

Reece swore under his breath. "I'll be up."

"Go check the apartment," I said to Angeline. "Everywhere. Every... Just go." The Filipino housekeeper moved off, her small, fast steps sounding as she disappeared.

There was a rap at the door. "Fast," I said, opening it to Reece, who came in swiftly.

"Are you sure?" he asked.

"Angeline's looking."

"What about the guy in the lobby?"

"I didn't know there was," I said. "You wait, I'll go."

I headed for the elevator I had seen McElroy and Mallet use and descended to the lobby. There was a small desk with a man behind. I wasn't sure whether he was intended as security or as a doorman or as someone who would perform any task he was called upon to perform.

"Bonjour, monsieur," I said, knowing that French was more likely to elicit a favorable reaction.

"Monsieur," he acknowledged.

"I'm with the Norden family." He nodded. "Have you seen Clementina—within the last ten or fifteen minutes?"

He shook his head. "Two men, but no Clementina."

"But you would recognize her if you saw her."

He smiled.

"You've been here all the time?" I asked.

"Of course, monsieur."

"You didn't..." I leaned closer, fixing him with a stare and not finishing the sentence.

The edge of his mouth twitched uncomfortably.

"When?" I asked.

"Ten minutes ago," he said apologetically.

five

Reece and Angeline were looking glum when I returned.

I wasn't sure whether they were glum because Clementina had disappeared or because the disappearance would send ripples through their worlds and upset the equilibrium. Or maybe they simply didn't have the patience for dealing with teenage tantrums.

Assuming this was a teenage tantrum.

"She definitely went on her own?" I asked Angeline. "No one forced her."

Angeline wasn't sure of the fine point I was trying to get at. "She was alone." In truth, this was probably all Angeline knew.

"Have you got her phone number?" I asked no one in particular.

"It's off," said Reece. "Could be switched off. Could be a dead battery."

"Has she done this before?" I asked.

Reece was noncommittal.

"How far did she get?"

"How far did she get when?" asked Reece, hesitation in his voice.

"Before," I said, not hiding my annoyance.

Reece exhaled slightly. "You seem to be saying she's done this before."

"Right," I said.

"Well, what is *this*?" asked Reece. "What has happened here?" He paused. "Do you see what I'm saying? You tell me what has happened, and I'll tell you if it's the same as something that has happened before, because at the moment all I know is that little Miss Snotty Cow isn't in her room."

Angeline said something.

"Isn't in the apartment," corrected Reece. "Do we know whether she's left the building?"

"No." My voice was dejected. "The guy on the door wasn't at his desk, so we don't have a clue." I tried a different tack with Reece. "Is she in the habit of going out on her own? Alone?"

Reece scrunched his face. I wasn't sure what he was trying to convey and what he was trying to hide. As far as I could tell, Reece knew there was trouble but didn't want to be involved because then he'd be sharing the blame.

"Do I take it that it's not unheard of for her to go out alone?"

"She gets to and from school on her own," he said. Seeing my confusion, he elaborated. "Lives with the mother. She doesn't indulge in quite the same way—they don't have...." He indicated himself.

I cursed under my breath. "Has she gone out on her own while she's been here? In Paris?"

"It's only been a few days," said Reece. "She hasn't really had the need."

"So why did she go out now?" I asked. The other two were remaining noncommittal. "How far will she get? Where will she go? Has she got any friends in the city?"

There was still no engagement by the other two. Reece pulled out his phone and tapped the screen a few times, shook his head, and punched the screen a few more times. "She hasn't posted anything." He put his phone back in his pocket. "She'll come back."

"She might," I said. "But I can't really protect her from the paparazzi if I don't know where she is, so I'd like to try to find her."

It seemed like they were both ready to volunteer to be the person who stayed home in case she returned.

"Do we have anything less conspicuous than the Maybach?"

Reece shook his head. "The car came with the apartment," he said by way of explanation.

"Have we got a photo of her?"

Reece pulled out his phone.

"A recent photo," I added.

"This morning?" asked Reece, fiddling with his phone. "Is that recent enough for you? Trying jewelry?"

"Send me the best one and let's get out and look."

Reece muttered and complained. I didn't have much patience for his protestations; however, once I got out of the building, I started to see his point. There were two options—assuming Clementina had left and was on foot. She could have gone left and followed the streets, or right and gone into the park that the apartment windows looked across: Jardins du Ranelagh.

I went left. It didn't take me long to realize my mistake. This was a largely residential area. Where much of Paris has stores at the ground level with apartments above, this quarter was different.

The buildings were set back with fences—mostly iron railings—to the front, and there were no stores or cafés. There was no obvious magnet to draw a teenager—even a teenager with a healthy credit card.

I returned and went into the park as if I had gone right when I first left the apartment. I soon understood the fallacy of this choice. "Alright, I should have listened to you," I said as Reece answered his phone. "Where will she have gone?"

"Beats the heck out of me," said the chauffeur. "Where are you?"

"The park...Jardins du Ranelagh."

"I doubt she would go away from the city," said Reece "If you go west, you'll get to Bois de Boulogne—she won't have gone there. South takes you nowhere. North is just more residential, so go east. It's the best suggestion I can make."

I hung up and continued through the park. It was a typical Parisian park—laid out on strict lines with regimented rows of trees instructing pedestrians on their route. It wasn't a bad place to be—you wouldn't tell someone not to come here—but I couldn't see what the attraction was, apart from proximity. If you were close, in the many apartment blocks built around the park—including the one in which the Norden family was renting—then you might come here for a walk. If you weren't close, then it wasn't a destination for a day trip, especially with the heavy traffic on the roads carving through the green space.

Passing the eastern edge of the park, the city took me into its warm embrace and offered a six-way junction.

I continued east—or at least what seemed closest to east, passing a row of upscale cafés and restaurants as I let myself be subsumed into the living and breathing city, rather than the stilted residential area I had left. The living, breathing city where a teenager might come. The living, breathing city where I didn't stand a chance of finding Clementina among the people who were filling the streets and the stores.

The next intersection only offered four options as two roads crossed. But there was a fifth option—a Metro station. I called Reece. "I'm at the Metro. Would she have taken it?"

Reece exhaled.

"I'm going down to take a look. Do you want to come and meet me here?"

For the tourists, they sell tickets for the Metro in packs of ten. I had bought ten that morning and used one to get closer to Place de la Concorde where Reece had met me. I slotted a second ticket into the machine and went down to the platforms. There was only one line through the station—one line, one pair of platforms staring at each other from either side of the tracks, which made it easy to confirm that she wasn't there, but still I waited for two trains to pass each way before I ascended.

Even in what is regarded an upscale district, the Maybach was sufficiently conspicuous to make finding Reece an easy task. He didn't need to say anything—his disengaged look communicated everything. "Have you tried calling?" I asked.

He nodded.

"And…"

Another nod. "I've tried it all."

"Rue de la Paix?" I asked.

"I haven't got any better suggestions," said the driver, firing the engine. "I'll take it slow down Rue de Passy." He saw my questioning look. "There are stores. And then…" He let the sentence hang as he pulled out.

Reece was correct—Rue de Passy had stores, the kind of stores that I might expect to excite a regular seventeen-year-old. I could even believe that these stores might interest Clementina in the way that bargain stores interest regular people; not because of their quality, but because there was so much on offer.

Twice I asked Reece to pull over and I went into the larger stores to look around. Twice I was disappointed. When I got back for the second time, the look on Reece's face had changed. He held his phone forward so I could see the screen, but not make out exactly what it showed. "I know where she was three minutes ago."

six

It was my second visit to Gare du Nord that day.

I had first been there when I arrived from Brussels that morning. Then, I had moved swiftly, without paying much attention to the building. Instead, I had been watching to ensure I hadn't walked into a trap.

I was now fairly sure there hadn't been a trap. This gave me the confidence that if anyone knew I was in Paris, they wouldn't know where in Paris I was. Yet.

Reece pulled up to the right of the station. The imposing frontage—columns and statues and arches carved in light-colored stone—had a small addition on this side, which looked like two large glass houses.

"Is she meeting someone or running?" I asked the driver.

He looked at his phone. "Don't even know she's here. She's gone dark again."

"I'll go look—can you get the car around the corner?" I pointed away from us. "The Eurostar platforms are on the far side. Assuming she's there, I want the shortest exit route."

Reece muttered his agreement as I got out of the car and entered through the glass houses. Immediately I was subsumed into a mass of human beings. It was something closer to a primordial soup than a collection of individuals each exerting his or her own free will.

Maybe a scientist who has studied currents could make some sense of what was happening, but for me, it seemed that there was a mass of people blocking my path whichever route I took.

There is a time to fight and a time to acknowledge that this was the busiest railway station in Europe—and indeed the busiest station in the world outside Japan. I gave up and left the building, reentering through an entrance that was closer to the Eurostar platforms, still fighting the crowds but finding a flow and the opportunity to look around.

Everywhere I looked people were taking photographs—mostly with phones, mostly selfies, recording joyful reunions and the last moments before a tearful departure. But there were also several serious photographers, earnestly taking considered artistic pictures of the crowds, the trains, and the architecture. What there didn't seem to be were any paparazzi with their long lenses and powerful flashes crowding around.

As I got closer to the Eurostar arrival platforms, there was a couple embracing passionately. Arms tightly holding each other, lips firmly sealed.

He was a thin and weedy guy, and she had something of Clementina about her, but was dressed differently from how she had been this morning. The jeans were different—a different tone and a different cut, and instead of a white T-shirt, this girl was wearing a dark floral top. If pushed I would have said peasant chic, completed with a large floppy hat that was tilted away from me.

The crowds jostled, the tide had turned, and I found the cross currents driving me away from my target. I lost sight of the couple but when I cut through, the two had separated and her hat was on the floor. She reached to pick it, turning toward me as she returned to the vertical.

Clementina.

Clementina and a guy.

I whistled. A single sharp blast; air forced over my bottom teeth. It felt like a thousand heads turned, including the one I wanted. Clementina saw me immediately, her cheeks flushing slightly.

By the time I reached her, the guy was gone. "Hi," I said. "I thought you might want a ride home."

"I'm not a child," she said, the crowd somehow giving us complete privacy for the first time since we had met.

"I know," I said. "I just thought you might find it easier to sit in a car rather than to fight through the crowd."

She didn't say anything.

"Put on your hat," I said. "It looks good on you." She fell for the compliment and complied as I led her toward where I hoped Reece had parked.

seven

As Reece pulled the Maybach into the parking lot, I was faster than I had been last time. "Leave us," I whispered to the driver as I followed Clementina out of the barely stationary vehicle.

Where Reece had led me to the service elevator, Clementina took the stairs to the lobby, where she called the main elevator. As the door closed, she spoke. "You're not going to tell anyone?"

"Tell them what?" I said. "My job is to keep you and the paparazzi away from each other. Apparently you don't play nice."

She forced a smile.

"And I'd prefer it if you didn't give me any more shit until bedtime."

The forced smile became a natural smile. "Agreed," she said. "No more shit until bedtime."

Clementina was the kind of girl for whom doors opened. We stepped out of the elevator and took the few paces to the apartment's door, which seem to open for her in the same way that the elevator's doors had. Angeline smiled meekly from behind the large lump of wood, and I followed the teenager.

As we entered the main space of the apartment, Clementina's voice took on a tone of excitement I hadn't heard from her. "Daddy bear!"

She rushed forward and embraced the man standing in the room. He was a little taller than her, maybe five-nine, stocky, and was losing his hair, although he had yet to fully give up the fight. I knew—thank you, internet—that he was 45, but he didn't look it. Emotionally he seemed younger; physically he had taken more hits.

"How are you, my baby girl?" he asked. His accent was English, which wasn't surprising given that he was born and brought up in England. But he clearly was not a London native—which again wasn't surprising, given that most English citizens don't live in London.

The two talked for a moment or two, then he said, "I need to speak to Leathan."

"Okay, daddy bear," she said, smiling broadly and tilting her head as if she were looking up to her father, before disappearing.

He watched his daughter leave the room before offering his hand to shake. "They speak highly of you, Leathan."

I got a better look at his hair. He had the same dilemma that the royal princes face. Their hair thins—and thins so that it is noticeable—but doesn't thin enough to make them fully bald. Most men in this situation choose to shave their heads or cut the hair short, but that always gives a certain look. A certain thuggish look that is inappropriate for a royal. And a look that a financier may feel is ill suited to his role.

So like the royals, Zackary Norden was living with thin hair.

"You've spoken to McElroy and Mallet?" he asked.

I bobbed my head to affirm.

"Did you talk money?"

"No," I said.

"Do you charge an hourly or a daily rate?"

"It's more complicated..." I began.

"What? Risk related or something like that?"

Something like that. I didn't want to say that I didn't know what to charge. I wasn't being trying to be coy—I hadn't thought about what I might charge. And part of the reason I hadn't thought what to charge was that I didn't want money. Sure, money is useful, but it brings its own problems—you have to store it, you pay tax on it, and people try to take it away from you. I wanted favors. I wanted people who I could trust and who could help me while I couldn't go back to London.

"You're here—you've started work, so I don't want to get into a whole great negotiation. Shall we say ten thousand euros a week?"

I hesitated. "Who's paying the tax?"

There was a wry smile on his face—he knew his first offer had been more than generous. "Fifteen, gross. You can pay the tax." He held out his hand as if to tell me he had made his final offer. He knew I had no intention of figuring whether I owed tax; it was just another way to ask for more money. "Please don't tell Reece—that first offer is far more than I pay him."

I shook his hand.

He indicated the long sofas where I had sat with the lawyer and the media relations man.

"You understand what is expected of you?"

"I understand what the two told me." We sat across from each other.

"But?"

"But I'd like to hear it from you," I said.

Norden leaned back on his sofa, spreading his arms, indicating that even if he didn't own it, this domain was his possession. "It's very simple—keep the press away from Clementina while she's in Paris."

I sat silently and waited for him to elaborate.

"If the press know I'm living here, then they'll figure I'm working on a deal, and if they figure I'm working on a deal, then they'll suspect which company I'm trying to buy and it'll mess up the price. Clemmy is like catnip to the paparazzi—pretty girl, rich daddy, and then there was that story."

He spoke as if everyone knew and had followed that story. I hadn't, but I had little wish to hear a father's explanation for his teenage daughter's poor choices.

When he continued, his voice was firmer. "Just make sure she isn't photographed while she's here."

"There are cheaper and easier ways to achieve your aims. You don't need to hire me," I said.

He lifted his eyes, indicating I should elaborate.

"If she stays inside or goes somewhere less pleasant than Paris."

He snorted. "I'm not locking up my daughter and I'm not asking you to be her jailer or my spy—just keep the press away. If she wants to go out, then Reece is here; he can drive unless he's driving me."

"Can she walk?" I stopped myself. "I mean, is the only way out of the apartment in a chauffeur-driven limousine?"

He winced.

"People—tourists—phones with cameras, social media," I said.

He winced again. "Stay close whatever she does, wherever she goes."

I waited a moment. He didn't seem to want to elaborate. He didn't seem to want to be specific. "You say I'm not her jailer, but you want me to stay close."

"No," said Clementina's father. "What I want is for you to ensure Clemmy doesn't show up in the papers. There is nothing complicated about what I want—you have one task."

He seemed to be becoming frustrated, so I tried to lighten the mood. "I just want to make sure I'm not going to get the blame if the gardener steals the family silver."

He half smiled. "There's no garden, and any silver doesn't belong to me." He let out a long sigh and muttered under his breath to no one in particular. "Clementina's mother will have taken any silver."

The thought of Clementina's mother seemed to have distracted him. There was little I really knew about my new employer. The internet had told me he was a financier but had given little detail. Instead, most of the virtual column inches had focused on his wealth and how that wealth had been split with his now former wife, Clementina's mother, in their divorce. The kind of divorce that the tabloids liked to call messy.

"Are we done?" he asked, bringing his attention back to me.

"Cash," I said. "It might be useful to have some. You know, if I need to...."

"Of course," said Norden, picking up on my implication as if offering casual bribes was an everyday occurrence. He stood. "I'll just get..."

He was back in under a minute with a stack of €50 bills. "There's a thousand. Is that enough to be getting on with?"

I nodded, taking the cash. "I'll return whatever I don't need."

He twisted his face dismissively. "Where are you staying?"

I shrugged.

"Where have you left your stuff?"

"I'm wearing everything," I said.

He wrinkled his face. "Stay here—I'd like you close. I'm..." He hesitated. "I'm out tonight. It would be good for someone to be around. Take one of the guest suites."

"Thank you," I mumbled.

"And go and buy some fresh clothes. Reece can drive you," said Norden. "He's got a credit card."

eight

When I returned, having bought new clothes as instructed, the apartment was quiet.

Zackary Norden had left—he had gone "out." An unspecified out, which I suspected meant it was either illegal or immoral, or most likely was something he didn't want his daughter to know about. The cook was still sick and it was Angeline's night off, although she did wait for my return before departing. She assured me that Clementina was still in the apartment, and the sound of running water suggested this was correct.

I poured myself a coffee and sat at the counter in the kitchen.

Eventually Clementina appeared. She had been re-perfected. Her hair was still slightly damp, and her face had been cleared of every trace of makeup.

She was dressed as she was when I first saw her, in soft cotton like any normal teenage girl. Unlike this morning, this soft cotton now displayed a pink and lilac mixture of hearts and flowers. Like my first sight, what she was wearing—and I wasn't sure whether it was general-purpose house wear or whether it was intended bed wear—was undeniably new.

"Do you want to go somewhere?" I asked. "I can call Reece."

She crinkled her face.

I lifted my eyebrows, inviting a response.

Her crinkle seemed more pained.

I waited.

She shook her head. A small movement from side to side. "Not with him."

I kept waiting.

"He stares at my boobs." She said it as one for whom it was an everyday occurrence to be leered at. She didn't seem offended and didn't seem to be drawing a line to more egregious behavior, but she clearly didn't have the energy to be stared at.

"We can walk," I offered.

She shook her head, her softening face telling me I didn't have to try so hard.

"Order in," I suggested.

"I'm not hungry," she said.

"Is there anything in the fridge?" I asked.

She twisted her mouth. The disinterested twist that only a teenager can muster.

I went to the fridge and opened the door. Her lack of commitment immediately became clear. It wasn't that there was nothing in the fridge—it was more a matter that there was so much that it was impossible to take in all the options and choices. There was an immediate and total sensory overload, and every permutation of every conceivable dish immediately came to mind.

I looked again. There was milk. There were eggs. There were fresh lemons. "Pancakes," I said, without searching out the flour. "Crepe-type pancakes—not those ridiculous thick things? With a bit of sugar and some lemon juice."

Her face brightened, with half a smile at the edge of her mouth.

"Or we can call your father?"

She snorted. "He's with his next wife."

I lifted the milk, two eggs, and a lemon out of the fridge, putting them on the island in the center of the large space, then turned to Clementina. I wasn't sure whether she wanted to talk, and her comment about her potential future stepmother was her asking me to invite her to elaborate, or whether she was stating a fact and we should move on.

I started opening cabinets looking for some flour and a bowl. Clementina half-snorted again, a slightly amused look across her face. "We have a competition at school for who has the worst stepmother—not that she's actually my stepmother, at least not yet."

I found a bowl and placed it next to the eggs, milk, and lemon on the island, which was probably bigger than most rooms in Paris.

"She used to be his secretary." Another snort. "She called herself his PA, but she was only ever a secretary."

The words were falling out of Clementina's mouth, but I suspected the author was her mother.

"She's only twenty-five."

It might be another woman's words, but I got the implication: She's barely older than his daughter.

"She's had a boob job." I'm a man. Breasts were mentioned—I couldn't not react. I met Clementina's gaze, distracting myself from the search for flour. "She keeps showing me."

A twenty-five-year-old who was keen to display her body. There were too many thoughts going through my head.

"They really messed it up." She paused. "Seriously. They're not symmetrical, and the shape is wrong."

I cracked. "How so?"

"Too big, too tight, and the bottom has been filled too much so her nipple's in the wrong place. And the scar..." She winced. "She keeps asking me what I think."

"And you think?"

"I think she's a freak show. I think you avoid surgery because they never get it right and even if they get it close to right, then your body will change. My mother's got a friend who had a nose job twenty years ago. I never thought much about it—I didn't even notice it when I was a kid—but as she's aged, her skin on her face has sagged." She stopped herself, seemingly worried about coming over badly about this other woman. "I don't mean *sagged* sagged. I mean, she's got older and her skin has lost some of its tone...some of its elasticity, but her nose is still the same. It's like changing one tile in a bathroom—it never looks right."

Again, I felt she was a ventriloquist's dummy for another woman—probably repeating the conversations that had started with her mother when she first gave a hint of teenage insecurity. But I also recognized that she had considered the issue, and this was more than a straightforward regurgitation of another woman's perspective.

Something shifted in her look—she looked uncomfortable, as if recalling being forced to look at something distasteful, which a botched boob job probably was. "Then she asks me if I think he likes them."

It took me a moment to follow where she had led the conversation.

"That's right," said Clementina. "She asks me whether I think my father will like her fake boobs. Do you see what I'm dealing with?"

I winced. I tried not to—we were, after all, talking about the woman who seemed likely to become my employer's future wife—but I failed. I couldn't disagree with Clementina's distaste.

Clementina seemed to want to comfort me. "She's always like that," she said, resignedly. "Usually she talks to me about blow jobs."

Again, I couldn't not react.

"She thinks she's good at blow jobs. Thinks she's some sort of expert. A PhD in getting her lips around a cock."

I remembered my search for the flour, hoping my distraction would distract my teenage charge, but Clementina carried on.

"She doesn't get that it's just something guys say." There was a short pause; then she continued, as if the pause had been a request on my part for elucidation. "Every guy says you look pretty, you give good blow jobs, and that you're great in bed."

This was turning into a conversation I didn't want to have with a seventeen-year-old, but it was too late to stop it now.

"They always say 'she's bad,' talking about another girl, 'but you're great.' A bit of rivalry, a bit of a compliment. She's just had some guy tell her that she's great at blow jobs because he wanted a blow job. Then she's told the next guy it's her specialty and he's said, 'Prove it.' She's gone down, and he's liked it—which he would, he's a guy."

I found the flour.

She caught my look. "Do you see what I'm dealing with?"

"I do." And I did, and her reasoning seemed sound. I just didn't want to talk about it.

"And then she wants to go shopping with me," said Clementina exasperatedly, as if the problem were obvious.

"I thought you liked shopping," I said weakly, finding a balloon whisk.

"I do. But I know what I'm looking for." I remembered the jewelry store and decided not to disagree.

She saw my hesitation.

"I like trying new things—sometimes they work. And I like to get my followers' opinions."

Followers. It wasn't the time to have *that* conversation.

"I can show them what works and what doesn't, and they love seeing inside stores that they wouldn't usually get inside."

"Those were the pictures today?" I had to scratch the itch. Just once.

She nodded, but seemed to have returned to her theme. "I don't mind that she doesn't listen when we go shopping. I don't even care that she has less style than you do. What upsets me is when she asks for my opinion and then ignores it or thinks she knows better. It's just a waste of time." Then quietly, "She only asks me because she wants me to be her friend, not because she want my opinion."

I tipped some flour into the bowl. I was sure there were scales in this kitchen that would have weighed the flour with an accuracy of several decimal points, but I was happy with what looked like eight ounces and dribbled in what seemed like about a pint of milk.

"So that's me," she said as I began whisking. "What about you? Why has daddy bear hired you?"

"To keep you and the paparazzi apart. He thinks they'll spoil his party."

"I know that," she said. "What I want to know is why *you*. Why did he hire you and not…I dunno…anyone else?"

"I guess he thinks I know how the press works," I said, "since I used to work for them."

"You were a journalist?"

I slowed my whisking and looked up at her, trying to shake my head but finding the movement hard as my hand continued to circle. "I used to work for journalists."

She frowned inquisitively.

"Journalists are bound by certain codes. There are things they're not meant to do; lines they aren't supposed to cross."

The inquisitiveness turned to confusion. "I thought journalists didn't worry about breaking the law—freedom of the press or whatever they say."

"Some don't. But some do. It's a gray world, and I did best in the gray world, doing the things that weren't quite illegal, but where journalists would like some deniability."

There was still confusion. "Why?"

"It was fun," I said. "And I believed in what we were doing. I've got no problem with bending a few rules to help expose a politician who's fiddling with his expenses."

"If it was so much fun, then why the babysitting?" she asked, pointing to herself as if to reaffirm how she viewed our relationship.

I cracked an egg into the milk and flour mix. The act felt like a metaphor.

"I fell in love."

I became aware that the room was silent, apart from my whisk folding the egg into the mixture. Clementina was staring straight at me, forcing her eyes wide to command me continue.

"I was working with a journalist called Sam, who was researching a story about human trafficking."

It was a broad term—Clementina just wanted to hear the love story. I got specific.

"Gangs bringing people—illegally and against their will—to the UK to work in brothels."

Her face fell. She had the look of a scared kid. Not scared by the subject matter, more worried that this was a world outside of her knowledge. She knew the topic was serious, but she might have to admit that however much of sophisticated worldly-wise image she wanted to project, on this topic she didn't know as much as she wanted.

"What were you doing?" she asked, her tone apprehensive, her delivery inquisitive.

"There was a Bulgarian gang. Sam wanted a guy on the inside—someone who could get him real evidence for the story."

She gasped. "You worked for the gang?"

"In a roundabout way," I said. "I was there to get evidence for Sam to write the story, so I had to do some things...see some things...."

Clementina stood motionless. She had wrapped her arms around herself and was looking at me with only one eye, as if trying to filter out the images that were playing inside her head.

"This wasn't just a story," I said. "We gave evidence to the police."

Telling her the police were involved seemed to be enough to bring the story back to some sort of reality that Clementina could understand or relate to. "You fell in love?" Half a question, half a plea to get back to safer ground.

"Mmm."

"With?"

I paused, watching the realization cross her face. Waves of disgust, then horror, then sympathy, then embarrassment at her reaction.

"We don't choose," I said softly.

"So where is she?"

I shrugged. "Deported."

Clementina had questions, but she had that look of someone not knowing what to ask.

"I couldn't deal with her suffering, so I took her and called the police. There were arrests and there were convictions, and she was there illegally—that's what happens when you're trafficked—so she was deported."

"Why...?" began Clementina.

"The Bulgarians. They'll kill me; they'll kill her." I returned to whisking my pancake mix. "That's why I left London."

nine

There was a scream.

At least, I thought it was a scream. I had been asleep, and whatever had made the noise had woken me.

At least, that's what I thought as I lay in what felt like the softest—and yet firm enough to offer just the right amount of support I needed—and most comfortable bed in the world.

As I felt the cotton wrap me, I tried to remember when I'd last been in a comfortable bed. The answer was obvious: in London. In my own bed. Since then? Certainly there had been clean beds. Most, if not virtually all, had been clean. Virtually all had been functionally acceptable—with a mattress, sheets, and something to keep me warm. Even the sofas I had crashed on had been comfortable enough and functional enough.

But this felt like the best I'd known for months: a perfect bed—there was no other way to describe it—in a bedroom with my own bathroom and my own dressing room.

A dressing room.

I had the clothes I was wearing when I got the call in Brussels. The same clothes I'd been wearing when I left Brussels. The same clothes I'd been wearing when I arrived in Paris. The same clothes I'd been wearing all day.

At Zackary Norden's suggestion—and on his credit card—I'd gone out before what might be called dinner, but what in practical terms was crepes, and bought a few bits: socks, underwear, and a few shirts. Even when added to everything I had been wearing for the past thirty-six hours, it wasn't enough to justify a dressing room. It might fill half a shelf in a closet, a whole shelf if I spread it out, but it wasn't enough for a dressing room.

And yet somehow I was tickled to have a dressing room.

I was far more appreciative of the bathroom, but amused to have a dressing room.

The bathroom had an immediate practical use and would have ongoing use. After dinner, Clementina suggested it was time to turn in. "I need an early night," she said. "And no offense, but you need a bath."

The allure of a bath was strong, but the thought that Clementina was going to bed for the night brought relief. The thought that she would be in her room—or her suite, as I'm sure it would be—and not causing trouble, not attracting paparazzi, had a powerful allure. I could be doing my job of keeping her away from the media while at the same time being several rooms away, soaking in a bath.

"No offense taken," I said. "I was thinking the same thing." She looked at me sideways, and I realized the ambiguity of my reply. "I was thinking that I needed to wash—not that you need a bath."

Her face relaxed. She seemed pleased that I was agreeing with her. Not that we had disagreed since I found her in Gare du Nord. Since then we seemed to have turned a corner—we had talked. I found out something about her, her mother, her putative step-mother, her relationship with her father, and she found why I had left London. I wasn't about to declare us BFFs, but by the time I got into the bath we had definitely taken a step forward, and a certain level of trust and understanding had been established.

I'm not really one for baths—I prefer showers. They perform the necessary function in the time it takes to run a bath. But tonight I was in the mood to sit, soak, go prune-like, and contemplate, while occasionally topping up with hot water.

When I got out, the choice of towels seemed almost overwhelming. I grabbed a large-ish one, dried myself, and then put on one of the toweling robes. The robe was cotton, but it felt like the softest thing I had ever worn as I dropped onto my bed and clicked on the evening news. Another unnecessary luxury. I don't need to know what's going on—most of it can be guessed, and if Europe goes to war I'm sure I'll hear—but it was relaxing to sit and watch what a bunch of television journalists thought was important.

After half an hour, maybe forty-five minutes, I was ready to sleep. I switched off the television and made a quick circuit of the main space of the apartment. I didn't need anything, but something told me I should at least look around.

So I did.

The large room was as Clementina and I had left it. I didn't switch on any lights, partly because I couldn't remember exactly where the switches were, but mostly because there was enough light coming through the windows. Somewhere along the corridor where Clementina had gone to her room there was a low light—the sort of light that pushes itself under a door and then struggles around a corner. Enough that you know a light is on, not enough that I needed to investigate.

Sleep had come fast in the comfortable bed, safe in the knowledge that there was nothing I needed to do to satisfy my employer. Sleep had been deep. The kind of deep sleep that only comes when you know you're safe.

But then something had woken me. I had thought it was a scream, but now, as I sat in the gloom, I was starting to wonder whether it was a scream in my dream that had woken me.

My uncertainty was clarified when I heard another scream. Not so much a scream, more of a yelp. But a yelp inside—not outside. A yelp—an expression without clarity.

I grabbed for a light switch.

There was another scream. It wasn't a long and agonized scream, but it was a scream, and who am I to judge how someone should scream or what the correct form of scream is when you're in trouble?

I put on and tied my sneakers—I can't kick with bare feet—and slipped on the robe I had worn after my bath.

It was a mistake putting my light on. It ruined my night vision. I went back and clicked off the light, hoping my eyes would adjust quickly. The alternate—switching on other lights—would alert anyone in the apartment to my prowling.

I made my way through to the main area and past the kitchen. It looked as I remembered, but my eyes were still readjusting to the shock of being awake and then blinded by the light. I had a vague memory of where I had seen a knife block and made my way around the large kitchen, feeling the countertop for direction.

My hand reached a large dark lump. A dark lump with knife handles pointing toward me. I moved the block into what constituted light—sufficient light to see the block and the handles. I pulled out a knife—too short. I replaced it and took another—too big, this seemed to be more of a carving knife. I was likely to hurt myself with this thing. The third blade was not too big and not too small—the kind of knife that Goldilocks might choose when she visited the three armed bears.

I felt the grip of the handle and the weight of the knife in my hand and headed toward Clementina's room. Her father had been clear: My job was to keep Clementina and the press apart. However, I wasn't sure how the conversation would play out with him: "Sure, Zack. I heard your little girl being murdered in her bed, but you told me I was only there to keep her out of the press, so I didn't investigate. I thought it wouldn't matter if she was murdered, as long as I kept it out of the papers."

I couldn't believe there was a world in which that conversation would end well.

I couldn't believe that I could live with myself if I let that happen, so I let my feet move me silently toward the sound.

As I turned the first corner, the light became brighter. Turning the second corner, I found the source with a thin line of light pushing its way under a door. A closed door. On the other side of the door there were noises. There was movement—furniture straining, the combination of low groans and fabric stretching and rubbing that only comes with the weight of a person moving. And there was something human—almost a scream, but not quite. The sound was smaller, more frequent, and higher-pitched. It was almost the sound of an anguished cry of fear.

I had a knife and I had a clear picture of Clementina in her room, whimpering in fear.

The door was the same as the door to my suite. Solid wood. I could kick, but I was unlikely to do much more than hurt my foot. The question was whether I could kick hard enough to break the latch or break the frame. Either option was pointless since the door was likely not locked.

I tried to still my heart and slow my breathing as I felt the knife in my clammy hand. On the other side of the door, I could hear Clementina whimper and then let out a small, feminine yelp. There was furniture straining and a second voice. Lower, male, commanding.

I threw the door open.

Clementina's long blond hair was immediately recognizable in the low light of the room. I had seen enough of the back of her head to be able to recognize her on sight.

I hadn't seen her naked back before.

She was on the bed, kneeling, as far as I could tell, in an upright position. Her head flicked round and she reached down, pulling the bedding toward her naked torso. She met my eyes. There was the look of a child—a child who had been caught. Then there was recognition of whom she was looking at, and her eyes narrowed. Even in the low light I would swear her eyes turned red.

"What the fuck, Leathan?" She spat venom as she half stood, one leg on the bed, one on the floor, pulling the bedding tightly around her, revealing a naked man lying on his back.

I looked to the guy and pointed the knife at him so he knew I was talking to him. "You. Out."

He was young—early twenties and had that scrawny vibe. But there was fear in his eyes. He didn't defend Clementina or argue with me—he pushed himself away from me as I pointed.

"What the fuck, Leathan?" repeated the surly teenager.

I said nothing. Her companion said nothing as he grabbed for his clothes, not taking his gaze off the blade. He got some clothes on—if not fully buttoned and straight—within moments. I moved the hand that was pointing at him to the door, becoming aware that I was gripping the knife and my fingers were going numb.

He complied with my instructions, moving through the door, but knocking into the doorframe as he kept his eyes focused on me. Me and my knife.

"Hoffman," said Clementina.

He didn't react.

I followed him into the corridor, closing the door on Clementina and slipping the knife into my pocket, blade up.

At the door I said, "Stay there," and quickly ducked back to my room and grabbed a €50 bill. I gave it to the skinny guy, who was re-buttoning his shirt when I returned. "Cab fare."

He muttered something as he took it. He muttered with an English accent.

"Were you at Gare du Nord this afternoon?" I asked.

He nodded.

I reached for the door. "You realize this is goodbye, not au revoir."

He grunted, and I shut the door behind him.

ten

I got up slowly.

I sat on the edge of my bed and flicked on the news. In the headlines there had been a suicide bombing in the Middle East. The human tragedy was horrific, but the story soon gave way to local story about a disabled kid who had met a football player.

Satisfied that the world hadn't ended and there was no obvious expectation of the apocalypse, I showered. A long, slow shower. Why? Because I could. Technically, I was already at work. I was doing the job I was being paid to perform. And better still, I could look forward to a breakfast prepared for me by someone else and funded by our employer.

I put on a new shirt. New shirt, new underwear, new socks—old jeans, old sneakers—and headed for the kitchen. The smell of coffee reached me before I arrived.

"Good morning," said Angeline brightly. "Coffee?"

"Please," I said. "Have they got you working in the kitchen again today?"

She said something—I couldn't really make out exactly what it was. There was the word "cook"; there may have been a suggestion as to what was wrong with her and perhaps some long-term prognosis.

Angeline busied herself, and I un-busied myself, enjoying the coffee and recalling last night's incident.

"You're not my father," Clementina had shouted as I returned from showing Hoffman the door.

"And you're not my daughter," I had said. A stupid retort on my part, but I was embarrassed by then. I had misread the situation and I had overreacted. Even though I knew I had overreacted—pointing a knife at a horny guy—I didn't apologize for the intrusion into part of Clementina's life that was clearly outside of the remit described by her father. And with the age of consent being sixteen in Europe, it wasn't as if any laws had been broken.

"You don't have the right to throw him out!" she continued, still shouting.

"And yet..." I looked at the closed door.

"That's Hoffman," she said, as if everything were explained by a single name that I wasn't sure was a forename or a surname.

But now it was morning. I had calmed down. I had realized my overreaction. I had slept. Now it was time for me to be the adult and to apologize.

"What time does Clementina usually get up?" I asked Angeline.

The housekeeper hesitated.

"Angeline?"

"She's not here," said Angeline.

It was my turn to hesitate. "What do you mean?" I asked.

"She's not here," repeated Angeline.

"When did she leave?"

"She wasn't here when I arrived."

"When was that?" I asked. "When did you arrive?"

"Six."

"Six AM?"

Angeline nodded as I started to count the ways I had messed up things last night.

eleven

The morning had a chill.

Not unpleasant, but enough to let you know that the sun had only just turned up at work and hadn't had its first cup of coffee. Enough to let you know that you didn't want to stand still and that if the wind did blow, then it would be cold.

I had the same options I had last time I left the apartment looking for Clementina—head toward the park or on the streets. I made the same assessment I had made before: I took the streets, although saying streets implies something gritty, grimy, and urban. In reality, taking the streets meant walking through one of Paris's more genteel residential districts, looking at the kind of properties that attract another zero on their rent.

The area had been outside of Paris when Baron Haussmann began his major urban renovations and so had avoided the recon-struction and imposition of uniformity that much of the rest of the city had seen. In some ways this was good—there was an interesting mix of architecture—but in other ways this was bad; some of that mix of architecture should have been demolished.

In Haussmannian Paris, I would be walking between solid walls where each apartment block joined the next, with stores on the ground floor and apartments on the next six floors. Here it was different. To my right, there was a rare sight for Paris—a house. A single dwelling—three stories, two of yellow stone and the third in the slate-covered mansard roof—not attached to any surrounding building. In the suburbs, a detached house wouldn't be uncommon, but in the city it was a rarity.

Across from it was a 1950s apartment block. It was ugly. I knew it was someone's baby once, but this block was ugly. Set over four floors with off-white stone and brown detailing, it had clearly once been intended as a sleek, sophisticated residential block. The intention hadn't come to fruition, and the block just looked shabby now.

The next block echoed the detached house, although it was an apartment block. Like the house, it had three floors—two with yellowed stone and black ironwork detailing, and the third floor in the slate-covered mansard roof with dormer windows poking out under the cover of an arced roof over them.

Unlike much of the rest of the city, these blocks were set back from the sidewalk, with a small strip of land to the front giving some distance and a black ironwork fence demarcating the line between public and private. As if to reinforce the message, thick trees and bushes were grown on the border, ensuring anyone on the inside was unaware of anyone on the outside.

The further I walked, the more disconnected I became. Each street was different, but rarely with sufficient character to be memorable. Each street was quiet—seemingly this wasn't the place where human beings congregated. It seemed accepted that the purpose of these streets was to act as an open-air parking lot, but occasionally there were streets that seemed to have been given over to the tedious business of driving.

Driving.

I pulled out my phone and called Reece. "I'll be back in five—can you meet me at the apartment?"

"Sure," said the driver and hung up.

twelve

"Good news, bad news," I said to Reece.

The driver sat with a coffee in front of him and said nothing, waiting.

"I'm hired; she's done a runner."

"Well, let's get out there," said Reece, standing and moving toward the door.

"Sit down," I said, remaining still until the driver relented and returned his seat at the counter. "That was my reaction, and I've just wasted ten minutes outside, achieving nothing apart from looking at a bunch of buildings and letting my mind think, 'She could be in there, or there...or there, or there, or there.'"

Reece nodded, seemingly understanding my basic point.

"It's pointless looking on the street—she's been gone for at least three hours. Just think about the search radius."

"She won't have gone..." began Reece before stopping himself. "You're right, she could be out of the country by now."

"Good news, bad news," I said, laying my phone on the counter.

Reece frowned.

"Good news, Mister Norden. The paparazzi don't think Clementina's in Paris. Bad news: They've just seen her landing in Moscow."

"You don't think?" asked Reece.

"That she's gone to Moscow? No. That was just..."

Reece stopped me. "You don't think she's left the country."

"I doubt it, but hold that thought," I said.

I turned and walked down the broad passage. The passage I had walked last night with a knife in my hand. Clementina's door was shut. I knocked, counted to ten, and then entered. The room was as it had been last night, but without a naked teenager having sex with her boyfriend. I ignored most of the room, looking at the flat surfaces. I saw what I was hoping to see on her nightstand—a trailing piece of wire.

At one end, the wire reached a transformer plugged into the wall. Following the twisted and knotted wire in the other direction, I found a small plug. The kind of plug that fits into the bottom of a phone to recharge it.

"She's still in the country and she hasn't gone far," I said to Reece as I got back to the kitchen.

"How do you know that?"

"She's left her phone charger."

"If you know that, then shouldn't we go and look for her?" asked Reece.

"Three points," I said. "First, she'll be back. When her phone runs out—when she thinks her phone is going to run out, she'll be back."

Reece wasn't convinced.

"Second, we have to be careful about how we find her. We found her yesterday when she posted a photo with a GPS tag." Reece nodded, and I continued. "We can be lucky once in finding her. We can be lucky twice. But by the third time, she'll realize what's going on, and if she knows how we can find her, then she'll behave differently, and we won't be able to find her when it matters."

"Doesn't it matter now?"

"No—we know she'll be back, because she's left the charger, and there's a third reason we're not going out." Reece's brow creased as he waited for me to explain. "Since I'm hired, I'd better understand all this stuff that Clementina uses. Give me her phone number and tell me what apps I need to install on my phone."

I spent the next ten minutes loading apps and drinking coffee, listening as Reece tried to explain.

"I know what these apps are called," I said. "What I'm trying to understand is how Clementina uses them."

Reece stopped trying to explain.

"So she's got text messaging on her phone, but she also uses this app because the cool kids use it because it avoids charges for SMS messages. It's not that she needs to avoid the charges; it's that she wants to be linked to people who don't want to pay the charges, and it's a way to include a group of people in a conversation."

There seemed to be a new understanding crossing Reece's face.

"And we can't access these messages because they're not public."

"That's right," said Reece.

"So it's of little use to us."

Reece shrugged defensively.

"Same with the disappearing photo thing."

Reece looked blankly.

"The messages aren't public, so let's not bother."

Reece considered the point, then seemed to accede.

"That leaves the three main social media apps. The first does short messages and images, and I can follow her, although she can block me."

I created an account in the name leathanwhoissorry. "I've created an account," I said to the driver. "Leathan who is sorry. All one word, no spaces."

"Are you sorry?"

"Not the point—I'm trying to turn down the temperature." I looked at the screen. "Holy heck! She's got thousands of followers."

Reece nodded wearily. "A lot of followers and sore thumbs."

"You're right—she posted hundreds of messages yesterday. Whole conversations about which earrings and which necklace she should buy." I found a post with a picture, a selfie. In the background, I recognized the person. He was out of focus, he was only half in the shot, like a bad photobomber, but he was me. "This was yesterday. All the time we were in the store, she was posting publicly."

Reece had that I-told-you-so look about him.

"You're telling me this is how the paparazzi found us."

Reece nodded wearily. Weary seemed to be his default emotion. "There are only a few photos there—try that other photo sharing app."

I opened the app, created an account for leathanwhoissorry, and followed Clementina's account. "Is there a photo from yesterday that she didn't post?" I asked, looking through all the selfies she took as she tried the jewels and the pictures of the various pieces that she had set on the counter.

I liked, liked again, favorited, liked a bit more, put a friend request in to another social media channel, and then sat back. "And now we wait. She'll see my name is there. It's her turn."

"Couldn't we call her?" asked Reece.

"Not now," I said. "I've let her know—on her terms—that I'm here. Now we can wait."

thirteen

I spent the next fifteen minutes watching as Clementina posted messages to her friends and followers.

I couldn't differentiate which were friends and which were total strangers. She seemed to treat everyone as if they were personal confidants she had known forever. Everyone was treated with love and respect.

As much love and respect as you can deliver in 140 characters with a bunch of emojis.

And with the constant flow, there was not one single photo. Not one single GPS tag or any hint of where she might be.

A phone chirruped. A single chirrup, and then stopped. Angeline Bautista rushed in, scraping her feet across the leather as she slowed before picking up the handset for the hidden phone. "Bonjour," she said in her mangled French. "Okay...okay...okay..." She hung up and then disappeared.

There was the sound of the front door closing, and a few moments later two sets of footsteps appeared. I didn't look around as I continued to watch the stream of posts from Clementina.

"He's for you," said Angeline, switching to English.

It took me a few seconds to recognize the skinny young man standing next to Angeline. The first time I had seen him, he had wrapped himself around Clementina near the Eurostar arrivals at Gare du Nord. The next time I saw him, he was lying on his back, naked, under Clementina, who as far as I could tell was also naked. The last time I saw him, I was throwing him out of the apartment.

"Hi," he said hesitantly. "I think we got off on the wrong foot. I'm Hoffman, Nat Hoffman." He held out a thin arm, offering to shake my hand. His other arm crossed his body, gripping the strap of the courier bag across his shoulder.

"Leathan Wilkey," I said, accepting the shake. "Pleased to meet you Nat."

"Hoffman. My friends call me Hoffman."

"Pleased to meet you, Hoffman," I said. "Come and sit down."

I showed him toward the main space of the room, pointing at the two large, curved sofas. He walked in front of me, allowing me to give Reece a wink and throw my head toward the door. Reece took the hint and left, taking his coffee with him, but not before mouthing, "Who is he?"

Hoffman sat without further invitation—the leather of his jacket squeaking against the leather of the sofa. He seemed unfazed by the detritus that had been left on the tables by Zackary Norden: a briefcase, papers, files, and a laptop.

"I wanted to say sorry for last night," said Hoffman, drawing my attention back to him.

"It's me who should be apologizing," I said. "I reacted...more than I should have done. I'm sorry."

"No problem," said Hoffman. His face dropped. "I'm sorry to ask this, but I left a sock. I was wondering if I could get it." He lifted his right leg and pulled up the hem of his jeans to reveal a sneaker worn without a sock.

"Do you want to come and look?" I said, standing.

Hoffman looked uncertain. "I know this sounds wrong...but it wouldn't feel right, going into Clementina's room without asking her. I know it's silly, but would you mind—or perhaps the maid?" His eyes looked past me as if searching out Angeline.

"I'll do it," I said. Clearly this was my penance for last night.

I returned to Clementina's room. The door was open; Angeline had stripped the bed. "Have you found a sock that doesn't belong to Clementina?" I asked.

Angeline's eyes went to three piles of fabric. I guessed lights, darks, and delicates. She scrunched her lips.

"I get it," I said. "Thanks anyway."

When I got back to Hoffman, he was standing by the kitchen, gripping his messenger bag. It was as if he were leaving.

"I'm sorry," I lied. "I can't find it."

"That's not a problem," said Hoffman. "I probably dropped it on my way out. I left in a bit of a rush." He smiled widely, trying to encourage some humor. "Thanks for looking; I'll be off now."

"Clementina's got your number?" I asked as he reached the door. He nodded.

"We'll call you if you we find it," I said, shaking his hand.

I shut the door on him, then dashed to my room to grab my jacket.

fourteen

It was the same dilemma I had each time I left the apartment block: streets or park. Previously, I had been looking for Clementina, but now I had to figure whether Hoffman had followed the streets or whether he had ducked into the park.

I guessed streets and jogged away from the apartment, careful to minimize the sound of my feet so I didn't alert Hoffman. Hoffman, the guy I had thrown out last night when I caught him having sex with my client's daughter. Hoffman, the guy who had come to that girlfriend's home this morning but didn't ask to see her.

Hoffman, who knew where Clementina was.

After ninety seconds or so, I hadn't seen Hoffman, so I spun and ran back in the other direction, passing the apartment before dropping into Jardins du Ranelagh. For all the green of the open space and the trees—the regimented trees standing in line—the park was noisier than the street with the broad roads crossing it. The rumble of traffic covered the sound of my feet as I picked up my pace, and within a few strides I had Hoffman in my sights.

He wasn't moving quickly, so I dropped back to a walking pace and found he was still moving slower than me. He stuck to the paved track, allowing me to duck behind the row of trees, keeping myself out of sight in case he looked back, which so far he hadn't.

Clementina might've thought he was great, but he didn't seem to be the smartest about not picking up a tail.

The messenger bag he had in the apartment was still slung across his chest. He seemed more concerned with it than he should have been. I thought the point of a messenger bag was you could sling it across your shoulder and forget it, but Hoffman seemed to be constantly fiddling with the strap that crossed his chest and back diagonally, and his hand kept dropping to the pouch as if the weight of the bag was insufficient to confirm that his cargo was still in place. Even keeping his grip on the messenger bag, he still managed to hold his phone to his ear with his other hand.

The route Hoffman was following was familiar and somewhat ironic. It was exactly the route I had followed yesterday when I was looking for Clementina, only to find that she had gone to meet Hoffman at Gare du Nord.

We reached the six-way junction, and Hoffman went straight. I felt like trotting up to tell him that the Metro would shortly be on the right, but there was clearly no need: Hoffman ducked into the building on the corner between the two streets meeting at forty-five degrees.

A café.

The café's signage was written in an Art Deco, Parisian-style font, and underneath a broad glass awning stretched out to shelter the customers who sat outside the café. A row of potted plants formed a wall separating customers from passing pedestrians who didn't have the benefit of the glass awning. Hoffman turned and sat in the row of seats against the café's window and facing out onto the street. As he settled himself and leaned back into his seat, I could see his companion: Clementina.

After the kind of greeting that only people who have just started having sex indulge in, he pulled open his messenger bag, flipped the flap, and showed her its contents. She smiled and threw her arms around his neck again, pulling him tightly toward her.

I pulled out my phone and searched for the number Reece had given me. When she released him, I called Clementina. Instinctively, her attention dropped from Hoffman and focused on her phone. She looked at the screen; there was a tilt of her head—a minor discombobulation as she was faced with a number that was unfamiliar to her. Was it someone new and interesting or was it a telemarketer?

"Hello," she said, choosing English.

"It's Leathan," I said.

"Leathan who is even more sorry now that I won't talk to him," she said and hung up.

She put the phone down on the table in front of her and returned her attention to Hoffman. I called again. She picked up the phone, looked to see who was calling, and with a single swipe sent me to voicemail before returning the phone to the table.

fifteen

"You've got a problem with your phone," I said. "It seems to cut out midway through calls."

Clementina looked up and sneered without saying anything.

Hoffman was lost. He wasn't sure how he should be reacting— should he be taking the lead or should he wait for his girlfriend to give him the signal? His head turned, looking to Clementina, then back to me, returning to Clementina.

As Hoffman's head turned back to me, I snapped my fingers, then pointed away from us with my thumb. Hoffman got the hint and disappeared, dragging his messenger bag with him. His phone was to his ear before I let my gaze drop. "See, I'm kind," I said, taking Hoffman's seat next to Clementina. "I've saved you the trouble of getting your phone fixed, and I've got rid of that annoying boy. That's two favors for you, and you haven't even said good morning."

She grunted. She desperately wanted to be that surly teenager, but she just couldn't quite pull it off. Maybe she was pleased to see Hoffman go, maybe she was embarrassed about being found, or maybe she knew that the subject of her disappearance was likely to come up—I couldn't tell. All I could tell was she wanted to be annoyed, but something was distracting her.

"How did you find me?" she asked.

I saw the waitress taking an order from the customers two tables down. "Café, s'il vous plaît," I mouthed. The waitress smiled, nodding her affirmation. I turned back to Clementina. "I'm sorry, you had a question."

"How did you find me? Have you been tracking me?"

"No." I let my denial hang and counted to ten before I elaborated. "Your boyfriend came to the apartment with some stupid story about losing a sock, and then he didn't ask to see you. There was only one reason he wouldn't ask to see you at home."

Clementina flushed.

"I followed him, and here we are."

She had the look of someone who didn't want to believe she had been tripped up so easily. It was too easy, and she was too sophisticated. "Really?"

"Really," I said.

"You didn't track me?"

"No," I said, feeling the edge of my mouth twitch. "Yesterday we tracked you—that was how we found you at Gare du Nord—but not today."

Her face showed conflicting emotions—she wanted to be angry that she had been tracked, albeit yesterday, and yet she wanted to hide for having been caught so easily. I faked a smile. "A big happy reunion. I can stop sending you messages on social media."

"Yeah, about that," she said.

"You don't need to say it. We're here; we're talking. I'll make you a promise..." I had her attention. "You agree to answer the phone when I call—and to talk with me—and I'll agree never to contact you on social media, ever. I'll delete the accounts here and now if you'll agree."

"Get deleting, tracker-boy," she said.

"And about that tracking..."

She grunted.

"You'd be doing us all a great favor if you'd turn off the GPS on your phone."

She narrowed her eyes—more confusion about the point I was making rather than aggression.

"If you turn off the GPS, then any photo you take won't have the location embedded. No location, no paparazzi following you. No papara... No paps and your dad will be happy...with me, at least."

She stared at me. Staring as if by staring hard enough she'd be able to see the angle she was sure I was playing. Her stare was interrupted by the waitress bringing my coffee.

"Think about this," I said. "If you turn off your GPS, then I won't be able to track you." There was a slow realization, and she tried not to show the smile that was spreading across her face. "Phone. Settings. GPS. Off."

She picked up her phone, looked to the screen, and then looked back to me. Something in her look told me she was sure this was a trap.

"If I'm messing with you, then you can turn it back on, right?"

She shrugged and started tapping her phone. "There. Done." She held the screen toward me as if to prove the point.

"Thank you," I said. "And I really am sorry about last night. I overreacted."

She half shrugged, half smirked—it was as if she took pleasure in my discomfort. She mumbled something. I think she said, "That's alright."

"I did apologize to Hoffman."

"Why?"

"I threw him out, remember? Having waved a knife at him."

"You gave him fifty euros, that was enough apology," she said. "We were...finished," she flushed and looked away, "and then he got paid. That was the best night of his life. Ever. You made him an outlaw hero in his own mind."

"Well, I'm sorry about that too," I said. "But are we friends again?"

"Again?" She was enjoying the tease.

"Are we cool?"

"I am."

I waited.

"Relax," she said. "Everything is fine. You don't need to worry."

"If everything is fine, will you come back with me? Your father left his stuff lying around..."

"He does," she cut across me. "You'll find out—he's the messy teenager, I'm the tidy adult."

"It looks like work stuff, so I'm guessing that he'll come back for it sometime."

"Sometime when he's finished with her, you mean," said Clementina.

"And when he comes back, I'd like to be able to tell him that I know where you are. Better still, I'd like you next to me so that he can see I've been keeping the paparazzi away from you."

She hesitated.

"When did you last charge your phone?" I asked.

She looked at the screen and grimaced. "Okay, but only because I need a charge." She became serious. "But you've got to promise not to mention Hoffman—not last night, not today. I'm still daddy's little girl."

"I'm here to keep the paps away from you. As long as Hoffman doesn't sell you out, then I've got no need to tell your dad."

She listened, weighing the implications of what I was saying.

"There's no problem with Hoffman."

"Good," I said. "I'll finish my coffee, and I'm sure you've got people you need to message. Once we're both sorted, then let's go back."

sixteen

"Daddy bear!"

Clementina rushed forward and wrapped her arms around her father. The confident young adult had transformed herself into a slightly needy child. A slightly needy child who I suspected was expert at being needy in order to manipulate her father for her own ends.

In the café she had been sharp, witty, looking to get what she wanted. In the apartment with her father, she was now the wide-eyed child cooing at her father and not expressing any opinions about what she wanted.

Zackary Norden met my gaze as his daughter released him from her embrace, but still clung to his arm as if he were her teddy. "We just went out for some air," I said, giving him a reassuring nod to confirm that everything was alright.

Norden was wearing a three-piece suit, although he had removed his jacket and laid it over the sofa on the right. The suit was a conservative shade of dark blue with the usual giveaway that it was tailored: no belt loops; a belt being unnecessary if the suit fits, and this did indeed fit.

I suspected his tie was a gift from the new woman in his life. An attempt to both mark her territory and reinforce what she saw as his personality. To me it looked like someone had eaten a child's coloring set and then vomited over a piece of silk. It was a mishmash of orange, brown, purple, and pink, with some lime green streaks to add to the seasickness.

Clementina must have seen where I was looking. "Is this new, daddy bear?"

"Mmm." He seemed embarrassed.

"Was it a present?" she asked slowly, but with just the slightest hint of tease.

He snorted. "No problems last night?" he asked, looking directly to me.

"None," I said.

"What did you get up to?" He had turned to his little girl, still hanging on his arm.

"We stayed in," she said. "Leathan makes the best—I mean *the best*—pancakes. So thin. So delicate."

"So I've hired another cook," muttered her father.

"No, daddy bear. These were the best pancakes."

"So no problems? No one came? Nothing happened?" His tone was flat, and he was trying to focus his attention toward me.

"No, daddy. We had pancakes. We chatted, then I had an early night."

Norden stared straight at me.

"I turned in not long after," I said.

"Have you seen my laptop?" His tone was businesslike. He pointed to the pile of files and papers scattered across the tables between the two sofas. "It was here when I left."

I didn't want to tell him it had been there this morning when Hoffman arrived.

"Have you lost your laptop again, daddy bear?" asked Clementina. "I think we need to have a search for the laptop." She released his arm and dropped to her knees, looking under the sofa. "Are you under there, laptop?" She crawled to the other sofa. "What about under here?"

Norden sighed.

Clementina stood up and lightly called, "Ninety-nine, one hundred. Coming ready or not! I'm going to find you, you naughty laptop." She then lightly skipped toward her bedroom.

"What's on the laptop?" I asked.

Norden hesitated. "The deal."

"What's on the laptop?" I asked again.

Norden scratched his head, a slight flush of color showing through his thinning hair. He looked straight at me and grimaced.

"Please tell me that it's encrypted."

"Of course," he said, "all computers are."

I felt sick. "No. Most computers aren't encrypted. Many have a password when you log in, but not encryption."

Norden looked at me blankly.

"If someone can get past your password—which, having worked with journalists, I know is quite simple most of the time—is the data on the machine encrypted? Or will anyone who can break your password be able to read everything that's there?"

Norden's color seemed to be fading, to be replaced by a ghostly white skin tone.

When I spoke, I kept my voice soft. "Please tell me your password isn't Clementina."

seventeen

I invited Zackary Norden to sit on the large leather sofa opposite me and leaned forward so I could keep my voice lower.

"Do you have people who handle this sort of thing?" I asked.

The color was still missing from Norden's face. When the color went, it seemed to have taken his ability to think. "What sort of thing?"

"Theft," I said. "Let's call it theft for the moment." Norden looked like I had punched him. "The theft of your laptop." He winced as if a second blow had landed. "Your laptop containing details of the deal you are working on that you are so keen to keep hidden from public view." He was punch-drunk from this third blow. "The laptop also containing other material—as yet unspecified, but I'm sure we'll be able to specify it quite well when it hits the internet and the papers report it." That was the knockout blow; Norden was on the canvas, and the referee was counting.

I sat back and waited, silently counting to ten. Norden was knocked out; I was declared the winner, but I was wounded. I had come into the ring wounded—wounded by my opponent's daughter. And those wounds left me vulnerable.

I had left London when I upset, to put it mildly, some Bulgarian people traffickers. Since then, I had been moving around Europe like a student with an InterRail ticket, staying in cities across the continent for a few days before moving on. From a practical perspective, the constant movement made me as close to untraceable as it was possible to be without dropping off the grid completely and living in the woods eating leaves and berries.

I thought I had reasoned with Clementina and shown her some good faith. I thought that by agreeing to cover for her nocturnal activities with Hoffman, it might build some level of trust between us. But in practice I provided an alibi for the guy who probably stole the computer.

I had become part of the crime.

And if I ended up in a French jail—accused of theft of industrial secrets—then it wouldn't be difficult for the Bulgarians to find someone to pay me a visit and return their thanks for breaking up their London prostitution business.

"Do you trust the people around you?" I asked.

Norden looked up, thinking.

"Are they competent? Can they maintain secrecy?"

Norden nodded. A cautious nod. More of an acknowledgement that he had heard and understood the question, rather than a suggestion that he was offering a definitive answer.

"Or is there a prince who thinks he should be king? Is there a lieutenant looking for advancement?" I asked. "I met your two guys—McElroy and Mallet—they both seem ambitious and unable to see the limit of their competence. That's a dangerous combination. They may not achieve their ambition, but they can damage you, fatally, and then let you take the fall."

Norden had the look of a man who was beginning to understand the point I was making, but he seemed to want more ammunition to convince himself. Maybe the earlier blows had sapped his energy?

"You talk to McElroy and Mallet—you say, 'Boys, my laptop has been stolen.' You've just lost face in front of them, right? Even if the laptop turns up without their involvement, you've exposed a personal failure and you've given them a get-out-of-jail-free card they can play in the future."

Norden nodded reluctantly.

"Take it further. You say, 'Boys, my laptop had something super-secret sitting on the hard drive.' What's their reaction? Are they really going to say, 'Sure, boss, we'll cover that for you...we don't need any reward for that'?"

Norden sighed, the sigh interspersed with silent curses.

"There is another option," I said.

I had Norden's attention.

I half-snorted. "I say option... Is it still an option if it's the only course open to you?"

I paused, letting the thought sink in.

"At the moment, I'm the only person you can trust."

Norden frowned.

"This was clearly a theft by someone you know."

He frowned harder.

"Was the door forced? Did they come in through the window?"

The frown relaxed.

"You've taken up references on me—you know I've got experience of looking into things—and until thirty-six hours ago when I got the call, I didn't know about you. So I didn't have time to plan this thing."

He exhaled, thinking. A finger raised to his mouth, and he bit his knuckle.

"I say I'm the only option—there is another choice," I said.

He lifted his eyebrows, holding his knuckle away from his mouth.

"You try and handle this yourself and let it all go to shit." I paused. "If you want to do that, then I'll leave now." I stood up.

Norden waved me down again.

"My fee is doubled," I said. "I need you to take this seriously— and I need you to know that I'm taking it seriously. But I'm not going to bankrupt you over it."

He shrugged like his teenage daughter. If he'd said "whatever," I wouldn't have been surprised.

"Everyone needs to think I'm still watching over Clementina."

He did that frowning thing again.

"Do you want to say, 'Hey! I've lost my laptop, and you're all suspects. Leathan's investigating'?"

He smiled sheepishly. "No." He looked up. "And you'll still keep the paparazzi away?"

"Yeah. I'll keep an eye on her," I said. "But you need to understand that I'm going to break things. You know the person who did this—you just don't know which of all the people you know did this. I'm going to have to upset people to get answers."

"Upset away," said the man who had just agreed to double my wages so I could keep myself out of jail.

eighteen

The bed had been made. The piles of laundry had gone, and beyond the obvious, the room looked tidier. I hadn't cataloged the untidiness when I spoke with Angeline, but it seemed that a layer of teenage detritus had been removed and a certain structure had been applied to that which was left.

Clementina sat, messing up the freshly made bed, focusing on her phone, tapping away intently and, like a car windshield wiper, brushing away her hair as it kept falling across her eyes. Apparently it was too much effort to cross the room and pick up one of the many, many hair things to hold her hair. There was a phone that required her full attention, and while it required her full attention she would give it that attention, even if there was a benefit to spending ten seconds tying her hair back. During those ten seconds of inattention, something might happen, and she might miss out.

"Congratulations," I said, stepping into the room. "You played me. You won."

She didn't look up from her phone. The frowning became deeper as she stared at the screen, but the tapping seemed to have lost some intensity.

"What have you got me into?"

"Huh?" She didn't look up.

I grabbed her phone and in a single movement, without looking at the screen, put the device in my pocket.

"Hey!" she said, her face showing something between shock and anger.

"Please don't tell daddy about Hoffman," I said in my best annoying baby voice before continuing in a more measured tone. "Hoffman who stole your father's laptop."

"No he didn't."

I sighed. "It was there on the table this morning. Hoffman sat next to it while we talked."

She showed no emotion.

"This is the same Hoffman who didn't ask about you," I continued. "Hoffman who walked straight from here to the café where you were waiting, with the laptop in the bag over his shoulder."

Her face had fixed a sneer.

"When he got to the café, he showed you the laptop in his bag."

"There was no laptop in there," Clementina said.

"Don't give me that."

"Did you see it?" she asked. "If you saw the laptop—if you saw Hoffman with the laptop that you say he took, then why didn't you stop him?" Even behind the sneer, she couldn't hide her pleasure at a well-deployed piece of logic.

"You're a spoiled little rich girl. If daddy's deal falls apart..."

"I'll be poor and on the street," she said, forced melodrama in her voice.

My tone was more measured when I continued. "It's daddy's money that lets you buy whatever you want, and because of daddy's money buying all this stuff, people are interested in you. Take away the money and they won't be interested in you."

She went to argue but held herself back, eventually whispering mostly for herself, "You're wrong."

"So where's Hoffman now?" I asked. "We need to get this laptop back."

"I don't know where he is," she said. "He's not picking up. He hasn't responded." Her upset refocused from the person ignoring her to the person holding her phone hostage, and her eyes narrowed. "And then someone took my phone away."

nineteen

"What do you mean, *not responding?*"

Clementina looked up from her phone that I had returned to her, drew on everything she had learned about sarcasm in her seventeen years, and focused on me, saying nothing but letting her visage communicate everything.

"Why have we got a problem?" I asked as Clementina returned her attention to her phone. "You saw Hoffman thirty minutes ago—I was there. I sent him away."

"There are rules," she said. "I call, he answers."

"And yet," I mumbled.

She drew her gaze away from her phone again and began talking as if she was the teacher in the remedial class. "I know you're not a creep like Reece." She paused. "But look." Her hand motioned toward herself, drawing my gaze to look at her face and then to slip lower down. "I am his Everest—there is no *up* from here."

"But isn't there something in this relationship for you?" I said. "I mean—he *is* Hoffman."

Her focus was back on her phone.

"You've fooled me twice," I said. "I'm really not keen on being fooled for a third time."

She put down her phone, exaggerating a sigh. "This is serious, Leathan. Hoffman doesn't just disappear. He lacks the creativity to think about disappearing."

She saw the incredulity cross my face.

"Hoffman is Hoffman. Something is wrong and you need to help me—I need to find Hoffman."

I let her think I was considering her instruction, which she probably thought was a request. When I spoke, my tone was soft, conspiratorial. "Then we're going without Reece."

She narrowed her eyes and waited for my elaboration. When it didn't come, there was a brief pause before she relaxed, a wicked grin spreading across her face. I hadn't said anything, but she had invented her own reasons.

"You also need to make yourself look as unlike you as possible." This time I explained. "We don't want you recognized while we're looking for Hoffman."

twenty

Clementina looked older and somehow more sophisticated without makeup or jewelry. While the end result of the application of makeup looked comparatively natural, the process of applying a synthetic foundation and then emphasizing and exaggerating before hanging a few pieces of expensive metal and precious gems detracted.

Without makeup, you could see that she was a good-looking girl with near-perfect skin that, quite literally, glowed. She wore jeans and a T-shirt, similar to what she had worn yesterday morning, but these were different jeans and a different T-shirt—inconspicuous jeans, apparently. The kind of jeans you can get anywhere.

Anywhere if you were prepared to pay $500 for a pair of jeans with a label that sounded Italian.

Her jacket was the same black leather jacket she had worn when we visited Rue de la Paix. It might have been fashioned in a style reminiscent of a biker's jacket, but the leather was the softest leather I had ever touched. "People know I never wear scarves," she had said, wrapping a gauzy piece of varying shades of tan, brown, taupe, and olive around her neck. "They're just so boho."

Her hair was pulled back in a ponytail. Not a simple ponytail pulling the strands of her long hair together. This began just above the meridian of her skull, so the ponytail arced out of the back of her head.

"Incognito," I said, still wondering how she had a scarf in her possession even though she professed not to wear scarves.

"When was I last in the papers with a ponytail?" she responded, ending the discussion. All that was necessary before we left was for me to find a key to get back in. Sure, we could knock, but I wanted to know that we could at least attempt to return without everyone recording our every movement.

We returned to the café on the corner and took a different table—still outside under the fixed glass awning, and next to the row of potted shrubs. I wanted to sit at 90 degrees to her so I could see her reactions when we talked. I wasn't convinced that I could read her, but I was sure I would see something in her reaction if I paid attention.

The waitress looked at us, recognizing and remembering us, and still not quite believing we were the same people who had been there so recently.

"This is where you last saw Hoffman," I said.

"Yeah. You know that—you were here, you sent him away, and you've been with me since then."

I let it pass. "Less than an hour ago."

She nodded.

"And you don't know where he is?"

She had a pained look as if to say: "Really? You're *really* going to ask me that?" Just the sort of reaction I would give in the hope of getting away with a lie—imply the lie, but don't say it. In some rulebook that gets you fewer black marks.

"You're convinced he's gone?"

"Are you going to ask me stupid questions all morning or are you going to help me find him like you said you would?" she snapped. Snapping is good—people tend to tell the truth when they snap, or at least they lie less.

The waitress seemed to be hanging back—unwilling to walk into the middle of an argument. I turned to her, "A coffee for me, please." I looked at Clementina. "Coffee?"

She nodded.

"Croissants?"

Another nod—this more vigorous, bouncing her ponytail.

"Two coffees and three croissants," I said to the waitress. She smiled and departed swiftly, clearly keen to avoid any further arguments.

"Three croissants?" asked Clementina.

"One each and I'll fight you for the third," I said.

She shrugged and looked away, her eyes lazily scanning the street with the morning traffic heading toward the center of Paris. "I thought we were going to—you know—*do* something," she said. "When you told me not to look like me, I thought that meant we were going somewhere."

"We are doing something and we have gone somewhere," I said. "We've come to the last place where you saw Hoffman, and we're going to talk."

She seemed unconvinced.

"We're going to talk, and we're going to hope that Hoffman doesn't do anything stupid in the time it takes you to come up with the truth—or at least something approaching the truth."

Her eyes narrowed.

"Can we just get past this?" I said. "You're not going to tell me that everything you have told me has been the truth, the whole truth, and nothing but the truth, so help you God?"

The side of her mouth twitched, and her eyes brightened. She looked down, dropping my gaze.

"Why did Hoffman go back to the apartment?" I asked.

"To get his sock." She was still looking down into her lap.

"Now the truth," I said.

"To try and do something to get you fired." She looked up. Like her makeup, all emotion had been wiped from her face. "He hoped he might get a picture of you pissing in a plant pot or have you admit something while he was recording you…"

"He recorded the conversation?"

"Oh yeah."

"Does your father know Hoffman?"

The tightening around her eyes said no.

"Know of?"

The slight relaxation in the muscles. "Maybe."

"Maybe?"

"I met Hoffman at something daddy bear made me go to."

"What?"

"I don't know. It was at the Opera House."

"Which opera house?"

"London," she said. "Covent Garden."

"You met Hoffman at the opera?"

"No. We met at the Opera House. It was some function—someone gave daddy bear a big award for being a big successful finance-whatever-he-is; he begged me to come."

I tried not to smirk. "When you say 'begged,' you mean he bribed you?"

"I had to look the part," she said defensively.

I was letting myself get sidetracked. "You looked the part. You turned up and Hoffman was there?"

She nodded as the waitress returned with our coffee and croissants, placing them on the table before quickly retreating.

"Why was Hoffman there?"

"Have you ever met people?" said Clementina incredulously. "You don't meet someone for the first time and say 'Why are you here?' You say, 'Hi, I'm Clemmy, pleased to meet you.'"

"So you said, 'Hi, I'm Clemmy.' He said, 'Yo, I'm Hoffman.' Then what did he say?"

"Not much."

"Something must have happened," I said.

"We had sex." She shrugged her left shoulder, fixing her gaze on me, defying me to react.

"There?"

"Not there, on the spot where we met... In the bathroom." She said it matter-of-factly. I tried not to let my face show any reaction and waited. She cracked first. "It was so boring, and he was the only other person under the age of ninety-five."

"The bathroom?" I asked.

"The disabled one," she said with a tone that suggested there was a significance to the choice of venue, but that the act itself was an everyday occurrence.

"But your father wanted you—begged you—to be there?"

"And I was, but that bloody secretary was all over daddy bear."

"Moving past that night," I said, pulling off a claw from the first croissant, "what does your father think about the nature of your relationship with Hoffman?"

"He doesn't know, and anyway there's not much he could say. He's screwing a twenty-five-year-old who's had a bad boob job and has got inflamed scars around her nipples. I've never done the parenting thing, but he's not really taking high moral ground, is he, Leathan?"

I didn't want to say she was in the right, but looked at from her perspective, I could see how her actions—or more accurately, her reactions—weren't as crazy as they might seem. Caught between two warring parents; treated simultaneously like an adult and a child; forced to make an appearance and then be ignored. She might have money, but I could see that Hoffman could be an answer.

"What does Hoffman think about your father?" I tried.

"It's weird," she said. "He knows so much about him."

I waited.

"He says he reads it in the papers."

"Hoffman didn't seem the sort of newspaper-reading type to me," I said.

"What do you want me to say?" asked Clementina. "He gets the information somewhere, and daddy bear is Hoffman's hero, apparently."

I took a sip of coffee. "How would you usually contact Hoffman?"

Clementina sighed and exaggerated the roll of her eyes as she held up her phone.

"You call?"

"Duh."

"Text?"

"What is this newfangled technology you talk of?" she said flatly.

"Just text or do you use one of those apps?"

She unlocked the screen and pointed to an app.

"Social media?"

She pointed to three apps.

"Messaging?"

Another app.

"Video call?"

She pointed to two apps.

"You use all of those to speak with Hoffman?"

She narrowed her eyes. "What are you asking, Leathan?"

"That's a lot of apps," I said. "Couldn't he have missed you?"

She shook her head. "You asked me what apps we use—we use all of those. Usually it's text. I texted him. He hasn't replied. That is a problem."

twenty-one

"Technically the Eiffel Tower is on the Left Bank. Technically Napoleon's tomb is on the Left Bank...."

"I get it," Clementina snapped. "The Left Bank is a big place, and you were a suck-up in geography."

We leaned against the balustrades, our backs to the river, watching the heavy traffic thunder past—two lanes in each direction, with scooters leading the charge each time the lights turned green.

"You said Hoffman liked it here on the Left Bank."

"Liked?" She twisted her lip and gave a small shake of her head. "He talked about...mentioned...the Left Bank. You know, intellectuals in cafés smoking dreadful cigarettes without filters while they talked about philosophy and drank coffee. That was pretty much it."

"Did he come here?" I asked.

She pushed out her bottom lip.

"Did he say he liked anything here?"

"I don't know," she said defensively.

"Did he say he wanted to see anything here?"

"Stop, Leathan. Just stop. Stop now. I don't know, so why do you keep hassling me?"

I waited a moment, letting my thoughts become crushed by the onslaught of traffic. Keeping my voice as soft as I could while making sure I was heard, I asked, "What is Hoffman into?"

Clementina thought for a moment or two. When she spoke, her voice was weak: "Me."

I stood and looked over the river toward Île de la Cité, the large island in the middle of la Seine and home to the gothic splendor of Cathédrale Notre Dame de Paris—or as everyone calls it, Notre Dame.

There's something calming about staring at a river. Something hypnotizing about the constant flow of water. I said nothing and waited for Clementina to follow my gaze. I hoped the river might put her in a trance too.

I let my gaze wander from the river and looked along the sturdy balustrade at the large green boxes that had been bolted onto the stone wall. Many of the boxes were open—the lid forming a roof to provide shelter to the guys trying to sell secondhand books from them. But it was October—with a chill when autumn gives winter a try—making it seem like a fruitless exercise to try to sell secondhand books.

"We're on the Left Bank," I said. "There are secondhand booksellers, and if you want to go inside and look at books, there's that famous bookstore somewhere down here; the Latin Quarter is just over there," I waved a hand loosely. "You've got everything you need for a bookish intellectual."

Clementina snorted. "So why d'you think Hoffman is here? He's not exactly—what did you call it—a bookish intellectual." I waited for her to elaborate. "He's smart...witty—dry more than witty—and he does that whole skinny thing that the intellectuals do. But he's not a big thinker."

I tried another approach. "Hoffman has to eat and sleep."

She faced me blankly, seemingly unwilling to admit that maybe Hoffman might need the basic human necessities.

"So where would he go to eat and sleep?"

"I dunno." Something in her tone said: "Why would I know that?" Something told me she had never been to his place.

"So what were the arrangements when he came over? Was he going to stay with you in the apartment?"

Clementina shook her head, her blond ponytail swishing behind her.

"But he had to go somewhere to wash?"

"Yeah," she said. "He's a boy, but he understands the basics of soap."

"So he would go somewhere to use soap, and then sit and wait for your call?"

"I suppose," said Clementina.

twenty-two

It was an unpleasant internet café, and somehow that amused me.

There was nothing positive to say about the place—the computers were old and dirty; the carpet, something of a rarity in Paris, was worn, frayed, and stained, in part explaining why carpets are a rarity in buildings open to the public; the desks once blond wood, with the look of the merchandise of a Swedish furniture store, were now pitted, worn, and covered in graffiti in any number of languages, only some of which I noticed; and most of all, the other people were loud, smelly, and didn't seem to respect personal space.

But the computer functioned, and the ambience—if I could call it that—distressed Clementina, and that amused me. I didn't know why it amused me, but I was definitely taking pleasure in her discomfort. When I had taken her onto the Metro to get to the Left Bank, she had seemed quite at home with public transport, but clearly public computing was a step too far for her and left her wanting to run back to the nice, comfortable apartment her father had rented.

I pulled up a map on the screen: the city of Paris and some of the outlying suburbs.

Clementina twisted awkwardly on her chair and looked down at the central row between the desks, her face registering repugnance.

"If you've got a better idea, then I'd love to hear it," I said.

Clementina's face remained sour as she looked up to the screen.

"Give me anything—any fact—about Hoffman. Where does he live? Where was he born? Where did he go to school? Has he been to university? Any fact."

Clementina continued with the sour face but didn't meet my stare.

"Anything," I said.

"I've only know him for a month," she said. "I call. He arrives. I'm not here to judge."

"You mean like you've already judged everyone else in this place?"

She gave a weak and helpless forced smile. It was an attempt at sarcasm that didn't hit its target and wasn't going to while I was enjoying myself. I drew her attention back to the map.

"Last night. You called Hoffman, and he arrived in thirty minutes."

She nodded.

"I'm going to make a guess that given the time he got a cab. He might have got the Metro, but I'm guessing he took a cab. Is that a reasonable assumption?"

Clementina exhaled. The exasperated teenager. "So Hoffman will have got a cab. What are we going to do? Ask every cab driver in Paris?"

"You know," I said softly, "that's not the worst idea I've heard all day. In fact, I would go as far as saying that is the most useful suggestion you've come up with."

She had the look of someone who wasn't sure whether to accept the compliment or be offended by the slightly sarcastic manner in which it was delivered.

"If he was there in thirty minutes—and he took a cab—then let's say it took five minutes from receiving your call for Hoffman to get out of his hotel and into a cab."

Clementina shook her head lightly. "I don't know."

"We're on mathematics," I said. "Thirty minutes total, less five minutes to get into the cab, gives us a total travel time of twenty-five minutes."

"And?" said Clementina, a hint of surly aggression returning to her tone.

"Look," I said, clicking on the mouse. "Start the journey at your apartment and travel to...the Eiffel Tower."

She looked as I clicked.

"Total distance two point three kilometers; travel time nine minutes in current traffic conditions; travel time without traffic—which you would expect at night—seven minutes."

She looked. She pondered. Eventually she spoke: "And?"

"And so it's unlikely that Hoffman is staying around the Eiffel Tower. If he had been, then he would likely have been with you in fifteen minutes."

Something clicked. "So he's probably staying further away," she said, her tone conveying that a light bulb had just come on. Then she thought a bit more, looked at the map, and pondered. When she spoke her voice was hesitant—she half pointed as she talked, as if that explained what she was thinking. "But he could be..."

"Anywhere in a very large city," I said. "I know. But let's make some assumptions and try to narrow things down."

She shrugged without commitment.

"I'm guessing he is staying within the Périphérique." I pointed to the Boulevard de Périphérique, the beltway that encircles Paris, demarcating the border between city and suburb. "Why would he go to the suburbs?"

Clementina was still refusing to talk or commit, but she stared at the screen as if by looking hard enough she would be able to see Hoffman.

I clicked the mouse, dragging out the route. "Eiffel Tower to your apartment, nine minutes." I dropped the end point somewhere into the 7th arrondissement, one of the twenty districts comprising the heart of Paris. "A fifteen-minute journey gets us here." I dragged a bit further to the near edge of the Latin Quarter. "Twenty minutes." Then a bit further. "Twenty-five minutes in a cab, thirty minutes to reach you, puts Hoffman here."

"Here?" She leaned forward looking at the screen.

I zoomed in. "Boulevard de l'Hôpital, near Austerlitz station."

"So you reckon he's there?"

I tried to hide my smile as my face softened. "Maybe. But what I'm trying to say is he's probably staying somewhere at this distance. Draw an arc with your apartment at the center of the circle." I pointed an arc on the screen. "He could be anywhere along this arc."

"But that's..."

"A big area," I said. "So we make guesses. And my first guess is that he's in one of three places." Clementina waited. "He's either close to Gare du Nord, or he's in Montmartre, or he's near the Left Bank."

"Montmartre?"

"The hill with Sacré-Cœur. It's trendy and arty around there. The sort of place a cool, skinny guy might hang."

Clementina's lips twitched as if agreeing that it was a possibility.

"If he's not in either of those two, then the third place is the only place he's mentioned—the Left Bank. So we start with the Left Bank since that's closest."

Clementina remained still. Something told me she wanted to argue—it was in her nature to argue—but she didn't know what to argue about.

"As I have said and will keep saying: If you've got a better idea, just let me know."

Clementina seemed to deflate.

"So the next question," I began, "is where would he stay? Did he give you any hints about his hotel?"

"He said something about a boring white box," said Clementina. "But I don't know what he meant by that."

"That's good. It gives us something," I said. "What about paying for the hotel? Did you have an arrangement—were you going to pay for him?"

"No." Clementina seemed shocked at the suggestion. "Hoffman always pays, wherever we go. He's like..." She stopped. Something was niggling. "He always pays—but he always gets a receipt. I mean, *always.*"

"And I can't believe you've let this happen without questioning him."

"Expenses." She shrugged. "He said he needs a receipt for expenses. I always thought it was a joke."

"And how does he pay?"

"Card," said Clementina, struggling to understand the question. "Never cash."

I might as well have asked her whether Hoffman was a mass murderer for the offense that was taken.

"What sort of card?"

"Plain, boring, plastic. Not gold. Not black."

She thought, then shook her head.

"Well that gives us something. Hoffman is in a boring white hotel that gives receipts, which is located somewhere along this arc. We haven't found him, but we've excluded most of Paris."

twenty-three

"Where are we, Leathan?" Clementina let her head slowly rotate as she took in our surroundings. "Where are we?" She articulated each word, clearly and with emphasis, as if that would add a layer of depth and context to her question.

"La Seine is over there." I pointed northward. "Over there, Gare d'Austerlitz. That's the kind of place where ordinary people take the train." I pointed through the gates toward the large, squat stone building with a raised bridge exiting halfway up its side; gray steel arches the only suggestion that it wasn't a regular bridge.

She half sighed, half growled. "Where are we?"

"No," I said. "That's not what you mean. You mean: Why are we where we are?"

Clementina stopped as she considered the tongue twister before her face relaxed. "So if you know I want to know why we are where we are, then will you give me an answer?"

"We figured Hoffman would have done one of three things—go local, so stay near Gare du Nord; go funky in Montmartre; or go near the place he mentioned."

"He didn't mention a station with the track coming out of a wall. I would have remembered that."

"But he mentioned the Left Bank, and..."

"And this doesn't look like the kind of place where you get intellectuals talking about philosophy and smoking cigarettes without filters," snapped Clementina. "This looks..."

"Like most of Paris," I finished. "Broad boulevards, lots of traffic, and a bunch of stores at street level. But more to the point..."

It was her turn to finish for me, her tone mocking: "It's twenty-five minutes' drive to the apartment." She looked with the unimpressed eyes of a teenager. "So what do we do now?"

"Bang on the door of every hotel that is plain and white—or at least might have plain white rooms."

She stared, incredulous. When I didn't respond, she sighed.

"This isn't punishment—this is how we find him. If we knock on every door in Paris, then we'll get there. Eventually."

"How many people live in Paris?" she asked.

"You mean how many residences are there in the most densely populated city in Europe?"

"Will you stop telling me what I mean?" she barked. "We're not going to go to every hotel in Paris and say, 'Have you seen Hoffman?'"

I started walking; Clementina waited until I had taken three or four steps then ran to catch me. "You're going to hear me say this quite a lot: If you've got a better idea, then tell me, and we'll do that."

I ignored the pained look I'm sure she pulled.

In less than three minutes we were standing outside a hotel. One of a chain that had many hotels dotted across the city, and many other hotels—all looking exactly the same—across most of Western Europe.

"This," I said to Clementina.

"What?" she replied rhetorically.

"A boring white box hotel. You wait here."

"Can't I come with you?" she said, suddenly becoming a simpering child.

"No. You need to wait here—out of sight." She frowned as I continued. "Don't let anyone see you. You're going to get us inside once we find the right place."

I ignored her look of confusion and proceeded to the reception desk.

twenty-four

"Hi. I'm meeting Nat Hoffman," I said.

The guy behind the desk had been dealing with a couple—hotel residents, I presumed—when I arrived. From his accent, he was French. My French is good—my French mother made sure that I learned the language before I realized I was learning the language—and yet I chose to speak English because as far as the guy behind the desk was concerned, I was just another English tourist. I could even forgive him for thinking me English when I was Scottish.

The hotel met all the criteria to be considered a white box hotel. It offered no frills, but on the flip side, you could be confident there were no horrors. It was clean but tedious. There would be all the limited facilities you would expect for the budget—which essentially boiled down to clean sheets, clean towels in the bathroom, air conditioning in public parts of the hotel, Wi-Fi, and breakfast if you wanted to pay the supplement. If you were on a budget, it was the kind of place that wouldn't rip you off, but it would probably sap your soul.

I was losing count of how many of these hotels I had been into in the last few hours. The reception areas were all exactly the same with a few minor variations. The space would be intended to be light and airy—it would achieve this through having the outside wall replaced with glass. The carpet would be a tone on a scale between light beige and biscuit, with maybe a hint of taupe. The desk would be a light-colored wood, but not too light—there would always be a hint of yellow in the wood—and it would be heavily varnished, although that varnish would be wearing thin where guests habitually rested as they checked in and out. At the opposite end from the desk would be a sofa or two. These would be covered in fabric and would demonstrate the hotel's identity and character.

At least, that was the story that had been told when sofas were bought for every hotel in the chain.

In reality, the sofa was a color that—if you squinted—matched the corporate color. Typically, it was a shade of burgundy or a tone of blue. If you kept squinting, you would see that the color of the fabric was close to the color of the curtains, even if the texture of the drapes was totally different from that covering the seats.

But then again, no one really was sure exactly what the corporate color was meant to be. These decisions were made by people who thought that choosing a different color made their hotel chain unique, when from my very recent experience I could tell them that their hotels offered not a single unique feature anywhere in Europe.

"Nat Hoffman," said the guy behind the reception desk in a heavy French accent. He glared at his screen and tapped a few buttons. Like every other hotel, the receptionist seemed to have to arm wrestle the computer system to extract even the most minor details required to perform his job. At the first hotel, I shrugged and assumed the guy behind the counter was new or lacked the intelligence to work the computer. When I found that every receptionist had exactly the same problem, I revised my opinion.

"Yeah, Nat," I said, pulling out my phone and looking at the screen. "I was meant to meet him here at one; it's now half-past."

The receptionist looked up from his computer with a slightly quizzical look.

"He's got a French SIM card," I said. "I haven't got his new number yet. Could you let me have it?"

The receptionist returned to arm wrestling with the computer. "Do you know which room he's in, sir?"

"No."

"And how do you spell the surname?" asked the thick French accent.

"H. O. F. F. M. A. N." There was a tap on the keyboard after I enunciated each letter. He mumbled something. "Nat—that's Nathaniel," I guessed, "N. A. T. H. A..." I trailed off as he looked up from his screen.

"So is he here?" I felt the anticipation that came with the hope that this would be the last hotel I would visit today.

The Frenchman look at me disbelievingly.

I realized the stupidity of my question and tried to correct. "Is he here now? He hasn't gone out?" Then I over-explained, adding hand gestures to amplify the fallacy. "I mean, obviously he's here—staying here—but I'm just checking that he's here, here, now. Now."

I was confusing myself. The other guy was already uncomprehending of my question, and while his grasp of English was good, he didn't speak the language as a native, and probably most opportunities he got to speak the language were as a lingua franca when it was the only common language he and a guest shared.

"I'll try his room," said the receptionist, lifting a handset.

I leaned forward, trying to get a view of the computer screen. There was a lot of text, and I wasn't at a good angle to read—or to parse what was corporate mess and what was the detail I was searching for. I scanned for numbers.

"I'm sorry, sir. He must be out."

"He's expecting me," I said, keeping my eyes fixed on the screen. "Could you try him again?"

The receptionist sighed and punched the number again.

On the screen, I had found Hoffman's name; there was a long number that I guessed was his phone, some dates, and some other text I couldn't read clearly. There was only one group of three digits. "Room two-two-three," I said, turning my attention back to the man on the phone. "Could that be it?"

The receptionist raised his eyebrows as if to agree, then put the handset down. "I'm sorry, there's no reply, sir."

"I'm late...he's probably gone already," I said. "I'll come back later."

"Shall I...?" began the receptionist.

"Tell him his Scottish friend came by—he's got my number."

Clementina had found a bench on the broad sidewalk. Her focus was on her phone. I stood to her right, casting her into shadow. "Next," she said. She was bored, but she was faking even deeper boredom.

"Why would we go to another hotel?" I asked.

"Because we're looking for..." she said, and then stopped herself as she realized her expectation and my reaction weren't in sync. Something had changed. She leaned forward—her lips pulled tight and twitching as she began to form a question. "Is Hoffman staying here?"

I nodded.

"Here? In this hotel? Now? Today? He's there?"

"He's staying here," I said. "But if he's in his room, then he's not answering the phone."

Clementina returned her focus to her phone. "He'll answer me," she said, punching the screen and holding the phone to her ear. As she sat, with her free hand she preened herself—straightening her jeans, tugging her T-shirt straight, and running a finger through her ponytail.

She lowered the phone, looking at the screen. "No reply." Her tone was flat, dejected.

"Voicemail?" I wasn't sure why I hadn't asked before.

"That's what's wrong," she said. "I'm not even going to voicemail. It just rings."

I sat on the bench beside Clementina. "That doesn't matter now. What matters is that you need to get us into Hoffman's hotel room."

"Me?"

"You."

"How?"

"However," I said. "You need to persuade anyone who stands between you and the door—anyone who can get you past the door—that they should let you past."

"And again, Leathan, I say: How?"

"Persuade them that you're waiting for your man," I offered weakly. "Tell them it's his birthday and you want to have a *special* surprise for him when he arrives."

Her eyes crinkled. "I thought Reece was the creep. What do you want me to do?"

"Use your imagination," I said.

"You think I should...?" The distaste in her tone was clear.

"Can I put this in simple terms?"

She nodded.

"I'm not suggesting you give the bellboy a blow job—not that they have bellboys here—but you might want to let him think you're there to give Hoffman a blow job. Am I making myself clear?"

She relaxed slightly, but she was still tense. "And you think I'd do that sort of thing...?"

"I think you had sex with Hoffman within a few hours of meeting him." I regretted the comment immediately. When I continued, I tried to keep my voice soft and reassuring. "We need to get inside his hotel room. It's the only lead we've got to Hoffman."

She stared at me, her eyes still crinkled. Slowly the pained look fell away, being replaced by a broad grin. "Then I'm going to need to dress slutty. We need to go shopping, Leathan."

twenty-five

"How do you know about this place," I asked as the cab pulled away.

Then the panic hit me—the detail I should have confirmed before I watched Clementina look at the map and direct our taxi over la Seine, past Place de la Bastille, and then along the path of Canal Saint-Martin as it made its way under the streets of eastern Paris before appearing in the 10th arrondissement. "Please tell me your GPS is still off."

"It's off," she said, not taking any offense—her attention having been drawn to her target, or at least what I assumed was her target.

For much of Paris, the buildings on either side of the road were a distance apart. It was no different here—the buildings on the other side were far enough that I had to squint to make out the details.

Baron Haussmann, Prefect of the Seine Department, at the behest of Emperor Napoleon, remodeled Paris, replacing narrow medieval streets with broad boulevards that now sweep across the city, bringing air and light. The new streets were fronted by buildings constructed in a uniform style, giving Paris a consistency and grace lacking in other major metropolises.

With the constant revolutionary fervor in France, small streets were easy to barricade. Broad boulevards were nearly impossible to block, plus an infantry could be marched down the street to quell any insurrection. The design clearly worked—there have been no further significant revolutions in France, and the streets have continued to perform their basic intended function, even now that the horse and carriage has been replaced by the internal combustion engine.

It's not unusual to have six lanes of traffic bounded by a further three lanes on either side dedicated to parking. But not here. Here, there was no central strip of six lanes. Instead there was water, Canal Saint-Martin, and as if to emphasize the point, a sand-carrying barge was passing—its cabin raised above us. I watched as it passed under the footbridge—an arched steel lattice crossing the canal—then turned my attention back to Clementina.

I had agreed to the shopping expedition because she couldn't immediately go into the hotel and ask for Hoffman—it would be too suspicious to have two people ask about the scrawny guy in less than five minutes.

But I hadn't been sufficiently questioning of Clementina's intentions. She had led us to a store that spanned three properties with residential apartments above. Each had a distinct frontage—one was painted baby pink, the second was lime green, and the third was bright yellow. Clementina seemed to be drawn to the lime green and was staring through the window.

"I thought you wanted slutty," I said, following her line of sight. "This looks more bobo."

"You mean boho," she said, exaggerating the "ho" and without turning from her focus.

"No, I mean bobo."

She spun to face me, frowning. "It's boho—short for bohemian."

"It might be in London," I said. "In Paris, they call it bobo. Bourgeois bohemian."

"Seriously?" she said.

"Seriously."

"No. I mean, seriously, you actually know something about style."

I let her have her joke. "French mother," I reminded her.

She lifted her eyebrows as the memory came back to her. Somehow to her teenage way of thinking I had acquired a few more cool points by virtue of my mother's country of birth. "Anyway," I said. "This looks bobo—at least to me, you can call it what you want—and you said you wanted slutty."

She sighed; in her mind I had returned the moral high ground to her, not that there was much moral high ground to be had in facilitating the acquisition of slutty clothes by a seventeen-year-old. "As your French mother would tell you, the French don't like *slutty* slutty—they like a more airy, floaty look."

She indicated to and along the windows within the baby pink, lime green, and bright yellow frames.

"Slutty was the wrong word." She stopped and closed her eyes as she gathered her thoughts. She opened her eyes and continued, "Slutty was the wrong word for you. The point I'm trying to get at is that whatever I wear has to say something, but it can't shout."

She moved in front of a dress. At least, I thought it was a dress—it seemed a bit too short and the gray fabric was too gauzy, apart from the white lace detailing around the neck and plunging in a V-shape.

"You don't get it, do you?" she said.

"It's a piece of gray gauze without shape. Gypsies and hippies used to wear this stuff and people would sneer, but now it's fashionable and everyone makes a fuss."

"No," she said. "You don't get what I'm trying to say."

I was still lost with the gray gauze. Its price tag was making me scratch.

"I can do the *obvious* look. Get a really hot dress—short, to show my legs, tight and shaped to show my figure. No underwear, of course. Something shiny, probably dark colored, as I'm blond. Heavy makeup with exaggerated eyes and poison red lips."

She conjured an image. I was thinking of someone else, but it was still a good image.

"But that's not what we need, is it? I need to be the girl who's there for her guy. She needs to be believable as the girl who's in control of her own life—but not so sophisticated that she would look out of place in a white box hotel. She needs..."

"I get it." I stopped her. She had a whole character in mind with a complete backstory, and she knew every piece of clothing this character had worn, every day of her whole life. "Shall we go in?"

The anticipation on her face was like a drug user knowing she was about to take a hit.

As she turned, I pointed at the gray dress. She answered the question I hadn't voiced. "Get some leggings, a dark bra, and you'd be set. Of course, you wouldn't need them if you were a slut." She was through the door and talking with an assistant.

By the time I got inside the door and had stumbled across the alien landscape of the interior of a bobo boutique, Clementina had sent the assistant scurrying away, periodically returning with hangers, from which dangled a range of different tones and textures.

"Can we buy something and get back?" I asked. "We just need to get you past the guy at the front desk and into Hoffman's room."

"Did I quibble with your plan?" she asked, holding a hanger at arm's length, inspecting a cream dress.

"Yes," I said. "You did quibble with my plan. Frequently. Vocally and through your body language."

"But I followed you. I didn't cause trouble." It was a stretch to suggest she didn't cause trouble, but I was losing the energy to argue. "I followed you because you were the expert—I understood that we were doing what you do."

It sounded like a compliment. I knew by now it was a lure—there to trap me. I stayed quiet.

"This is what I do," she said defiantly.

"You're still at school," I said, immediately regretting the harshness of my put-down.

"Have you seen how many social media followers I've got?" She seemed prepared for my kind of cynicism and was responding by telling me I was old and irrelevant. She pulled out her phone and held it toward me—moving the dress in her other hand to hang in front of her. "Take a picture."

"We don't have time for this," I said.

She was focused on her phone. "I don't have the battery for this."

The assistant arrived with armfuls of smocks, shirts, dresses, and trousers. "You can try," she said, in heavily accented English, pointing to a small area cordoned off by two louvered doors, arranged more like the entrance to a bar in an old western.

"Merci beaucoup," said Clementina, taking the bundle and heading for the changing room. She had dropped the bundle and was slipping off her sneakers as I arrived. "You need to take photos, Leathan. Your phone can take photos, yes?"

Before I could argue, the assistant appeared with four pairs of boots—each a slightly different shade of brown and a marginally different style. Clementina cooed before thanking the assistant, who disappeared as quickly as she had arrived.

"We need to hurry up," I said. "We need to find Hoffman before he does anything stupid."

"I am hurrying, and the faster you take photos, the faster we get out of here."

twenty-six

The cab pulled away.

Clementina had changed in the store and had given me the bag holding the clothes she had been wearing when we left the apartment. She was now dressed in a red smock with yellow and orange streaks, and on top a white waistcoat, unbuttoned and open at the front; blue jeans—apparently the blue jeans she had been wearing were the wrong shade of blue, the wrong cut, and had the wrong wear pattern—held by a thick brown leather belt with a chunky yet ornate buckle; and brown boots—slightly aged, slightly distressed, and with a heel. A coat that was fuzzy and an indistinct mixture of brown and tan. A small bag—cream and brown embroidered fabric, with leather detailing and leather handles—hung from her arm.

"How do I look?"

She looked like the kind of girl every young guy would want to have waiting for him in his hotel room. Sexy but not slutty.

I nodded slowly, taking in the details. It didn't seem that I needed to add words.

"You're sure?"

"Sure," I said. "But not sure that you needed to tip the girl in the store."

"She helped."

"So you tipped her with my money."

"And who gave you that money?" asked Clementina. She saw my awkwardness and seemed to want to change the subject. "So this is really what you do for living?"

"Not quite," I said. "But it's better than working in an office."

"Don't apologize," she said. "This is fun."

"We've just been shopping—that's what was fun, for you."

"That wasn't shopping," she said. "I'm in disguise. I'm a secret agent—I'm about to get into a hotel room. Best fun ever. Ev-vah. Seriously, ever."

And she did seem to be buzzing.

"You understand the plan," I said. "You need to get into Hoffman's room, and once you're there, call me and I'll come up."

She nodded.

"Tell them you're waiting for Hoffman—you want to surprise him. You've got that?"

"It's not exactly the hardest plan. Smile and walk through a door—I think I can handle that," she said. "What do I look for when I'm there?"

"You don't," I said. "You let me in and I look."

"Okay... What are you looking for?"

"If I knew that, I wouldn't need to look for it," I said.

She seemed deflated. "Oh."

"Just get me in—remember, it's room two-two-three. I know you can do it."

She nodded and gripped her bag before turning and heading through the doors into the hotel reception.

twenty-seven

It was nearly five minutes before Clementina called. "I can't find anything," she said.

"I'm coming up," I said and hung up.

The Ancient Greeks had myths about people lost in mazes. They spent endless time describing how the passages were long and dark. They could have just said he got lost in a chain hotel where every floor, every corridor, and every door looked exactly the same. I was sure I should be accorded minor hero status for finding my way through the faceless white box to room 223.

Clementina opened the door when I knocked, letting me into another white box within the larger white box.

There was a built-in closet with sliding white doors—the left one was slid over the right, and Clementina had placed herself in front of the open closet, rummaging through the shelves. "What are you doing?" I asked.

"Looking. Isn't that what we're meant to be doing?"

"Have you found the laptop?"

"Why would it be here?" asked Clementina, turning away from the closet to stare at me. Her tone was sharp as she continued. "I told you, Hoffman didn't have the laptop."

"Are you saying Hoffman didn't have the laptop—or that you didn't see the laptop when you looked in his bag?"

"He didn't..." she began, then stopped.

"Did you check everything that was in Hoffman's messenger bag?"

"No," she said regretfully.

"So it might have been there, it might not have been there. All we can say for certain is: One, it disappeared around the time Hoffman was in the apartment; and two, Hoffman might have taken it, but we have no evidence to convict or prove him innocent."

"Innocent until proven guilty," said Clementina.

"Hoffman? Innocent?" I didn't need to add more. She half smirked, shrugged, and returned to the closet, sliding the doors to the left to reveal the other half, where trousers, shirts, and jackets hung.

There was a built-in desk-cum-dressing table-cum-place to put the obligatory coffee-making facilities present in every chain hotel room. "Is this how you got in?" I asked, picking up a keycard that had been left next to the kettle.

Clementina looked over. "Yeah," she said, returning her attention.

I slipped the card into my back pocket and looked to the drawers under the counter. In the top drawer behind the obligatory hair dryer, which had its cord fixed inside the drawer, was a stack of papers—a mess of receipts, cards, ticket stubs, and scraps of paper.

I cursed under my breath and took the top receipt, straightening and flattening the creases before laying it on top of the white easy-wipe surface of the unit and photographing the document with my phone. "This may take a while," I said, flattening the next receipt. "Have you found anything?"

"An iPad. It was under the mattress."

"You're taking this seriously." I snapped a business card without reading it.

"You're missing the point," said Clementina. "Hoffman doesn't own an iPad." She caught my frown as I glanced around. "If it doesn't fit in his pocket, then it has no place in his life."

"So a phone, scraps of paper," I said, flattening the next receipt, "but not a tablet or a laptop."

"Yeah."

"Then why the messenger bag?"

"Don't know. This morning was the first time I saw it."

"I don't suppose you've found the messenger bag?"

"I found an iPad, Leathan—isn't that enough?" She paused. "Do you want me to look through the bathroom?"

"Yeah," I said, snapping the next picture. "I've still got a way to go."

Clementina went into the bathroom and came out again, waiting until she had my attention. "It smells wrong."

"The room smells wrong or there's something fishy going on here?" I said, mock dramatically.

She sighed. "The room smelt wrong when I came in, and I've just noticed it again going into the bathroom."

"Wrong how?"

"I dunno." She shrugged. "It doesn't smell right." She paused, thinking. "Hoffman's clean—he washes. He doesn't care what soap he uses or anything like that, but this doesn't smell clean. I can't explain it."

"Housekeeping with poor hygiene?" I offered. She returned to the bathroom. "Once you've finished in there, we should get moving," I said, looking at the reducing pile of receipts still to photograph.

twenty-eight

We left through the kitchen, such as it was. It was a small room in the back of the hotel—a space big enough to store the food for the breakfast that the hotel included in the price of a night's stay and to prepare the meal. There was also enough space for the dishwashers to clean the breakfast dishes and the cups from the coffee-making facilities in each room.

It was more of a fuss to find the kitchen and leave that way, but I thought it would be better to leave by the door that was less likely to have a CCTV camera and better to pass people who were usually hidden from guests. There was a reason they were hidden.

"Where do we look now?" asked Clementina.

I ignored her question for a moment, taking in the city. I was seeing color again. I was hearing sounds that weren't the white noise of air passing through a cooling system. I was seeing people who didn't wear uniform vests with their color chosen because it matched the corporate color that was also evident on the fabric covering the sofas and the drapes in the hotel lobby.

"We don't look. We go back to the apartment."

"But Hoffman." Clementina looked at me insistently, as if she had just made the winning move and was waiting for me to admit defeat. I could out-wait her. Slowly, she noticed that I was waiting. "You've got another idea, haven't you?"

"It's not really an idea," I said, feeling the weight of the bag I was carrying that held the clothes Clementina had been wearing when we left the apartment a few hours ago. The bag that now weighed a bit more—the additional weight coming from the iPad Clementina had found in Hoffman's room. "It's more common sense."

She looked quizzically at me.

"I've taken photos of Hoffman's receipts and the other scraps of paper." She nodded as I continued. "I want to have a look at those photos and see if I can figure what Mister Hoffman has been up to, where he might have gone, and who he might have been talking with. Once I've done that, we can get out and look a bit more."

"What am I going to do?"

"Your people need you," I said. "Your many, many, many social media followers need to see the pictures of you trying on bobo rags."

"Can't I...do something...to help?"

I thought about how to answer. I could find work to keep her busy or I could lie. In the end, I decided to half tell the truth. "Hoffman's missing, right?"

She had a look as if to say: "Why are you patronizing me with rhetorical questions?"

"There will be a reason why he's missing—and it will probably be trivial. But if he sees that you're suddenly not posting, isn't he going to think that something's wrong?" I softened my voice. "You need to let him know—you need to show him—that everything is normal."

She wasn't convinced, but she couldn't find a way to argue. "If you say." She looked around. "Where do we get a cab?"

"Let's get the Metro. It'll be quicker."

I wanted to get a cab, but I wasn't lying that the Metro would be quicker in the pre–rush hour buildup of traffic. Also, the lack of any sort of privacy would discourage Clementina from asking questions when I wanted to think.

Reece was sitting forlornly at the kitchen counter when we returned; an empty coffee cup in front of him. He stood up, ready to leave on his client's command now that his client—or at least, his client's daughter—had returned. Clementina half smiled at him and Angeline before heading toward her room. "Come on," she said to me.

"I'll be with you in a moment," I said.

Reece sat down again, slumping over the counter. A driver who doesn't drive isn't really a driver anymore—he's just the guy carrying the car keys. "Where have you been?" he asked flatly.

"Keeping her occupied. You will notice an absence of social media postings."

Reece nodded. He hadn't even been able to find out what was happening at second hand.

"There's about to be a flood of postings." I stepped toward Clementina's room. "But first we're going to braid each other's hair."

Reece seemed to deflate further, if that was possible.

"We're not going out, so if you want to go back to your apartment..." I let the thought hang as I left him.

twenty-nine

"Photos," she said, her eyes wide, a broad grin across her face.

In the time it had taken me to exchange a few words with Reece, Clementina had changed, putting on a pair of leggings and a knitted beige sweater that swamped her, especially around the neck, where the rolls of the collar were like a pillow to support her head on a flight or after a car crash.

I shut the door behind me and rested the bag I had been carrying next to her bed, removing the iPad first. "Yours."

She had laid the clothes she had been wearing on her bed. The red smock with yellow and orange stripes was wearing the white waistcoat—the sleeves sticking through the armholes, the buttons on the front still not fastened. "I like it," she said pensively, "but I'm not sure it's me."

There was any number of smartass retorts I could have thrown. For once I managed to overcome and settle for a few facial contortions to suggest I was considering what she had said.

She broke the quiet. Her voice was weak—the child in her needed reassurance. "Are you sure we shouldn't be out there looking for Hoffman?"

I exhaled slowly, feeling the pressure blowing out my cheeks. "I'd like to be out there—but now that we've been to his hotel, I'm not sure where *there* is. I'm not sure where we look next."

The child that needed reassurance now seemed frightened.

"I'm not sure where we look next yet." I said. "Yet."

"But you will?" There was hope, but caution in her voice. I nodded once. "And you think I should be posting pictures?"

"I think you should behave normally—you need to show Hoffman that everything is normal."

I watched as she argued with herself: Should she worry about Hoffman or should she get with her friends and followers and discuss the clothes she had tried on today? One of the few things I had learned during the last few hours was that Clementina with something to do was much easier to handle than Clementina when she was bored. "Do you want the photos?" I asked.

She hesitated, then the excitement overtook her: "Show me!"

"You have seen these—you looked at every picture I took in that store and made me delete anything that made you look fat, dorkish, plain, ugly, unhappy, too happy, too perfect, too…"

"Shh," she said, leaning over me and flicking through the photos on the screen as I clutched my phone. "That one. Not that one. Not that one. Yuck. Double yuck. Ha! That one."

"Shall I send them all, and you can choose?"

"Do that," she said, holding her phone, which had now acquired a lead and was recharging. "Hurry up."

I selected all the photos without any landmarks. I figured the baby pink, lime green, and bright yellow would be instantly recognizable, but also any views through the window where the canal was present in the background. I hit send. "Remember—don't mention Paris or give any indication as to where you are."

"That'll be fun," she said. "Guess where I am?"

I shook my head. "No guessing. Someone might get it right. Someone else is bound to say, 'Well where are you?'"

"Alright," she said. She didn't even need to sigh—I understood the teenage exasperation.

Her phone pinged as the photos started to arrive, and she jumped onto her bed, seemingly forgetting the clothes she had been wearing, which now lay under her legs. Her head went down, looking at the screen as her fingers started tapping, and her hair fell forward on either side. There were a few laughs, some groans, a giggle, a muttered sentence or two.

There was a two-person sofa. Unlike the hotels we had visited today, I suspected this came from a very short run and probably cost more than every other sofa I'd seen today. I lowered myself and started looking through the photos I had taken in Hoffman's room, zooming in to read the detail of each receipt.

There were several meals, and unless Hoffman had a crazy caffeine habit and a wasting illness requiring him to eat double, there was more than him at these meals. I checked the times—lunch and dinner. Several lunches, several dinners.

Next up was a business card. I knew the name—I was surprised that Hoffman had the card.

Another lunch. Two more dinners. In Paris.

"How long have you been in Paris?"

"Huh?" said Clementina, her head lifting but her hair still forming a curtain on either side.

"When did you arrive in Paris?"

She thought, then looked down again at her phone. "This is day six," she said, formally terminating communication.

I went back to my photos. There were a few scribbled notes—none meant anything to me—and another lunch.

"Before yesterday," I began.

Clementina muttered.

"When did you last see Hoffman?"

She came up from her screen, like a diver coming up from the depths. "Two days, three days before we left." She was noncommittal and uninterested.

"Why no tearful farewell on your last night?"

She shrugged. "I don't know."

"Why did it take five days for you to call Hoffman to heel?"

Another shrug. "I suppose he had things to do." She dropped her eyes to the screen.

"Clementina," I said.

She looked up, her eyes narrow. "You can call me Clemmy—only my parents call me Clementina."

"Sorry," I mumbled. "This is important."

She shrugged again.

"Yesterday at Gare du Nord—when Hoffman arrived, did you see him get off the train?"

"Of course not," said call-me-Clemmy. "He was way back in the cheap seats."

"But did you see him come off the platform? Did you see him in that sea of people who get off the train?"

"No." She had the look of someone who had been asked a stupid question and who wasn't bashful about communicating her disdain.

"You didn't see him. You didn't wave to him as he came along the platform."

"No. He saw me—he said he waved, but I was looking in completely the wrong direction."

"So the first you saw of him was when he was standing next to you."

"Yeah." Her hair fell forward as she nodded; then she looked up, a single finger clearing her gaze. "Why?"

thirty

"You know that creamy, browny dress I tried?"

"With the puffy sleeves?"

"That was pink. No, the one with…"

Clementina's rebuke was interrupted by a firm rap on her door. Angeline stepped inside, keeping hold of the door with one hand. "They want you, Mister Leathan." She disappeared, leaving the door open.

"You tell all those people on the internet that it's pink, not brown," I said, leaving before Clemmy could spit poison at me.

I shut the door and wandered to the kitchen. Angeline pointed with her eyes to the main area. Johnson McElroy was sitting on one of the sofas, holding a sheaf of papers, a briefcase open beside him. "Leathan," he said before throwing the papers into the case and standing to greet me.

I sat across from the lawyer, noticing that Angeline had disappeared.

"I wanted to check everything's going alright," said McElroy.

"It's going good," I said.

"What have you been up to?"

"Oh, you know," I mumbled. "This and that—I've been occupying her." McElroy leaned back and waited. "We've seen some sights—I've shown her a few different places—and of course, there was some shopping."

His lips tightened. "Of course there was shopping. There's always shopping with Clementina."

It wasn't an attractive look that he displayed.

"You didn't take Reece." The lawyer was making a statement but asking a bigger question.

"I tried to slow things down—make it about the journey, not the destination. And while she's been having to walk around, it was much harder to use her phone." I tried to smile, hoping he would mirror. "It was a basic distraction technique."

"Yes, yes," said the lawyer, himself distracted and seemingly uninterested by what I was saying. "What's this I hear about this Hoffman character?"

I wanted to say: "What, the same Nat Hoffman who has your business card in his room?" But I didn't. I feigned indifference.

"Reece blabbed," said the lawyer in a matter-of-fact tone.

It was my turn to sit back and relax in the sofa. "He was here. The three of us went for coffee this morning, and then Hoffman scooted." When the lawyer said nothing, I added a metaphorical full stop and end of paragraph mark. "We went shopping—you know the rest."

The slight rise and fall of the lawyer's chest told me he was still breathing. If it wasn't for that movement, I could have been sitting across from a waxwork. He spoke eventually. "What time was this?"

"Nine-ish."

"Nine AM, this morning?"

"Around nine—I didn't check the time."

"That was the last time you saw this Hoffman person?"

"Yup."

"And since?"

"I haven't seen him since."

"Clementina?"

"She was with me the whole time—she hasn't seen him," I said. "I think she might have tried to call him once or twice."

The lawyer reached out his hand to close his case without breaking eye contact. "We've got a problem, Leathan. You need to come with me."

He stood and was moving toward the door before I could ask what the problem was.

Angeline was holding the front door for us. "Keep an eye on Little Miss Pain-in-the-Ass," he said to the Filipino housekeeper as he led toward the elevator.

thirty-one

Reece let the Maybach drift out of the parking lot. I sat on the back seat next to Johnson McElroy. None of us spoke.

The Maybach found its way to Boulevard Périphérique, the beltway encircling Paris, making it clear when you're in the city and when you're in the suburbs. Even with four lanes in each direction, the traffic was heavy and sluggish.

When we got to the southeast corner of the city—with its tower blocks and Chinatown—we turned north, heading back toward the center of the city.

We might have been within the bounds of the city, but this wasn't the Paris of picture postcards. This wasn't the place where you came and locked a padlock on a bridge as a symbol of your undying love. This wasn't the Paris that Baron Haussmann had imposed his will upon. The buildings were newer than most in Paris—1960s, maybe 1970s—but had become tired and unloved. Concrete and brick hastily erected and now covered with a layer of internal combustion engine fumes.

We didn't get much closer to the city. Within three hundred yards we turned into a narrow street. To the right was a concrete-constructed block, put up cheaply in the 1950s, when it was last shown any love. At the ground level were boarded-up stores.

To the left, a squat red building, dwarfed by a residential tower block behind it, which in turn was dwarfed by a circular office tower that looked like the kind of place you worked in my worst nightmares. In front of us were four high-rise white concrete towers and several sprawling mid-rise blocks, all residential.

I refocused on the red building—a school with a high brick wall running the whole block with a few windows and an entrance about halfway. I wasn't sure whether the security was to protect the local residents from the kids or to keep pedophiles away.

The building across from the school gave way to a small park—in reality, more of a green space than a formal park. An area had been fenced off in the park, and a children's play area constructed with a slide, low swings, and something to climb on.

McElroy threw his head in the direction of the park—a jungle of trees and shrubs—and broke the silence that had sat over the three of us since we left the underground parking lot. "It was closed for maintenance today." He slumped back in his seat, falling quiet again.

We turned into an even narrower road. The blocks on our left were little higher than most buildings in the heart of Paris, but with a sidewalk that was only a few feet wide, it felt like we were in a ravine.

Another mid-rise block had chewed into the corner of the green space that found its way behind the blocks and to the street. By the gate to the park, a police officer stood.

Reece pulled the car to the side and stepped out, shutting the door behind him. "The Hoffman kid is dead," said McElroy. "To be more accurate, there's a dead kid in the park—he was found a few hours ago—and the working assumption is he's the Hoffman kid."

The lawyer let himself out of the car without further explanation and came around to open my door.

The narrow street was swollen with the official vehicles: several marked police cars, a few unmarked cars—the kind of cars that only a governmental agency would purchase—an ambulance, and several vans marked with official insignias. There was a range of people, but all seemed to think they had a connection with the crime—uniformed police officers; people in white all-in-one suits, some carrying cameras; and a few others without uniform who seemed to have command.

McElroy led me toward the gate—the choke point through which all activity passed, where the officer I had seen earlier stood guard. The lawyer stopped a few steps short of the gate, looking around as if searching for someone.

Deeper in the park he caught sight of a woman—mid-thirties, long dark hair, wearing a light brown coat. He raised his hand to acknowledge her. She signaled back: three. In three minutes—three minutes spent in silence, watching—the woman, a detective I presumed, was with us.

McElroy offered no greeting. "This is the guy looking after the Norden girl," he said. His French was functional, but not great.

"With me, please, sir," she said in English. Her English was worse that McElroy's French.

I followed as she led into the park, ascending a shallow concrete staircase. "I speak French," I said in French. The detective seemed relieved.

"It's just over here," she said, pointing to a cube-like white tent—the only pure white object I had seen since we left the Périphérique. There were three crime scene techs outside the tent, one with a large camera hanging from his neck. The detective muttered something to the tallest of the three, who mumbled something that sounded like agreement.

The detective led me to the entrance to the tent and turned, holding the door open and encouraging me to come close, but not too close. "Can you identify...?" she said, her voice trailing off.

I looked inside and felt an urge to puke.

It was Hoffman—I could recognize the right side of his face, even with the cut under his left eye. The left side of his face was a mass of cuts, burns, bruises, congealed blood, and dirt. His fingers—they had all been straight this morning when I suspected he had stolen the laptop—were now twisted and bloodied, and his jeans were filthy. It was easier to focus on the filth, not on the angle his right leg made in the middle of his thigh.

"There's a bone pushed through his jeans," I said to the detective, making a rudimentary observation without ascribing any order of priority to the injury.

She nodded, understanding the point I was making about the force necessary to rip denim. With a tilt of her head, she invited me to step away from the tent. As we left, the crime scene techs reentered.

"What happened?" I asked.

"That's their job," said the detective, pointing at where the three white-suited scientists had been standing. "Do you know that man?"

"We met for the first time this morning," I said, the images of the man still fresh in my memory. "His name's Hoffman. Nat Hoffman. I presume Nat is short for Nathaniel." She scribbled some notes. "He's my employer's daughter's..."

The detective looked up.

"The kid is seventeen. She knows this guy. She's fond of him...I'm not sure when you call someone a boyfriend and when you acknowledge there's a formal relationship."

"You saw him this morning?" asked the detective.

"Nine o'clock, roughly. We had coffee—me, the daughter, and..." I pointed to the white tent.

"What happened after that?"

"Hoffman left—he went off on his own. I spent the day with the daughter." The detective looked up at me. "We saw some sights... went shopping... What does a teenage girl do in Paris?"

"Did you see...Hoffman again?" she said. The word Hoffman didn't fit well in her mouth.

"No. Clementina tried to call him several times, but I guess now we know why he wasn't picking up."

She asked some more questions; I wasn't sure what, as my power of speech seemed to have disconnected from the rest of my nervous system, which only seemed capable of projecting images of Hoffman.

The detective led me back to McElroy, who silently guided me back to the car. "I need to speak to Zack," I said, "before I see Clementina."

thirty-two

The Maybach wiggled through some side streets and headed north on the main road. The silence we had shared as we journeyed here before I had seen Hoffman had returned.

I recognized Place d'Italie—a large circle where roads converged. Five main roads met here. Two were part of an orbital boulevard—another, smaller, ring around Paris. This ring demarcated the inner and outer arrondissements—a convenient barrier to tell you whether you should be paying more rent or less. The outer arrondissements with the high-rises and social housing, the inner arrondissements welcoming Baron Haussmann's flatter, broader vision for Paris with uniform architectural design.

There were three main arterial roads, leading to and from the heart: the road we had just followed; Boulevard de l'Hôpital, the road that starts at Gare d'Austerlitz, where Clementina and I had begun our search for Hoffman's hotel; and the third road. We took the third road, Avenue des Gobelins, purring along its four lanes—two in each direction, one of which was dedicated to buses and bicycles. The sidewalks were wide—as wide as the road in the middle—with seating for restaurants and cafés dotted along the street.

The car slowed and turned onto a side street, pulling to a halt. McElroy exited and opened my door, making a clicking sound to invite me to step out. As I found my feet, he closed the door and started walking briskly. I followed behind, like a child trying to keep up without showing I needed to run.

The lawyer turned the corner back onto Avenue des Gobelins, passing a pizza delivery restaurant and a brasserie with its customers sitting on the sidewalk under a large red awning stretching from the building.

There was a brown double door in the wall next to the brasserie. Like most double doors in Paris, it was wide enough for a car, and as the lawyer led through, I saw that, like most double doors in Paris, it led to a small courtyard that was overlooked by the apartments above the brasserie.

We ascended two flights of stairs that wrapped around an elevator before the lawyer led me into an apartment. It had the look of a residential apartment—the kind of place you might see anywhere in Paris. The kind of place I had seen many times as a kid when my mother would visit her friends in Paris. Friends who were now mostly long gone.

The lawyer led me through the entrance hall and into what I guessed was the main reception room. The sofas had been pushed back against the walls to open the floor, and in the newly created space, two desks had been set up. Cheap but functional desks that had the look of having been sourced from a chain office supplier.

"We've got a problem," said McElroy.

From behind one desk Zackary Norden looked up, first looking to the lawyer, then looking past him to me. "Hi, Leathan. Welcome to the beating heart of our operation. When they talk about big finance, remember what you've seen here—a plastic desk set up in a rented front room."

He indicated the sofa against the wall opposite him. "We're keeping it low key," said McElroy, slightly shamefully, as I sat.

Norden leaned back in his seat and lifted his eyebrows, looking to the lawyer.

"Your daughter's boyfriend," began McElroy.

"You're going to need to be more specific."

"The kid she met at the Opera House—Hoffman."

"He's a boyfriend? I thought he was a...buddy." He had the look of someone trying not to say "just some guy my willful daughter likes to have sex with."

"He's dead," said the lawyer.

I tried to read Norden's reaction—I could interpret it in a number of ways. There was disbelief—but this seemed more to be disbelief about the state of the world. There was frustration at the attention this might draw. There was irritation that this would require time and resources.

That's what I saw cross his face, but I waited for him to say something. I waited for him to give voice to whatever was going on inside his head that would prove I was right or wrong in how I read his reaction. I waited for the questions: Are we sure? How? Where? When? What the hell? How is Clementina?

But none came. Just a slow exhalation and grimace.

"Do you need detail?" asked McElroy.

"No," said Norden, his voice lacking any emotion.

I shifted to face the lawyer. "You and Mallet are going to squash anything that's out there?"

Norden fixed his gaze on the other man as if he was endorsing my suggestion. The lawyer stood and spoke hesitantly. "Yeah."

thirty-three

Johnson McElroy went to search out the company's media relations man, Orville Michael Mallet.

I listened to the footsteps of the lawyer on the floorboards as he walked away, then stood and closed the door. The large piece of wood told a story of age—there were dents and scratches, and where the door would have stuck or rubbed, the sharp corners had been worn away. The detailing around the four panels in the door had been lost in many coats of paint, each added without removing the last, the most recent itself showing chips and discoloration.

I moved the door from its position against the wall, spinning it through an arc of 180 degrees, its hinges clearly unused to such movement. "These round handles always make me twitch," I said to Norden as I closed the door, indicating the well-worn round brass door handle.

"Vampires scare me," said the financier. "Door handles, less so. I thought you were good at the practical stuff."

"It's practical that makes me twitch. A door lever, literally, gives you a lever. The principle of moments, and you can get the door open. A knob requires that you grip. Make that knob slippery, and you delay your exit by a few seconds."

Norden's gaze was fixed on the doorknob. "I'd never thought of it that way."

I dropped back into the sofa across from Norden's desk and took in the room. It was a reasonable size, but with windows only to one side—the front. They were narrow and partly obscured by the drapes hanging to either side, giving the room an after-hours vibe, even when there was still full daylight outside. The butterscotch-covered walls suggested that the last person to decorate—who had probably painted the walls when the door was last painted—was going for that warm feel.

"What's on your mind?" asked Norden.

"I'm worried that what I said to you this morning could be misinterpreted. I wouldn't want you to have the wrong impression."

Norden snorted, a broad grin spreading across his face, and his eyes glistening in the orange light of the room. "Then you'd better un-misinterpret me, Leathan."

"Hoffman was at the apartment this morning. He might have taken the laptop."

Norden cursed under his breath.

"I'm not saying he did," I said. "What I am saying is: Hoffman was there, he was sitting next to the laptop, I followed him when he left, and when I got back you were there, but the laptop wasn't."

"Why did you follow him?"

"I didn't trust him."

"It's a shame you didn't mistrust him enough to stop him taking my laptop."

I ignored the comment. "Have you told McElroy?"

"I see what you're doing there," said Norden, grinning and pointing a finger as if indicating directly how I had twisted the conversation.

"I'm just doing what you told me," I said. Norden dropped his finger but didn't respond. "You've told me to do two things—look after Clementina and find your laptop."

"Implicit in that must be an instruction not to lie to me," said Clementina's father.

"Now you're just splitting hairs," I said. "We can have that conversation if you want, but there's a bigger conversation we need to have."

I could hear Norden's breathing as he sat staring at me. He had the look of a man figuring the permutations and having a conversation with himself. "Okay," he said, sighing and leaning back.

"After I saw him, Hoffman disappeared this morning. I saw that as a good thing—Clementina less so."

"Let me guess," said Clementina's father. "He didn't return her calls." I nodded—he tightened his lips in acknowledgement.

"We've spent the day searching for Hoffman."

Norden's still tight lips twitched, "What?"

"It gave me a way to watch Clementina and to search for your laptop—I figured she would know as well as anyone where Hoffman was." Norden went to speak, but I continued. "We found his hotel room and had a look."

"You did what? With Clementina?" Norden leaned forward, one hand on his desk, the other raised as if pointing would aid my understanding of his implied commentary on my choices.

"Have you seen a single inappropriate post on social media today? Have there been paparazzi following her around the city?"

Norden remained stiff in his position, slowly thawing. "No. No, I haven't."

"Well done Leathan on a job well done," I said. "I looked around Hoffman's hotel room. There was no laptop, and the messenger bag he could have used to carry the laptop wasn't there."

I stood, wandered to the window, and looked through the dirty glass over the red awning of the brasserie to Avenue des Gobelins. "Food any good?" I asked, indicating the brasserie.

"Yeah," said Norden, shaking his head as if coming back from a daydream. "Don't have the fish, but everything else is good. Apart from the noise."

"McElroy wanted me to identify Hoffman's body."

Norden's face was blank. He stared past me. He wasn't questioning why McElroy would know—or suspect—who the dead guy was, and he didn't seem interested in how McElroy had found out about Hoffman's death.

"He didn't have the messenger bag with him," I said.

Norden continued to stare past me.

"A small observation," I said.

"Huh?" Norden's gaze returned to me.

"If McElroy had anything to do with the disappearance of the laptop, then he knows that it's been missing for eight hours and you haven't mentioned it."

I dropped onto the sofa and waited for Norden to process my previous thought. He cursed under his breath.

"I'll keep looking for the laptop, but the reason I came..."

"You mean you didn't come to tell me that you lied and that I shouldn't trust McElroy?"

"His eyes are too close together," I said. "And it's not me who doesn't trust him. You haven't told him about the laptop, have you?"

Norden looked away. "Can we just say that there's stuff on it that I don't want anyone to see?"

"You can say whatever you want—you're paying me," I said. "But the reason I came is to make sure you're alright with me telling Clementina about Hoffman."

His brow narrowed, questioning.

"You don't think it should come from you...her father?"

He shook his head once, then returned his gaze to the papers spread across his cheap desk, which looked even more out of place than it had when I entered. "Just find the laptop," he muttered without looking up.

thirty-four

"Look, I'm sorry," said Reece.

The Maybach crawled through the early evening traffic. The expertly upholstered leather cuddled me and the climate control kept me at a perfect temperature.

"Dropping you in it with Johnnie. I'm sorry."

"Johnnie?"

"Johnson," said Reece, using the lawyer's full given name. "Telling him about Hoffman being around this morning."

"It's not a problem. You didn't tell him half of it," I muttered.

"Huh?"

"I'm mumbling—ignore me," I said, recalling my first introduction to Hoffman—last night, when I had found him naked, underneath Clementina, who was also naked as far as I could tell. I had withheld this detail—from Reece, from Angeline, from the man Reece called Johnnie but who I thought of as the lawyer I didn't trust, and from Zackary Norden.

Mostly I shut up because what a seventeen-year-old girl gets up to is her own business, but I also kept quiet because I still didn't know what was going on and where the loyalties lay.

That was why I had kept quiet about Hoffman having McElroy's—or as he now was, Johnnie's—card with him. In Paris. Paris, where Hoffman had been hanging out for several days before faking his arrival to Clementina. At least, he seemed to have faked his arrival—there was still the possibility that he had been on the train and that he had been picking up fake receipts to defraud someone, probably Johnnie.

And I'd also kept quiet about the laptop. I wasn't sure whether the driver beside me knew about its disappearance. If he didn't, there was no need for him to hear it from me.

"Tell me about Johnnie," I said. "You're mates? He looks after you?"

"He's the coming king," said Reece. "Zack's a good guy—and he's been good to me—but he's too distracted."

"How so?"

"The divorce. His new girl. That daughter causes a lot of hassle—as you know. He's doing too much, spread too thin. He'll burn, and Johnnie will take the throne."

"Does Johnnie want it? Is he pushing for it?" I asked.

"No, no... He just wants to be ready—to make sure there's continuity if Zack stumbles...for the investors. There's a lot of money involved, and he already runs things." He seemed to be weighing how to explain the situation. "You have a fire drill—not because you want there to be a fire, but just in case."

"And Johnnie's the fire officer, making sure we're ready?"

thirty-five

"You are all over—I mean *all over everywhere*."

"Me?" I shut Clementina's bedroom door behind me.

She had changed again since I left and was now wearing the red smock with yellow and orange splotches on top of a white T-shirt. I couldn't see the waistcoat, nor the brown boots. She put on a pair of sunglasses with five-point star lenses toned amber. "Quite the hippie look, huh? Do you like it?"

"Yeah," I said offhandedly. "You were saying about me, everywhere."

"The internet loves—I mean love, love, love, love, love, *love*, love, loves—those pictures you took of me. Did I mention they love the pictures? Seriously, everyone thinks that gear is so incredibly cool and retro, and..."

I sat on the sofa. Clementina noticed I wasn't sharing in her exuberant excitement.

"Put these on." She held out the starry amber sunglasses. "I'll take your photo—it'll be funny."

"Sit down for a moment." I hated to burst her bubble.

"Let me take your photo first," she said.

I ignored her.

"Leathan. Oh, Leathan. This is your sense of humor calling. Please come back to me—I'm lost in space." I stood and grabbed her phone. "Hey!" She made a grab—I held up my arm to restrain her. "Give me back my phone."

"Sit." I pointed to her bed. "We need to talk."

"What's this?" she said, then took on a mocking tone. "You need me to be very grown up."

I put the phone down on her dressing table, losing it within a cluster of small jars, tubes, and brushes, and then returned to the sofa. "I've already asked you this question, but I'm going to ask you again. I'm asking you again because this is important—life and death important."

"Life and death, huh? You've been watching too many movies."

My breathing was slow and deep. I could feel my shoulders rising and my spine straightening as I inhaled. I kept my focus locked.

Clementina sighed theatrically. "I get it. It's serious. You're a serious person doing serious stuff—so serious you've got to take my phone away."

I said nothing, leaving my fixed gaze to discomfort her.

She pulled up her legs and dragged a sheet around her, like a kid's blanket.

"Just talk, Leathan."

"The laptop."

The focus across her face dropped. The exasperated teenager was back.

"I don't care what you said before, but I need to know—did you see it? Did Hoffman mention the laptop?"

"No. Seriously Leathan, no." She hesitated. "I'm not saying it wasn't in the bag—I didn't check the bag—but I did look in it. All I am saying is when I looked in the bag, I didn't see a laptop, and Hoffman didn't mention it before you came and shooed him away like an unwanted tomcat spraying in the garden."

It was her turn to fix me with a stare, her head tilted to one side.

"Tell me again how you met Hoffman." My voice was barely above a whisper.

"How I met him..." she smirked, looking upward as if withholding an amusing family story.

"The Royal Opera House, Covent Garden," I began. "About a month ago."

"Daddy bear was getting some sort of award."

"For what?"

She shook her head with a small movement. "I dunno." She looked straight at me. "Enough with the third degree, Leathan—I don't know. I can't tell you what I don't know—ask Awful Michael Mallet." She flopped her tongue out of her mouth as she said her version of the media relations man's name.

"Did he organize the bash?"

"No. The law man did."

"Law man? You mean Johnson McElroy."

"Yup. The man whose parents hated him in so many ways. Seriously—who calls a kid Johnson?"

"You're saying McElroy organized and Mallet invited?"

"I presume Awful Michael Mallet did," she flopped her tongue again as she said his name. "What else do media relations people do apart from invite people to parties that they're running for their clients?"

"Did Mallet invite you?"

"Awful Michael Mallet? No. The law man did. He said I needed to be there to support daddy bear. He was insistent...but I suppose if you've got a name like that, then you're going to grow up to be an angry man."

"Do you know why McElroy wanted you there?"

"Photos." She shrugged. "He told me I had to be there."

"Photos?"

"I presumed they wanted me in the photos rather than the slut who was off having her tits groped by a shitty surgeon in Harley Street. I don't want to be bitchy," I let it pass, "but I take a better picture than her." She shrugged. "Sorry—it's true. I always look good in photos—she looks like shit, but that's probably because she..."

"Enough," I said. "Tell me about the guests."

"Boring men. They were either ancient—you know, forty or something—or they were perverts who thought they owned the world. My ass got pinched so much. You know what those City boys are like."

"So how did Hoffman get in? Who invited him?"

"I dunno."

"Why was he there?"

"Still don't know, Leathan."

"He wasn't a business contact of your father? He wasn't the kid of a business contact? He didn't work in the City? So how did he get in there?"

"That wasn't really the question that was on my mind," said Clementina. "He was the only person there who wasn't an asshole. Daddy bear excepted, and even then..."

She noticed that I was thinking.

"Why do you keep asking me these questions, Leathan?"

"Bits of paper in Hoffman's room... Conversations I've just had..." I mumbled.

"And?"

"And," I said. It was my turn to shrug. I tried a different line. "We were together in the café this morning when I sent Hoffman away."

"Yeah."

"That was the last time you saw him, and we've been together ever since."

"Except when I peed, yes," said Clementina. "And apart from the last two hours."

I couldn't see the clock, but I was sure there was one in the room.

She seemed weary. "Why do you keep asking me these questions, Leathan? I just want to see Hoffman."

I held my lower lip between my teeth, becoming aware of the feeling of nausea in the pit of my gut as the image of Hoffman's mangled body floated in front of my eyes.

"You know something," said Clementina. "You know something about Hoffman." She half smiled—a look of hopeful anticipation crossed her face. The kid who knew she was about to be told something good—she just didn't know how good. "You do know something, don't you, Leathan?"

The acid in my stomach gurgled, and I felt the clamminess of my hands. The air became thin, making me feel light-headed. I tried to move my face—to soften it, to suggest some sympathy—but I felt the power in all my muscles fading.

"Leathan? What's up, Leathan?" Her tone had changed—thinner, sharper, aware that something was wrong, but holding back the panic while she sought reassurance. "Leathan, where's Hoffman?"

I found the power to shrug, but nothing more.

"What's happened, Leathan? Leathan? Tell me you know where Hoffman is and that he's alright." I wanted to say something, but my jaw wouldn't move. "Tell me he's alright."

When I looked up, Clementina's face was white. Her eyes were glistening with moisture. I shook my head—a small movement.

"No," said Clementina, her voice high-pitched and strained, a tear starting to roll down the side of her nose. "No, Leathan."

"I'm sorry, Clemmy." A hoarse whisper was all I could manage.

The sound she made was somewhere between a shriek and a moan of pain that precedes death. Then she pulled the sheets around herself and cried and cried and cried.

thirty-six

I rapped on the door with my knuckles.

This door was the opposite of the door to the apartment. Where the door to the apartment was big—technically it was a double door, but I had only seen one door open—this was a regular-sized door. The apartment door was natural wood, carved, and detailed. This was flat, without ornamentation, and painted white.

Reece opened the door. "You look like shit." He stood back, inviting me in.

Clementina had started crying. I didn't blame her: She had just found out that her boyfriend—the term I was going with, even if no one else was—was dead. She had started crying and I wasn't sure when she'd stop, or even if she would ever stop.

After I had briefly confirmed that Hoffman was indeed dead, I needed to be anywhere else. I needed to think. I needed to be distracted. I needed to be pulled away from the image I had of Hoffman's burned and bruise face, and that twisted leg with the broken bone ripped through the denim.

I left Clementina crying—I felt like I was intruding. I felt like I would be intruding to disturb her by leaving, so I sat, watching her cry. But that felt like I was intruding even more, so I had left. I mumbled that I would stay close and she should call if she wanted anything. She didn't respond.

I didn't say how close I'd stay, but the driver's apartment wasn't far away.

"Seriously like shit," said Reece as he led me into a reception room. It was small and windowless. The walls had been painted a shade of cream and were featureless. A flat screen television was attached to a wall. Underneath was a stand with a DVD player and a game console—a sprawling mass of wires of different colors, twisted and knotted, connected the devices.

The image on the screen was frozen—the view from the cockpit of a fighter jet. Reece held up a game controller. "Do you?"

"Nah."

He indicated the sofa and sat himself in a large chair placed directly in front of the screen. As he sat, he reached beside him and pulled out something. The screen went blank. "Talk," said the driver, letting a still fall over the room.

"Did McEl...I mean, did Johnnie tell you about the kid who was here this morning? The one who was looking for Clementina."

"No."

"His name is Hoffman," I said. "Or to be more accurate, his name *was* Hoffman—he's dead and Clementina is in freefall, as you might expect."

The driver exhaled slowly. "You just tell her?" I nodded. "That's why you look like shit." He exhaled again and leaned back in his chair—the back lowered and a footrest came up from under the seat. "Were they doing it? The girl and Hoff?" He had clenched a fist as if to imply "it" was a sexual act.

"Were they having sex?" I asked. "I seriously doubt it."

I left the lie without embellishment.

"Was this where we drove?" he asked, his finger pointing as if to suggest the trip we had taken with the lawyer.

"With the cops," I said.

"Why's he dead?"

It was my turn to exhale. "It looks random...wrong place, wrong time, I guess. But McElroy might know more."

He nodded sagely, sitting back in his seat, his curiosity seemingly sated.

I counted to five before I continued. "The reason I'm here... You got me thinking."

"Me?" He seemed shocked that I would engage with him on a cerebral matter.

"If you had to hide something around here, where would you hide it?"

"How big?"

"About the size of a phone directory."

"Wow, grandpa! Tell me about your war stories too," said Reece. "You're aging yourself there."

"Okay, something about this big," I said, indicating something the size of phone directory.

"Hide how?" said Reece. "Hide a birthday present or hide...?"

"I don't trust Clementina," I said.

Reece pulled a face that would have befitted a teenager. He didn't need to use words, his face said: "Well, of course, who would trust that stuck-up little bitch?"

"There's an absence of trust on my part—it's not that I positively mistrust her—but the jury is still out."

Reece snorted. "I'll save you the wait."

"If I need to dig into Clementina's life—outside of her room, where would she hide things? For instance, would she give them to Angeline, and get Angeline to make them disappear?

Reece exhaled slowly.

"Come at it another way—where would you hide things? Where would Angeline hide things?"

The driver was still exhaling. "Too many places, my man. Too many places." I waited for him to elaborate. "In the apartment." He caught my eye. "Do you think that Clementina or Zack knows where the ironing board is kept?" He waited out his own rhetorical question. "Precisely. You could put stuff in a closet and those two wouldn't find it—they wouldn't even find the closet."

"Where would Angeline hide something from you?" I tried.

"Behind a closet—the closets and the cabinets might be fitted very nicely, but they're ugly behind. Lots of gaps, lots of filler. It'd take a long time just to check the obvious. That's before we talk about her apartment—it's the mirror of this—and then there are the storage rooms in the basement and all the hidey-holes in the parking lot." He waited a moment. "Or maybe she would just use the linen room."

"There's a linen room?" I asked.

The driver nodded slowly. "But I doubt Angeline would put herself out—at least not that far out—for Clementina. She does her job, but there's no love between the two. What are you looking...?" He let his question trail off.

"I don't know," I said. "But I'd like to do something—to find something—to impress McElroy. If he's the prince across the water, then it's a smart move for me to impress him. And we both get suck-up points if I can show that the two of us have been playing nicely."

The mention of being awarded suck-up points without doing any work had distracted Reece. He was busy figuring how he would spend his next bonus. "Been meaning to ask," I said. "McElroy and Mallet—where are they staying while they're in Paris?"

"Above the office," said the driver. "They've each got an apartment in that block."

thirty-seven

I walked up from Reece's apartment and leaned against the wall outside the Norden family's apartment, phone in hand, searching the internet.

It only took a few moments for the search results to give me a list of left luggage lockers in Paris. It took me a few minutes of fighting with websites designed to be seen on a full-sized computer monitor to find the nearest and to make a booking. Seemingly, I couldn't just turn up—I had to book, and therefore pay, first.

I completed the transaction and waited for the email to come confirming my booking, then I went in.

I tapped gently on Clementina's door and entered without waiting to be invited. She was sitting in exactly the same position that she had been when I left. Her eyes looked like they had been bathed in acid, but the tears had stopped flowing.

"Have you got a bag I could borrow?" I said, indicating something small.

She threw a hand toward a door leading off the room. "Over there," I think she said. "Second door."

The room was a dressing room, similar to the one in my room, but larger. The second door opened a closet that as far as I could tell had one purpose—to store bags. I took out several before settling on a leather backpack.

"I need to go out," I said, moving to the sofa. I slipped the iPad into the backpack and looked up at Clementina. Her head was bowed. "I need to find more about Hoffman."

The tears began to flow again.

thirty-eight

The storage lockers were a ten-, maybe fifteen-minute walk.

I slowed my pace: I needed to hold the phone steady as I looked at the photograph I had taken a few hours earlier when I thought Hoffman was missing. In reality, by then he was probably already dead.

I zoomed in, squinted, read the number, and then flipped to the dialer. I was back at my full walking speed before the phone rang.

There was a grunt at the other end of the line—the sort of response people give when they don't know who's calling. Before caller ID, anyone answering would clearly state who they were, or at least state the number. With caller ID, an unrecognizable number was an invitation to ignore the call or at best to be evasive in answering, and to put the responsibility onto the caller to identify himself first.

"It's Leathan," I said, holding the phone with one hand and gripping the strap of Clementina's leather backpack now containing the iPad with the other.

There was a pause. I knew what McElroy was thinking—Leathan who? Once he'd got through that loop and figured it was me, then his brain would leap to the next question: How the heck did Leathan get my number? And then he'd try to play it cool—he wouldn't want to show that this was unusual.

"Leathan," he said, in a tone of voice that told me he was struggling to show no emotion, but he really wanted to know why I was calling.

"Clementina's going to be crying until the end of time," I said, "so I'm going for a beer. A beer, singular. Then I'll be heading back to the apartment where I'll be sitting in my room for the rest of the evening, just waiting around in case she needs me."

"That's...good," he said, as if he had been the person to hire me and I had just provided him with evidence that I had performed my job to a satisfactory standard. I guessed it still rankled that I had been hired directly by his boss. He might have told me what was expected—but his boss was paying me and was the one who actually yanked my strings.

"Is there anything more useful I can be doing instead of sitting around?" I asked.

"We've got it all sorted, thanks Leathan."

"You've got a lid on everything?"

"Yeah."

"Mallet has made sure that Hoffman stays out of the papers."

"Mallet has made sure it's a nonstory," said the lawyer.

"What about the big guy? Has he run to the call of his woman?"

"He's left for the evening," said the lawyer, "but I'm sure he'll come past you at some time—maybe tomorrow morning."

"So everything's sorted?"

"Yeah."

"Great," I said. "So how about dinner? Could I...?"

"I'm sorry, Leathan. I'm already booked for tonight."

"Maybe a quick aperitif?" I tried.

"I need to get ready."

"A nightcap? I could sneak out."

"It's likely to be a long dinner—it's business as much as pleasure."

"No problem," I said. "I'll catch you tomorrow."

thirty-nine

The brasserie with the red awning looked inviting, and it was too long since I had eaten.

The pizza place next door seemed less inviting, but while I was hungry, that wasn't the issue that mattered to me. I pulled out my phone and dialed the number written on the sign outside the pizza place.

"I'll collect," I said in better French than the guy who answered the phone spoke, and hung up. My prop—which might become dinner—would be ready in fifteen minutes. I leaned back against the tree—one of many forming a straight row helping to mark the border between the sidewalk and the blacktop—and looked across the four lanes of Avenue des Gobelins.

Another delivery boy left. He placed his insulated bag into the box on the back of his scooter, pulled down his helmet, and fired up the engine. The European Union seems to have legislated on every area of our lives—I can never understand why that legislation doesn't extend as far as the noise that scooters make. The noise was about as socially acceptable as throwing a bucket of shit in church.

The diners under the red awning of the brasserie jumped as one as the high-pitched engine imposed itself into their dinner. I looked down the street; three restaurants down, and diners were twitching with the intrusion. They might not know what the problem was, but they knew something was wrong.

The kid on the scooter rolled it forward and off its stand, twisting the throttle as far as it would go. The shout of the engine became a scream, and he took off. Doubtless he felt he was going fast—for those of us tolerating his noise, he didn't move fast enough.

Within two minutes, there was the sound of a scooter returning. Similar but different—equally intrusive, but with a different timbre of engine scream. The kid pulled the scooter onto the sidewalk outside the pizza place, lining it with the other scooters, and killed the engine before lifting his helmet and unzipping his leather jacket. His jeans were dirtier than mine, but we looked close enough. Or rather, I could pass for a delivery boy if I had a helmet.

I let my gaze shift to the brasserie and up above the red awning. There was no light in the room Norden was using as his temporary office. This didn't prove he wasn't there—it just proved that I couldn't see a light in that room. The floor above had a light, and the one above that was in darkness. None of which told me which was McElroy's apartment or whether he was out.

I spent another five minutes staring at closed windows, hoping for something. I got nothing, so I walked down the street before crossing, taking my time to make sure I saw Norden, McElroy, or Mallet—or anyone else who might recognize me—before I saw them. I kept close the building frontages as I walked back up to the pizza place and ducked in.

"Monsieur Lapin," I said.

The guy behind the counter said nothing but tapped the touchscreen of the till in front of him, then turned to a stack of pizza boxes on the counter beside him, each with a printout stuck on the edge. "American hot," he said, pulling the box from the middle of the stack.

"Yeah." Our conversation was nearly as detailed and as wide-ranging as the one I'd had with the girl behind the counter when I stored Clementina's leather backpack holding the iPad.

He punched the touchscreen and held out his hand, letting me know he wanted payment. I handed him €50. He dropped the change on the box and passed me my prop. I took the square cardboard and moved over to the door, waiting.

It didn't take long until I heard the scream. I was familiar with the process by now and watched as the kid drove up onto the sidewalk, sliding into the row between the other scooters, then kicked the stand.

I was with him before his helmet was off. "Fifty euros," I said to the kid—his skin shining with a fine layer of sweat and his wiry hair messed up.

He sneered and ignored me, but moved slowly—slower than the kids did returning from a run.

"One hundred," I said.

"For what?"

"To borrow your helmet. Five minutes—one hundred euros."

He stared at me. He was a kid with a dilemma. The dilemma wasn't whether to let me use the helmet—the dilemma was how much he could charge me before I walked away.

"No? Okay."

"Wait," he said.

"And I need a knife." He looked blankly at me. "Don't tell me you go out without some sort of protection." Still no reaction. "You don't need a knife to sit on your ass and wait for five minutes." His visage was unmoving. "One-fifty, the helmet and your knife." The muscles across his cheekbones tightened. "Do you know the code for the brown door?" I pointed across the brasserie.

"Of course." He seemed offended that I would even ask.

"Final offer: The code for the door. Your knife. The helmet. Two hundred." He looked me up and down. "Going in five, four, three..."

"Stop counting and give me the money," he said, a grin finally spreading across his face.

I pulled out €100. "Helmet," I said, looking up. He got the hint and held out the helmet. I exchanged it for the pizza box and pulled it over my head, feeling the kid's now cold sweat get wiped over my face.

I retrieved the pizza, led the kid toward the brown door, and pulled out two €50 bills. I moved out of the sight of the diners in the brasserie and held out the first €50. "Knife." I felt something metallic with a bit of weight touch my hand as he took the bill. I accepted the lump of metal and slipped it into my back pocket. "And finally," I nodded toward the door. He punched the keypad and there was a click. I gave him the last €50 as I stepped through. "I'll be back in five."

He snorted. He didn't believe me either.

"Okay, ten." I let the door drop behind me and proceeded under the arch to the small courtyard, which was overlooked by the apartments surrounding the block. I pulled out my phone and hit redial, then wedged the phone inside the helmet next to my ear.

McElroy answered.

"Shit, I'm sorry. It's Leathan; I dialed the wrong number," I said. "You must be out by now."

"I'm just leaving my apartment," said the lawyer.

forty

I held the door for the man who was coming out from the stairs, which wrapped themselves around the old elevator. His descent had not been quiet—not that it was possible to quietly descend wooden stairs surrounded by hard surfaces reflecting every tiny sound and amplifying every large sound.

"Bonsoir, monsieur," I said in perfect French.

"Hi. Thanks," grunted McElroy. Even his English seemed limited.

"Madame le Jeune?" I asked.

"Don't know her," said McElroy, sticking with English

"Which floor are you?" I asked in English, faking a heavy French accent and not making eye contact from under the helmet. "So I don't tap, tap, tap, tap..." I mimicked knocking on a door.

"Third," said the lawyer, who departed without any further comment.

"Merci," I said to no one in particular, safe in the knowledge that I knew which door was now double bolted against me.

I stepped back through the courtyard and placed the pizza box and the helmet under the mailboxes that were bolted against the side wall of the tunnel connecting the gate to the courtyard. I didn't have any further need for either—but the slice of pizza I took was surprisingly good.

From a brief survey—completed with my slice in one hand—it was clear that the staircase wrapped around the elevator had small windows bringing in a limited amount of light. The windows were small and were set below the level of the windows for the apartment on the floor to which each flight was rising.

The windows for the apartments were mostly, but not exclusively, in need of repair or replacement. All had security shutters—from the look operated by a crank set inside each apartment. From the look, all of the shutters were in greater need of repair than the windows.

Like most apartments, the apartment on the third floor hadn't closed its security shutters, assuming they still functioned. And if the shutters had broken, then they had broken in an open position. Whatever the case, the third floor looked inviting.

I finished my slice, wiped my fingers on my jeans, and proceeded to climb the stairs.

forty-one

I rapped firmly and loudly on the door, listening as the sound echoed inside.

I wasn't hoping for a response, and I hadn't prepared a lie in case the door was answered, but I figured there was little to lose in checking and a lot to lose if my assumption was wrong.

Silence.

I returned to the stairs, taking the four steps down to the window. The window lever was painted shut—a bit of scraping and prodding with my newly borrowed and frighteningly sharp knife fixed that.

It was an awkward jump to the windowsill—the window was raised from the height of the stair from which I jumped—and as I sat down, my body outside, my legs inside, the frame cut into my thighs.

The lack of use had left the opening window with some structural strength—enough strength to balance my weight as I moved myself to a standing position, with only the tips of my toes left inside.

Now that I was standing on the windowsill, the view to the cobbled courtyard below—a vertical drop—took on a different perspective. Silently I cursed French security arrangements: heavily bolted doors, but lightly guarded windows if you can get over your fear of falling.

I scrambled up and across to the next windowsill, gripping the thick tongue that ran along the bottom of the window as I retrieved the knife from my back pocket. I managed to get half a foot onto the sill—enough to help my balance, not enough that I could relax.

Getting the knife out of my pocket was easy; unfolding the blade was less so with one hand still gripping the windowsill. With encouragement from a combination of lips and teeth, the blade opened. The sharp steel easily fitted through the small gap in the metal frame and pushed the catch, letting the glass swing open.

Or at least, the glass could have swung open if its arc wasn't blocked by my body—I shifted to let the pane move.

With some groaning, some cautious shifting, and some heaving, I pulled myself through the window, finding myself panting, but standing inside, looking back at the window I had just pulled myself through.

I was in a bedroom.

The sort of bedroom that always suggested to me that the resident only uses the room for one purpose: sleeping. The room was a purely functional box. The resident would enter, de-robe, get into bed, and sleep. Come the morning, the resident would wake, dress, and leave. It wasn't a room for entertaining the opposite sex or the same sex, and it wasn't a place to read or watch television, or a sanctuary away from the world. It was a box into which the resident went in order to sleep.

If this was McElroy's room, then I suspected he had never looked out of the window. The window could be bricked up, and he wouldn't notice the difference.

The wall parallel to the window wasn't a wall as such—it was a row of floor-to-ceiling closets. I started from the left, opening the tall white-painted piece of wood to reveal a closet that McElroy had probably only opened once and would never open again. At a guess it was the utility storage closet for the apartment—the place where all those things that are infrequently needed are stored. The items that a landlord needs to provide in order to rent out an apartment, but which the resident will never want to use.

Two vacuum cleaners, an ironing board, a broom, a dustpan and brush, and on the shelves above, there was an iron, a laundry basket, and that was the point at which I closed the door, moving on to the next closet.

The double doors opened on hanging space. There was a full rail of suits, jackets, trousers, shirts, and sweaters. I reached for a dark blue sweater and felt—cashmere. At the bottom of the closet, angled probably so that the door would close, was a large suitcase. I suspected it wasn't large enough for all the clothes, but that wasn't my problem.

I jumped: footsteps. Fast, running footsteps. Moving right to left across the third wall. The wall shared with the bedroom and the stairwell. I hadn't noticed when I came in, but as I now paid attention, I could see that the wall was curved to follow the curve of the stairs.

The feet continued to the landing outside the apartment and then began their descent of the flight below. I returned to the closet, opening the next double doors to reveal shelves. Floor-to-ceiling shelves, each between eight and twelve inches apart. I started at the bottom—the rows were empty. At about three feet off the ground, I found the first filled shelf—papers. The next shelf up, more papers. Above that, socks. One further, underwear. Then one of those shelves with the detritus that would usually be spread across the top of a chest of drawers or on a dressing table.

There were footsteps again, but this time ascending. Two sets. One leading, confident, heavy; the other less regular and slower in pace—I suspected taking two steps at once. I closed the doors on the shelves, letting the wood shut silently, and listened.

The feet reached the landing but didn't begin the next ascent.

Shit.

There was the sound of metal tapping on metal—a key missing the lock, but eventually finding where it wanted to go and zipping into place. A satisfying thunk as the lock turned and the deadbolts were released from their task.

Shit.

A hinge groaned as a door opened. A voice, a second voice—less clear.

Shit.

I opened the utility cupboard and squeezed myself next to an upright vacuum cleaner—its handle sticking into my ass as I closed the door behind me, offering a silent prayer that my pounding heart couldn't be heard by whoever was coming through the door.

There were more footsteps—leather on wood. I guessed the wood floor in the bedroom extended to the rest of the apartment. There were voices—one voice moved, becoming louder and softer as the footsteps became louder or softer; the other remained consistent. A door opened—a closet, a kitchen cabinet perhaps—then closed. More movement. More talk. Then slam. The front door closed.

I cracked the closet door and listened to the even more satisfying thunk as the lock was turned and the deadbolts resumed their duty of preventing me from passing through that door. Footsteps on the landing, and then the four feet began their descent.

I was at the window before the two reached the floor below. With the pump of adrenalin, their final descent and appearance in the courtyard felt like it took weeks. In reality, I was looking out the window for a few seconds when Johnson McElroy came out of from the stairwell and into the courtyard.

As I had seen him a few minutes ago, the lawyer was wearing a blue business suit. I wasn't close enough to see his shoes, but I was sure that if I continued looking in the closet I would find something similar.

The lawyer held the door for another man. My first impression: he needed to wash his hair—the grease parted his hair. Second impression: younger than McElroy—he seemed to carry himself as if he was always ready for a fight. Third impression: a dark-brown leather coat. Three steps and they disappeared under the arch. I listened for the slam of the brown door and turned away from the window before heading toward the front door.

There was a smell. Nothing strong—just a memory of something unpleasant. The kind of smell that maybe a teenager would be unable to explain—the smell not being one that could be purchased at an expensive perfumery.

The apartment was arranged with a hallway running toward the bedroom, which was next to the bathroom. A third door opened onto a living room with a kitchenette in the far end. I stepped back into the hallway. By the bathroom was a small cupboard—functionally little more than a side table with space underneath.

I opened the door of the small cupboard. It was the storage for soap, shampoo, and handwash. Pushed into a space at the top was something black made of rip-stop nylon. I pulled it out, laying it flat on the floor.

A messenger bag. A familiar messenger bag. I couldn't be certain it was the same bag, but it looked the same as the one that had been slung across Hoffman's shoulder that morning. I didn't need to look—the weight and the way the bag had been scrunched up already told me there was no laptop.

I pushed the bag back, silently wishing I'd paid more attention to how it looked before I pulled it out. I spent five minutes more looking and didn't find a laptop. There may have been many things that would have interested me, but I wasn't going to hang around—I had pizza to eat and a helmet to return.

But first, there was a window to climb out of.

forty-two

An officer was standing outside the gate to the green space—the garden in the middle of the blocks that towered around it.

Having returned the helmet and the knife to the pizza delivery guy, I went to the only other place in Paris that I knew for certain McElroy had visited. "They say there was a murder," I said to the officer.

The officer met my gaze—not in an aggressive manner, not in a way that seemed likely to intimidate, but more as a basic courtesy in the hope that I'd go away sooner. He pulled in the side of his mouth, flattening one cheek against his teeth. It was a small, subtle movement, but the message it conveyed was clear: "I don't care. I'm just doing my job. Now go away."

"Have they taken the body?" I asked.

He tilted his head forward and backward as if agreeing and in a blank monotone said: "What body? I don't know what you're talking about, monsieur."

"Anyone see anything?" He met my gaze and gave a small shake of his head. His first unambiguous communication. "There was a white van."

"And that's all you've got?"

He returned his stare to somewhere in the distance.

"Thanks," I muttered, then turned back. "Do you want a coffee or something?"

"I'm fine," he said.

With my first visit, I'd noticed an older-style block, but then I'd focused inward—looking toward the white tent. Now I looked outward. Running along the bottom edge of the garden was a residential block. It had the smell of something intended to move the area upmarket, but in that smell, the whiff of modernism was clearly present with its boxy construction and stark white tiling covering the outer surfaces.

The face fronting the garden was flat. Where a room overlooked the garden, its wall was constructed from glass—floor-to-ceiling, wall-to-wall glass. Between the rooms, there were balconies—instead of a platform hanging off a wall, these balconies were more like rooms where the architect had forgotten to specify the materials for the outside wall and so an open space had been left.

Doubtless on the architect's plan, this was described as a luxury feature allowing residents to sit on their balcony and look over the garden with an uninterrupted view. And this might work, but the balconies also looked at the low-rise block to their right.

This low rise had the look of an attempt at social housing but taking account of lessons learned somewhere else. The pure white modernism seen in much of Paris wasn't there—instead, the block was something that I was more used to seeing in London. Designed to be cheaply constructed, faced with near-orange bricks, and with a steel fence around the perimeter to give the residents some feeling of ownership in the hope that a small measure of pride would seep through. It was a cheap ploy to save on the cost of hiring people to look after the shrubs.

Two sides with windows overlooking the garden. To the third side was the kids' playground across from the red-bricked school I had seen when Reece first drove us there. The officer looked at me, a look that said: "Please, no more questions. Please don't do anything that would require me to take any action. Please just go away."

"Sure you don't want a coffee?"

"I'm fine," he repeated and took a step sideways to reveal what passed as a trash receptacle—a steel pole with a ring at the top, the ring holding a clear polythene trash sack. At the bottom of the sack were several disposable coffee cups. "Really, I'm fine."

"If you change your mind," I said and headed toward the third side, walking along the cobbled path between the frontage of the intended upscale block and the steel fence of the garden.

At the end of the block, on the corner of the garden, was an old Haussmannian block. Eight floors of 1850-something Parisian architecture. Parisian architecture that had upset someone enough that the neighborhood had been flattened; apart from this block and the one on the diagonally opposite corner of the garden, the old streets had been dug up, and the new blocks had been imposed. But this block had been left, standing free and about twenty yards closer to the garden than the rest of the row.

Getting into old blocks isn't necessarily difficult. Trying to find someone who has seen anything is. I spent half an hour or so knocking on doors and talking. I looked out of a few windows and soon reached a conclusion that no one would have seen Hoffman's last moments with any clarity from these windows. That was, unless I got lucky and found someone with x-ray vision who could see through the trees.

But I carried on—there was a chance that someone had been walking by or had heard a rumor.

Most of the residents were older. They seemed keen to tell me that it wasn't like it used to be. They seemed keen to point the finger—apparently it was obvious who would commit a murder. Them. The newer arrivals. They didn't need to look further; they didn't need corroboration, because they knew who it was.

I suspected they were wrong.

If one of them had mentioned a white van, I might have had a different opinion. Not that the white van was a given—but it was more of a lead than an assumption based on social or racial prejudice or anxieties about changes.

Leaving the block, I gave up on that side. If you couldn't see the garden from this block, then you weren't going to be able to see it any better from twenty or thirty yards farther away. I headed back along the southern edge of the park, passing the intended upscale block, looking for any way to get in.

But upscale and newer also meant more emphasis on security—locks, codes, doors that wouldn't open just by leaning on them heavily. Sure, a single apartment would be easy from the outside, but getting into the public areas without the cops being called would be harder.

As I passed the corner, the cop had gone. I didn't look hard, but I suspected he was somewhere in the trees of the garden, taking a quick leak after drinking too much coffee.

I found the entrance to the block obscured from view. Clearly an opening door might offend some architectural sensibilities, and so the door had been hidden down a narrow and dark passage. A narrow and dark passage that only had one function—to provide access to the block.

I stood away from the path—someone had to pass at some point.

I had waited fifteen minutes before someone turned into the passageway leading to the apartment block entrance. I nearly missed him—I was distracted counting the number of floors in the tower that you couldn't miss as you left this apparently upscale block.

I wasn't sure whether there were thirty or thirty-one floors in the block. Whichever was right, there were a lot of people in one block, and the heap of trash—mattresses, tables, a bicycle with one wheel—stacked against the perimeter fence did little to enhance the ambience of the block I was waiting on.

He was a younger guy—twenty-something—wearing a suit that probably cost a reasonable amount but had since been worn shiny, and carrying a briefcase. I followed him in. He took the elevator, so I headed for the stairs and started banging on doors, working my way down from the top floor. The story here was fairly consistent: I didn't see anything, my spouse/significant other didn't see anything, we were at work.

On the second floor I rapped on a door. The response was immediate—a baby howled.

The sound of the baby became louder, and the door opened. A woman stood, holding a baby—a howling baby. "What?"

In the face of unmitigated anger and hostility—when that hostility is richly deserved since you have just woken a sleeping baby—there is only one sensible option: Tell lies. "I'm with the police."

She had a look of suspicion, heightened by her natural protective instincts. Her natural protective instincts that focused her attention on the howling. She gently rocked the baby, mumbling soft encouragement to return to sleep.

"I'm civilian staff," I tried. "I don't know if you saw—there was an incident in the garden. I'm just trying to find anyone who saw anything. If you did, then the detectives can come and see you tomorrow, and get a statement."

She half looked up, but her attention was focused on the baby, who had stopped howling and was now gurgling.

"Budget cuts," I said. "It's cheaper for me to knock on doors rather than the detectives." I didn't know whether I had convinced her, but I had convinced myself that the Paris police should have civilian staff to go knocking on doors. "Did you see anything?"

"Early afternoon?" she asked.

"Yeah."

"This one had started howling, and I was..." She rocked the baby gently in her arms. "I was walking and staring aimlessly out the window. It wasn't much..."

"That doesn't matter," I said. "You can only say what you saw."

She hesitated. "I didn't see much—I don't know that I saw anything—but it's not what I saw so much as it was unusual."

I waited.

"There was a white van, but the guy who got out didn't look like the guys who usually drive those things for the mayor. He didn't have overalls—he was wearing what looked like a brown leather coat. Then he went to the back of the van, opened the doors, and it was like he pulled out this other guy. This other guy looked like he'd been in a fight—he couldn't walk on his own, the man with the coat had to help him."

I waited.

"That was all I saw," she said. "This one had calmed down, so I laid her back in her cot."

I waited.

"That was it. I'm sorry."

"Don't apologize," I said. "That's very helpful. I'll tell the detectives."

She frowned. It wasn't a frown to express disagreement, more than something wasn't right for her. "This is going to sound crazy, but I'm sure another man got out of the van."

"From the back?"

"No—from the passenger seat in the front. And that's what really struck me—there was the man in the brown coat, and the other one was wearing a suit." She stopped herself. Her voice lost its hesitation, taking on a lighter tone. "Look. I was focused on this one. He could have been someone just walking by—ignore me. I can't be certain."

forty-three

It was hard to be certain that this was the right hotel—there had been so many, and they all looked the same. In the dark it was harder still. I needed to scratch around looking for the back entrance—or the back exit, as it had been for Clementina and me—to be sure I had the right place.

There were no police, at least none that I could see. Within a block in each direction, there were several white vans, and even more vans that you might call white or think were white if you weren't paying attention. Most were without occupants, and in those that had a driver, the driver wasn't wearing a brown leather coat.

I spent another while watching the hotel, looking for any sign of anything out of the ordinary—always hard when you're looking at a hotel that is the very definition of ordinary and that infects everything around it with ordinary, making even the extraordinary just plain ordinary. I pulled out my phone and called the hotel. "Mister Hoffman, room two-two-three."

"Putting you through."

That was a good start.

The phone rang. And rang. And rang. And rang.

It kept ringing until I saw a group of four or five tourists aimlessly shuffling in—pausing halfway in and halfway out of the entrance, keeping the automatic doors open as they discussed the finer points of something I didn't care about. I hung up, crossed the road, and as they resolved their issue, I joined the back of the group, slipping into the hotel with them.

They greeted the porter behind the reception desk in a language I didn't recognize, but in a tone that was jovial and respectful. As they moved toward the elevator, I slipped past and took the stairs, finding my way to the second floor and room 223.

There was no sign that anyone had linked the room to Hoffman—no officer standing guard, no crime scene tape, no notice on the door. It looked exactly as it had when Clementina and I left.

I tugged out my shirt and wiped the knob before dropping the keycard into the slot and waiting for the lock to click.

I closed the door behind me as quietly as I could, then wiped the knob with my shirt. I leaned on the light switches with my elbow, and while the low-energy bulbs coughed to life, I made my way to the bathroom and found a hand towel.

As I stood in the bathroom doorway, looking into the main room, it looked exactly as I remembered it from a few hours ago, which is much like saying one white sheet of paper looked how I remembered the look of another sheet of white paper. But there was certainly nothing to suggest fresh disturbance, and whatever smell Clementina had smelled had now dissipated.

I started with the nightstands. Clementina had searched here. In one there was a bible, in the other a well-hidden dried lump of chewing gum—at least I hoped it was chewing gum. I wiped down the nightstands then moved to the closets Clementina had searched, sliding the left door over the right to reveal shelves.

She hadn't lied. There was no laptop here. I had a more than cursory rummage and slid the doors to the left to reveal the other half, where trousers, shirts, and jackets hung. A swift rummage through the dead man's pockets revealed nothing further, so I took the towel, wiped the doors of all fingerprints, and returned them to the closed position.

My reinspection of the built-in desk-cum-dressing table-cum-place to put the obligatory coffee-making facilities was swift. There was nothing that I hadn't seen on my first visit, but this time, instead of photographing the receipts and scraps of paper, I took the bundle before wiping down every surface, every handle, and everywhere that anyone might look for a fingerprint.

I looked under the bed, between the mattress and the box spring, in the bedding, and everywhere a laptop might be hidden—or anything else that might interest me. There was nothing. In locating the iPad, Clementina had found everything that was there to be found.

A final scan and I saw a few last places to wipe—the switches by the bed, the TV remote, the faux-leather seat by the dressing table, the television itself. Having wiped everything, I moved to the bathroom and washed my hands before I finished my wipe-down of the room.

The white noise of running water and the focus on getting the dirt from under my nails distracted me. I didn't realize I wasn't alone until a moment before the fist came at me. There was a change in the light as he came across the door, his fist uncoiling, but without sufficient preparation he mistimed the blow, glancing my shoulder at the maximum extent of his reach.

I felt the potential but not the power as I turned, trapped in a tiled white room, in a white box, stacked with other white boxes, in a bigger white box.

The doorway presented a challenge to the man in the brown leather coat. It wasn't wide enough to get a good swing, and he didn't want to get closer to me—I had grabbed the first thing I could find, the toilet brush, and was holding it toward him like a small sword. It might not have much effect, but I knew he wouldn't want a shitty brush coming at his face.

He stepped back, moving out of my sight, then reappeared, holding the faux-leather backless dressing table seat, its legs toward me. He threw the seat and followed it into the small room.

Two of the legs hit me before the seat fell to the floor, slamming my left foot between it and the white tiles.

The first blow hit me on my left temple; the second was a gut shot, landing squarely and winding me. The third glanced my shoulder as I stumbled forward, tripping on the upturned seat, and ramming one of the seat legs into my kneecap as I fell on the bath, slamming my elbow on the plastic.

I tried to breathe, sucking all of the air that I could pull through my mouth and into my lungs, becoming aware of a bitterness, a mustiness in the taste and the smell of the air. Becoming aware that I had dropped the brush without noticing. Becoming aware that I was losing my focus.

As I tried to stand he spread his feet, finding his balance, and let his right fist swung; I ducked. He threw a left. As it came, I grabbed his hand and pulled, letting his momentum pull him over as I got to my feet.

He cursed at me and tried to kick out.

I unleashed a retaliatory kick between his legs, and as he howled in pain, I ran.

forty-four

I left through the front door. I didn't have time to search for the kitchen or some other back route. My priority was to be away from a man who was stronger than me, used to fighting, and angry that I had been lucky.

I walked through the lobby, and as I got outside I began to jog, trying to convince myself that the pain I was feeling was because I was doing physical exercise. I lost the argument with myself and stopped. The blows had hurt. Where he had made contact would show a bruise, but the real damage seemed to be where I had fallen: Hard tiles on the floor and walls, a hard porcelain toilet, and a plastic bathtub that had no flexibility.

At the time I hadn't been aware of making contact, except with my elbow on the tub, but now I could feel the pain. I started moving farther away from the hotel and toward the Latin Quarter, trying to stop myself limping and flinching as the pain pinched.

I pulled out the mess of paper I had photographed on my first visit and retrieved on this visit and started to sort it. Anything with an address in the Latin Quarter would do. I found a receipt with an address that sounded familiar—a café. The kind of place that would serve the medicine I felt I needed.

After a ten-minute limp following the directions given to me by my phone, I dragged myself to the bar in the café. "Whisky and a coffee, please."

The woman behind the bar hesitated.

"Whisky. Coffee." I said. "Separate. Not together. Not Irish."

She relaxed and poured the coffee in front of me.

"Have you got any painkillers?" I asked, feeling a twinge in my knee and the thump at the side of my head.

"Sorry," she said.

"I'm not a tourist," I said, making sure she noticed I was speaking French.

Her face softened and she turned away, returning a few moments later, dropping a blister pack in front of me. "If you steal one of those while I'm getting your whisky, I'll be very angry with you," she said mockingly.

I wasn't sure what the right dose was, but four is always a good number.

When she returned I had the bundle of receipts and scraps of paper on the bar and was spreading them. There were only three other customers—a couple and a guy on his own—so I figured I was safe.

"You look like you need a double." She put the glass of amber fluid next to my coffee. I was pleased for the consideration, even though I knew I was likely to be faintly disappointed—the French never get Scotch right, in much the same way that the English never get food right.

I passed her a €50. "Thank you. Keep the change."

She took the bill and hesitated. "This is..."

"I know."

She looked at the bill, then to me. I gave a nod—as reassuring as I could. "Thank you," she mouthed and turned toward the till.

I ignored the scraps of paper for a moment. I pulled out my phone and sent a text to Clementina: ?

She responded within thirty seconds as I was flattening another receipt: :-(Then a second message followed immediately: "Wher RU"

"Near. Do you want me to come home?" She might not put a value on correct spelling and adherence to the rules of grammar, but I at least tried.

"No. Just wanna no UR close." The message came back in less than fifteen seconds.

"Sleep tight and I'll see you in the morning."

"U2 xx."

The whisky went down more quickly than I would have usually drunk, but usually I would have chosen something less cheap. But who was I to complain—no one goes to Paris to drink Scotch, and the coffee was good.

"Another?" asked the waitress, indicating my empty tumbler. I shook my head. She didn't argue but instead made a small sweeping gesture with her hand, as if to say: "Then can I help you with your task?"

"I'm looking for the local places," I said. "A friend's gone...I don't want to say missing, but I can't find a better word."

Her face had a look of shock. "How long?" she asked.

"Two days," I said. I wasn't expecting a question to follow my lie and wasn't sure what the appropriate answer should be.

"Oh," she said. Clearly she wasn't sure why she had asked the question either.

"Do you recognize any of these places?"

She looked across the scraps of paper, picking up the receipts each in turn before holding on to four or five. "These are close." She placed each in turn, giving detailed directions. By halfway through the explanation of how to get to the second café, I was lost, but my phone would give me directions.

"Here's the guy," I said, showing her a picture of Hoffman I had found in one of Clementina's pictures. "Do you remember him? He was here."

I offered her the phone and the receipt from this café.

She stared at the screen. Her head began to move slowly—a horizontal rotation. "I'm sorry, no. Good-looking guy, but...no, I don't recognize him."

forty-five

Five cafés. One whisky, a double. Five coffees. Two I drunk, one I started, one went cold, and one watered the plant. In the third café when I showed the picture of Hoffman, there was recognition. "I saw him. Four or five days ago." The receipt was dated four days ago.

The remaining details were sketchy: "Evening" was the closest I could get to a time. The receipt was timed at just after 8 PM, and the clock on the cash register was within five minutes of being accurate. "Sitting, drinking." Again, nothing that the receipt hadn't already told me—in fact, the receipt told me that four beers had been ordered, two bottles of two different brands.

There was no new information, but the scrap of paper suggested to me that the café owner had a pretty clear memory. I wondered how much further the memory could be pushed: "Tell me about the other guy," I said.

Two different brands of beer—it seemed logical to me that there had been two guys. Sure, Hoffman may have changed beer, but most guys who change what they're drinking change after their first beer. Then they stick with the new beer, return to the original, or try a third. A guy drinking on his own would not have two beers, change, and have another two beers.

"He had his back to me." I waited—this guy had remembered details, there was more to come. He threw out the few details his brain could retrieve. "Brown jacket—might have been a coat—leather. Greasy hair." He exhaled, lost in thought. "I didn't see a face." He wrinkled his nose. "There was a smell."

That was all he could offer, but that was more than I got in all the other cafés combined.

The immediate pain of my introduction to the guy in the brown coat—when he threw a seat and his fists at me while I was in the bathroom of Hoffman's hotel room—had passed, leaving in its place a dull, lingering ache that would be with me, reminding me, slowing me, for the next few days.

When I sat in a café, the ache came back; when I walked to the next, I felt the stiffness as I began to move, but it soon passed. I'm sure my muscles probably needed some time to rest and recover, but

I had more work to do, so I walked back to the apartment in the 16th.

It took me about an hour. An hour of stretching my muscles without stressing them. An hour of wandering through the mostly deserted streets, thinking. Thinking but not finding any conclusions. Thinking, but finding my thoughts drawn to my situation, not to the missing laptop.

I had left London several months ago after upsetting, to put it mildly, some Bulgarians. Since then I had behaved like a student with a rail ticket—every few days I had moved on. I wasn't certain what reach the Bulgarians had—who they could bribe or how they could find me—and I wasn't sure what digital trail I was leaving behind me, but I was wearying of the constant movement.

I figured I would be sleeping in a different bed every night for the next few years, but it would be good if I could settle on a city. I was in Paris, looking for a laptop, and I had no one I could call—no friends, no contacts, no one who owed me a favor. In short, no infrastructure, no support system. If I didn't stay in a place for longer than a few days, I wouldn't build up those relationships, and at some point I would run out of money.

Maybe Paris was the place to stay. It's easier to hide in a dense crowd than it is to hide in the middle of an empty field, and I speak the language. But first, there was a laptop to find, and I still wasn't sure who had taken it. The obvious answer was Hoffman—but he was dead, making it hard for him to come to his own defense.

The porter seemed surprised by my arrival. Surprised being another way of saying shocked into wakefulness by my arrival. "Bonsoir, monsieur," he mumbled groggily before knocking his coffee across his desk. He cursed under his breath and went to search for a cloth.

He went right; I turned left and headed toward the underground parking.

Whoever had designed the apartments, the person who had designed the parking lot had made the exact opposite decisions. The apartments were airy with high ceilings; the parking garage was cramped with a low ceiling. Instead of white plaster walls, there were bricks. Instead of a leather-covered floor, there was cement painted with a rubberized gray paint.

I heard my feet squeak on the painted gray surface as I let the door swing behind me. There were spaces for six cars. Two spaces had been allocated to the Nordens' apartment. The Maybach spanned both spaces—the line between the spaces perfectly aligned under the center of the large car. Three of the other spaces were filled—two with Range Rovers, one with BMW's reimagining of a Range Rover.

I walked to the far end where the security grill was lowered and looked back, letting my eyes scan the space and search out anywhere a laptop could be hidden.

Walls, pillars, floor, surface-mounted electrics spreading ugly strip lighting across the ceiling. Nothing that said laptop. I walked half a circuit of the space, following the wall as closely as I could, careful not to disturb the cars, which were probably all alarmed. Reaching the door, I returned along the center aisle and completed a sweep of the other side.

Nothing. Not even a hint.

When I got back to the lobby, the porter was still mopping his coffee. "I thought there was somewhere to…I need to have a leak. I don't want to wake the family."

"Use mine," he said, lazily pointing with his thumb.

I followed where he indicated. The door led to a narrow passageway with white emulsion walls and what looked like nylon carpet. I understood the rules now: Narrow passageways with no natural daylight, decorated cheaply, were intended for staff. Broad, airy, spaces with luxury finishes were intended for residents. The parking lot seemed to have a dual character. Clearly it had been designed for staff, but when it was designed no one had figured that it was quicker to get to the apartments from the parking lot than it was from the street outside, plus why would residents want to alight from their chauffeur-driven car into the rain?

On the left of this staff passageway there were two locked doors, and at the end was a small room. Some might call it tiny. There was a toilet—its positioning within the small room blocked the door from opening properly—and a sink with a surface area the size of one of my hands. A tattered blue towel hung beside the sink.

Two paces back from the entrance to the restroom was another room, which seemed to be the office and break room for the porter. A functional desk had been inserted with shelves above it. Against the far wall, there was a sofa and to the left sat a table with a coffeemaker.

Nothing looked like a laptop, but I quickly checked the drawers in the desk. Even more swiftly I regretted my action when I found the porter's dirty underwear stuffed into the bottom drawer—the perfect hiding place for a laptop. Except it wasn't there. And it wasn't on the shelves. I stood on the desk, quickly checking all the box files and lever arch files filling the space.

I jumped down and headed back toward the porter, but stopped and returned to flush the toilet before leaving. I had to pretend...

"There's a storeroom somewhere," I said, pulling out the keys I had taken when Clementina and I had left the apartment this morning. "I said I'd get a few bits out."

The porter had finished mopping and seemed to be readying himself to return to sleep. He grunted, his thumb pointed to the corridor I had just left. "Yours is the first door."

"I thought we had two," I said.

A single shake of his head, which was little more than him finding a more comfortable position to sleep.

"Who's got the other?" I asked.

"Floor below you." Clearly I was interrupting his sleep.

The third key I tried opened the door. There was a slight chill as I stepped into the room, reaching clumsily for the light. I hit the switch and the strip lights buzzed; after a few lightning flashes, they came to life.

The room was white apart from the floor. The walls and ceiling were plaster, painted with white emulsion. The floor, like the floor in the parking garage, was painted with gray rubberized paint, making the surface easy to clean.

There were freestanding shelves on either side. Cheap, pine, but sturdy. And the shelves needed to be sturdy—I wasn't sure how long the apartment had been rented, nor what was here before the Nordens arrived, but someone was clearly preparing for the apocalypse.

The toilet rolls came in packs of 24. Floor to ceiling, eight packs could be fitted, and there were three stacks. My mathematics was never fast, but that was 576 toilet rolls, and I knew there was a supply in my bathroom and suspected there were many other supplies throughout the apartment. There was no laptop hidden behind, under, or between any of the packs of toilet rolls.

There was bedding. Sheets, duvets, pillows. All new. All still wrapped in cellophane. None hiding a laptop.

The bathroom and cleaning products seemed to be intermingled—there was bleach, soap, cleaning sprays, toothbrushes, cloths and scourers, more cleaning sprays, and cleaning liquids for different purposes and of different abrasions. Then there were the tinned foods—rows of tins. I didn't look at what was on offer—I just made sure there was no laptop.

And there was no laptop, so I headed for the apartment.

As I passed the porter, he was snoring.

forty-six

It was 3:30 when I got to bed, having spent most of my evening looking for the laptop and failing.

Sleep came fast.

The sleep was deep.

But sleep was disturbed, by Zack at around 5 AM. He turned on the overhead light and sat in the chair. Unlike Clementina's room, I only had a single seat chair, not a sofa. Then he waited.

"What's up?" I asked groggily, sitting up in bed. Neither of us seemed to bother with the courtesy of a good morning, nor wanted to be bothered with the tedium of an apology for the inconvenience and the need for me to say "it's not a problem." I assumed the explanation would make itself clear soon enough.

"Did you find the laptop?"

"No."

He swore under his breath.

I sat up straighter, feeling the dull ache in my muscles, reminding me of the man in the brown coat.

"I do have a hunch," I said. "Whoever wants it doesn't have it."

"I don't understand," said my employer.

"Someone wants that laptop and has made efforts to get it," I said. "But I'm wondering whether it has been intercepted on its journey to them."

He shook his head mournfully. "No, Leathan. They've got it."

"How do you know this?" I asked.

"Because I've had the threat," said Norden.

I wasn't sure how long he had been awake, but something behind Norden's eyes had died. His body was functioning, but all emotion had been disconnected. He was a human robot—he had the ability to think but lacked the facility to empathize or show any emotion about his own situation.

"The threat?" I asked.

"They want me to quit," he said. "They say if I quit, then they'll play nice."

"What does that mean?" I asked, growing increasingly uncomfortable with the notion of having a conversation with my employer while I lay naked and in bed.

"It means they promise that they..." said Norden.

"And who is they?" I asked, immediately regretting my interruption.

Norden seemed to be unable to name his tormentor.

"McElroy?" I tried.

Norden's response was swift. "No. He wouldn't spread dirt on me."

Two questions answered in one reply—they thought they had dirt on Norden. "You know that whatever dirt they think they've got on you, it won't go away by you quitting. You're just as vulnerable whatever you do—you can't retroactively immunize yourself."

Norden sighed. "You're right."

"We need to figure what we do next," I said. "You put some coffee on, and I'll get dressed."

forty-seven

There were two cups of coffee on the kitchen counter, and the smell of a fresh brew was filling the space. I sat on one of the high stools. "The beginning," I said.

"McElroy called."

"So it is McElroy?"

Norden winced. "He said they contacted him."

"They?"

"Whoever has the laptop."

"And *they* want?"

"Me to quit as managing partner," said Norden.

"Who benefits?"

Norden went silent, seemingly unable to utter the name.

"Let me rephrase that question," I said. "Is there anyone apart from Johnson McElroy who would benefit from your departure?"

He remained silent, refusing to name his tormentor.

"Can't you fire him?" I asked.

"No," said Norden. "We're a partnership, and he's a partner." He snorted. "And a lawyer."

"And if you quit, then you'll still be a partner?" I phrased it as a statement but delivered it as a question.

"I'll still be a partner, but someone else will have their hands on the controls. If you're the person whose signature is needed, then you have a disproportionate amount of control."

"And if you don't stand back as managing partner?"

Norden spent a moment gathering his thoughts and taking a sip of his coffee. He had switched on some of the lights in the kitchen and one in the hall. The main space with the sofas and the dining table was cast in shadow, only lit by the lights making their way from the kitchen and the streetlights that had pushed their way through the windows.

"The partnership agreement provides that the managing partner can be removed as managing partner in certain specific situations." I waited for Norden to continue. "Insanity or physical inability to perform the task—for instance, if I was in a coma. If I were in jail, but there are terms around bringing the firm into disrepute, which would kick in first."

"What constitutes disrepute in your world?" I asked.

"Illegal behavior—financial fraud, tax evasion."

The terms were broad, and he wasn't pointing to anything specific, but it was enough to give me a hint about what might be on the laptop.

"Question," I said. "Where else would McElroy keep the laptop? It wasn't in his apartment."

I watched Norden's face. He seemed ready to argue about whether McElroy was involved, but then his brain had told him his ears had just heard something they weren't expecting. And the message the ears had heard didn't quite make sense to the brain. "What do you mean it wasn't in his apartment, Leathan?"

"The laptop isn't in McElroy's apartment," I said quietly, but articulating each word, emphasizing *isn't*.

Norden's brain was still trying to process the new information it had taken in.

I helped him understand. "I looked—the laptop isn't there."

"You looked in Johnnie's apartment?"

"Yeah."

"When?"

"Eight, ten hours ago."

Norden seemed to be struggling to fit the details together. He had too many questions all needing to be answered at once.

"The laptop wasn't in McElroy's apartment," I repeated. "I don't trust that guy. I'm sure he's up to something—but I'm not sure that he's got the laptop." I paused to give some emphasis to my next statement. "I do know that he wants it."

Norden's mouth was moving, but no sound was coming out.

"How specific was the threat?" I asked.

"Specific," said the other man.

"Specific in what they want from you—or specific in what they're threatening you with?"

Norden frowned.

"Were they specific about what they're going to disclose?" I asked. "Or did they just say, 'We've got the laptop and we're going to put the details out there,' and leave you to fill in the gaps?"

Norden inhaled slowly but deeply. Inhaling as if he had a hidden pressure relief valve that allowed him to continue sucking in air.

Finally, he stopped. "You're right—he hinted, I filled in the blanks." When the exhalation came, it was a short burst. "But that doesn't mean that they...he...whoever doesn't have the laptop."

"True," I said.

"And you really think Johnnie is behind all this?"

"When we last spoke—back in your office—you said that Johnnie didn't know about the missing laptop." I paused as Norden made the link. "Now he does—and he hasn't mentioned the discrepancy."

"You don't think that he's got too much to lose by taking me down?" tried my employer.

"I think he's got a lot to lose if he damages the partnership—but so far he's not tried to do that. He wants you to walk away quietly, and he's using his knowledge and your weakness to get there. It's a smart play."

Norden stared at his coffee, seemingly unable to meet my gaze.

"If we can find the laptop, it puts you in a better position," I said. "And I've got an idea."

"I've..." began Norden.

"I get it," I said. "You've got a deal you need to sort."

Norden hesitated. He wanted to explain, but he didn't know which was more important—the laptop or the deal.

"I get it," I continued. "No deal, the laptop becomes irrelevant. Get Reece to take you to the office—I'll do some more digging."

forty-eight

A faint light squeezed under the door.

I put my ear to the wood and listened. Silence. A tap with one finger. Silence. A hand on the handle, a delicate rattle. Silence. I opened the door, holding it ajar for a few seconds before fully opening it and stepping in.

Clementina was asleep. She was still wearing the red smock with yellow and orange splotches on top of a white T-shirt and had messily wrapped her bedding around her, looking like an animal that had made a nest for winter hibernation.

There was a three-drawer chest of drawers near her bed; on the top, a lamp that seemed cheaper and kitschier than would be Clementina's choice. An eight-year-old without a rich daddy might have chosen the plastic monstrosity—but not Clementina, unless she was trying to make an ironic statement. The shade—a plastic reimagining of a stained glass lampshade, with greens, oranges, and blues—trapped the light inside, only letting out a gentle illumination. Enough to see by—enough to act as a nightlight—but not enough to glare.

I moved the hair out of Clementina's face with a single finger.

"Mmmm..."

I dropped to my knees to lower my face. "How are you?"

"Shitty," she said, pulling the bedding tighter around her. "What time is it?"

"About six."

She opened her left eye and stared at me. "Six. In the morning?"

"I need a favor," I said.

"If you weren't such an asshole who thinks it's acceptable to wake people up at six in the morning, then I'm sure you'd find a friend who could do you a favor." The eye was closed, and she snuggled more tightly.

"I need a favor from you," I said.

The eye opened again. "Now?"

"Soon."

"Tomorrow?"

"Today. This morning. Soon."

The second eye opened, and Clementina wriggled up the bed as if trying to sit, then gave up. "What?"

"I want the apartment cleared."

"Then tell everyone to get out and let me get back to sleep."

I shifted on my knees.

"Or shout fire. That should clear the apartment quickly."

She closed her eyes again.

"I need a clear apartment—and I need to know that the people who might walk in on me aren't going to be around for an hour or so."

Her eyes were open. Wide. "What are you up to, Leathan?"

"An itch that needs scratching."

She reached out a hand, putting her fingertips on top of my head and letting her nails work their way through my hair to scratch my scalp. "Itch scratched," she said, withdrawing her hand and closing her eyes again.

"If Hoffman didn't take the laptop," I began. The eyes opened. "I've looked—I've looked in lots of places. It's not there. And if Hoffman didn't take it, then someone else did."

Clementina sat up, pulling her bedding around her. "What do you mean you've looked?"

"A quick bit of breaking and entering," I said. "I'll tell you more later, but first..."

"You need a favor," she sighed. "What have I got to do?"

I paused. "Go and visit the place where Hoffman was found. Say you want to see it."

Her eyes misted. Even in the muted light it was clear that her eyes were filling.

"He's not there—I just want you..."

"I don't have to look at dead bodies," said Clementina, interrupting.

"No," I said. "You just need to insist. Reece will drive you there." She lifted the side of her lip. "And I'll send Angeline with you too."

"Why do I want her?" said Clementina, her lifted lip turned into a snarl. "She's..." The look was enough to express her disapproval.

"She's there as a female to offer emotional support, so you can cry on her shoulder," I said slowly.

"I'd rather cry on your shoulder," she said, then stopped abruptly. "You think...Angeline?"

I said nothing.

"Reece?"

"Keep them away for at least an hour—I'm going to get nosy."

forty-nine

Zack Norden had departed for the office with instructions for me to meet him there as soon as I had found anything. Reece had driven him to the office and had just returned by the time Clementina was ready.

I sat at the counter drinking coffee as I watched the three depart.

Clementina had been insistent. "I need to see where he died," she wailed. She played the role well—her mix of genuine upset at Hoffman's death and role-playing insistence had been a powerful combination.

Reece seemed pleased not to be spending a second day sitting on his ass and was clearly excited by the responsibility he had been given. He was only being asked to do his job—to drive a car—but when I added the words "I'm trusting you, Reece," the task seemed to take on a new dimension.

Angeline was reluctant.

I wasn't sure whether that reluctance was about the time she would waste that should be spent doing the job she was actually paid to do and that she'd still have to do, as well as filling in for the cook who was still sick, or whether she didn't want to spend the morning dealing with Clementina—a blubbing Clementina.

The door closed, its noise like a starting gun telling me to begin searching for the keys. While the driver and the housekeeper had a right to privacy, the service apartments belonged to this apartment, and accordingly, there would be spare keys somewhere. In the hallway by the front door, I found a closet I hadn't previously paid attention to—it was the coat closet, and while it had an intended purpose, it was bigger than some bedrooms I had known.

Inside the closet, hidden behind some coats, was a key safe: a metal case about twelve inches wide, twelve inches tall, and three inches deep. Ironically for something that is described as a safe, it was unlocked. Some of the keys were labeled, others not. I started with the labeled keys and soon found the keys to the service apartments.

I began with Angeline's apartment—it seemed to be the same size as Reece's apartment, but it didn't have the electronic gear that the driver's did.

I passed through the main room and into the bathroom. It was tiny but spotless. And there was no laptop.

I returned through the main room and entered the bedroom. A windowless box with a single bed—a wood frame with a mattress, a freestanding closet, and little space to move. I opened the closet doors. Monochromatic, near-uniform clothes hung. No laptop.

The bed had been made—there was a precision to the art. I took out my phone and photographed the bed, then patted it down before lifting the mattress.

No laptop.

I lowered the mattress and proceeded to replicate the state the bed had been in when I arrived, holding my phone in one hand and pulling the sheets with the other. Under the bed was a suitcase, I dropped it on the bed, then cursed at the work I had just created for myself in disturbing the made bed again.

The lid unzipped to reveal an empty case. I re-zipped the lid, then opened the pocket on the front. It had been stuffed with pieces of paper. I hesitated for a moment trying to figure whether there was a system to the stuffing or whether I would be able to return the papers.

If there was a trap to show that the papers had been disturbed, then I couldn't see it; and if there had been a trap, I'd probably already tripped it. I pulled out the papers and started to pore over them.

It seemed to be Angeline's financial records. There were bank statements, pay slips from several employers, and receipts for money transfers. None in any apparent order.

I looked at a pay slip. At best, the hourly rate could be described as modest by European standards. But Angeline worked long hours and, with accommodation provided, had low overheads.

I found the bank statement that covered the period of the pay slip. Her pay went straight into her bank account. Three days later, 90 percent of that amount was debited from her account. I flicked through the receipts for money transfers—the money had been transferred to an account in the Philippines.

So far, so logical—many overseas residents work in Europe and send money home. Angeline was clearly working hard to support her family back home, and 1,000 euros or 2,000 euros would go a long way in the Philippines—certainly much further than it would go in Paris.

I kept flicking. More statements, more pay slips, more receipts for money transfers. But there were also receipts from a different institution—her bank had a blue logo; the second set of receipts had a yellow logo. I looked harder, reading the details. These transfers were recent—within the last few weeks—and were for cash transfers; no payment had passed through her bank.

So she got paid in cash.

I flicked to the next receipt, and then I noticed. The transfers from the bank had been for modest amounts—significant amounts for Angeline, but in the context of the money that Zackary and Clementina were spending, modest: 1,000 Euros or 2,000 Euros. These cash transfers were for 10,000 Euros and 15,000 Euros. That was more like a year's salary for Angeline, and she had made three such transfers that month.

I laid out the receipts, the bank statements, and the pay slips and photographed them before returning the papers to the suitcase and making the bed again, double-checking with the photo on my phone of its state when I arrived.

The main room gave no hint of there being a laptop hidden anywhere—or anything else of interest. I was out of the door and into Reece's apartment within fifteen minutes.

Where, apart from a pocket in a suitcase under her bed, Angeline's apartment showed discipline and order, Reece's apartment was like an indulgence for a teenager. I ignored the main space and headed for the bathroom.

From a brief examination of the floor, I deduced that this morning Reece had showered, shaved, and had a piss or two. The small shelf under the mirror was filled with cheap but numerous perfumes, deodorants, hair products, shaving creams and gels, moisturizers, and razors and hair trimmers.

If there had been a laptop in there, it had drowned or it had died from the smell.

The bedroom was the same size as Angeline's, but the antithesis. Some jackets and trousers had been hung in the closet, but at the bottom was a heap. I wasn't sure whether this was his laundry or how Reece stored his clothes. Gingerly I picked my way through—no laptop.

The bed hadn't been made, but there was a laptop. A laptop, not *the* laptop.

The laptop lying on Reece's unmade bed was larger than the one I was looking for, and where I was looking for something aluminum or silver in color, this had a red plastic lid with stickers on it.

I lifted the lid, hit the power button, and continued my search of the bed as the machine fired up. There was nothing—apart from dirty underwear, which did not warrant further investigation.

I carried the laptop out to the main room and sat in the chair facing the television. Before I did anything, I sent a message to Clementina: ? Then I turned my attention to the laptop, trying to guess the password.

There was no password—I went straight to the home screen.

My phone pinged. "Nott three yt. In trffc." I took it that they were not there yet because they were stuck in traffic.

I returned my attention to the laptop. As far as I could tell, it had a single purpose—games. And Reece seemed to like anything that involved fighting or shooting. While it did have a single purpose, it clearly performed other functions for the driver.

I opened his email. Most of the emails seemed to be about games—advertisements for games, confirmations that he had bought games or credits or something in games, and password resets for games' forums. Apart from some spam and three emails from his mother, there was nothing.

His web browsing history was largely to be expected: games and pornography. It would appear that Reece had a taste for women who dress as schoolgirls and who then undress.

I was about to shut the machine down when on a whim I opened the photo app.

I suddenly felt very uncomfortable. I had sent Clementina with a man and a woman. The woman was sending money home—money that in a month was well in excess of her salary for a year, and for which there was no obvious source. And now I had found that the man who I had entrusted to protect Clementina had photographs of Clementina.

There was nothing illegal about the photos, as far as I could tell—Clementina was clothed in all of them—but they creeped me out. Especially the ones of her in a bikini, which I couldn't look at. Every photo seemed to have been taken without her knowing that she was being photographed—there wasn't one photo where she looked at the camera and smiled. Each picture was from an angle, a low view, a high view, a side view. Usually alone, sometimes with friends, and all seemingly taken on a mobile phone. I scanned the dates—there was more than a year's worth of photos.

I recalled Clementina's comment: "He looks at my boobs." She was wrong—he looked at everything. He probably also coveted, but he hadn't acted on his impulse—at least not yet, from what Clementina had told me.

I returned the laptop and finished the scan of the main room before leaving. Reaching the apartment, I continued my search for the laptop. After forty minutes I convinced myself it was not to be found.

"Update." I hit send. Did I mean update me on your expedition or update me on your two escorts, I wondered.

"Just arrvd." The reply was swift. The reply also made me remember that Clementina had lied. I spent five minutes in her room—it was long enough to tell me that I would need a small team and two weeks to get through the suite.

fifty

"Did you find the laptop?" Zackary Norden opened the door to the apartment that was doubling as a low-key office while he and his team were in Paris completing some super-special, super-secret deal.

"No, no laptop," I said.

Norden swore under his breath and led me to his room overlooking the red awning of the brasserie below. He indicated the sofa across from his desk and took the seat behind his desk.

"Where's McElroy?" I asked.

"I don't keep tabs on him—we don't sign in and sign out."

I remained standing. "Can I look...?"

"I'm ahead of you," said Norden, waving me to the sitting position. "I've looked—his space, Mallet's... There's nothing. No laptop."

"Do you trust Mallet?"

"I don't think he's got the gumption, and he's got less to gain—he's not a partner." He paused. "Anyway, he went to London this morning. He'll be back tomorrow afternoon."

The butterscotch-colored room fell quiet—the only noise was the sound outside of traffic two floors below us.

"I was sure that Angeline had taken the laptop...or at least was involved," I muttered more to myself than to Norden. I had spent the journey—a combination of fast walking and the Metro—trying to process what I had found and put some sort of order around it. There was an obvious reaction—fire both Angeline and Reece—but I wasn't sure whether that was the smart play. I hadn't even figured whether I should tell Norden—if I'd misunderstood what I had seen or there was an innocent explanation, then I was potentially getting Angeline and Reece fired over my stupidity.

"Why Angeline? asked Norden.

"The laptop wasn't with Hoffman, it wasn't in Hoffman's hotel room, and it wasn't in McElroy's room. That suggests that maybe Hoffman didn't take the laptop—and if he didn't, then there were three other people who might've. The three people at the apartment when it disappeared: me, Reece, and Angeline. I know I didn't take it, I don't think Reece has the competence, and that leaves Angeline."

"That sounds weak, Leathan."

"It is weak," I said. "But I don't trust her—and you shouldn't either."

Norden cocked his head and raised his eyes, waiting for me to elaborate.

"Who pays her?" I asked. "As I understand she comes with the apartment—so is her cost part of the rent?"

"Not quite," said Norden. "I pay seventy-five percent of the rent for the apartment. The partnership picks up the other twenty-five percent because we meet there. The partnership pays for the staff." He saw my confusion. "If I was in a hotel, the partnership would pay one hundred percent of my cost—I meet a chunk of the rent because I wanted the bigger place so Clementina could stay."

"Who did all the organizing?" I asked. "Your secretary?"

"I'm...between secretaries at the moment," said Norden. "Not that she would have organized it anyway—this is Johnnie's province. His people sort this stuff—there's a lot of paperwork, so it's best to get someone with a legal mind." He paused, then looked up. "Why the interest in admin? How does this relate to Angeline?"

"We need to have a serious talk about what I found—in Angeline's room and Reece's—but I want to do some thinking first. If I've got this wrong, then I'm throwing around serious allegations, so I want to make sure I'm right."

Norden seemed to accept my reticence. "While you figure that out, I'm going to call Johnnie and confront him. He knows I'm being blackmailed."

I winced.

"What?"

"Could you hold off on that? Give me two hours—I want to speak to Clementina, face to face, to find what she found out this morning."

Norden sighed lightly. "Two hours—I want this sorted, Leathan. There's a deal to be done, and I don't want you getting in the way."

"Two hours," I said.

fifty-one

I wasn't entirely sure why I didn't want Zack to talk with Johnnie—it would have been a quick way to flush out what the lawyer knew—but I knew I couldn't control the consequences of that discussion. And given what I had found in Angeline's and Reece's apartments, I wanted to talk with Clementina first to see if they had let anything slip while she was distracting the two of them.

"Oh, Mister Leathan," said Angeline, mispronouncing my name, when I let myself into the apartment. I tried to read her reaction. Was it surprise? Shock? Fear? Uncertainty? Guilt that she wasn't working? Or was there something I was missing?

"Is Clementina in her room?" I asked.

"No." This reaction was different—this was confusion. "You said..."

I stopped her. "Where's Clementina?"

"Shopping," said Angeline.

"Shopping, where?"

Angeline shook her head—more of a vibration.

"Where's Reece?"

"Driving Miss Clementina," said the housekeeper. "You..."

I held up a hand to stop her and pulled out my phone. I went through to voicemail. "Clemmy, it's Leathan. Call me as soon as you get this message."

I returned the phone to my pocket. Angeline pushed herself against a kitchen cabinet as if trying to move away from me. She seemed to be drawing her body in as if minimizing her physical size to reduce the chance of injury if she was attacked.

"Was I not clear?" I asked, letting the question echo in the big space.

Her head was still vibrating. I wasn't sure whether it was fear or whether her default position when cornered was to deny everything. "But Mister Reece said..." she began.

"What did I say?"

"Miss Clementina said it was alright," said the housekeeper in her mangled English.

"What did I say?" I repeated.

Angeline looked down, her yellowed skin flushing pink at her cheeks. She mumbled something. It might have been an apology; it could have been an explanation. I wasn't really interested in either—I was figuring out whether I needed to be worried about Clementina being with a guy who liked taking pictures of her. It was one thing when I was ignorant, but now that I knew what he had been doing, I needed to review.

On balance, Reece was—to put it mildly—a creep. But he seemed to be a protective—albeit misguided and only protective for his own selfish reasons—creep, and Clementina was ahead of me in knowing just how much of a creep he was.

"Tell me about the money you send home," I said to Angeline.

She looked up, indignation burning in her eyes. "It's my money. I work hard."

And I didn't disagree. My arrival a few moments ago was the first time I had seen Angeline not working.

"What about the cash?" I asked.

"It's my pay," she said. I waited—she was riled and wanted to be believed. I needed patience to wait for her to make a mistake. "Mister Johnnie gave it to me."

I was surprised the mistake came so quickly. McElroy paid Angeline through the partnership, making deposits directly into her bank account on a weekly basis, and then in addition gave her cash—large amounts of cash—with no associated pay slip.

"It's funny how the cash came at the same time that Clementina found herself in the press." I wasn't sure I was being entirely fair or accurate, but I wanted to see how she reacted to the accusation.

"I did what I was told," said Angeline. "Ask Mister Johnnie."

"McElroy told you to call the press?" I asked.

"I didn't call the newspaper."

"So what did McElroy pay you to do?"

"I did what I was told," insisted Angeline, her lips pulled tight and her arms folded across her chest.

I counted to ten, waiting to see if she would elaborate. She offered nothing. The fixed look on her face became a glare, and the arms folded across her chest seemed to get pulled tighter.

"We can't trust you," I said, trying to hide the hesitation in my voice. "You're leaving."

The housekeeper didn't react.

"You're leaving—now. Your job here is finished."

fifty-two

Angeline was still wailing.

I had thought Clementina had played the histrionics well this morning when—at my request—she had insisted on going to see the place where Hoffman's body had been found. Clementina's reaction was nothing when compared to what I had seen from Angeline in the last ten minutes or so.

The housekeeper—now former housekeeper—had started by crying. She soon mopped the tears and came over to me like a simpering child. "You can't say this."

"And yet I did."

"You don't mean..." She was like a child trying to be brave; her eyes were glistening, and her cheeks damp.

"I do."

"My family. Please, my family."

"What about Mister Norden and his family? Don't they matter?" That was the moment that I saw the panic in her eyes. She had played her trump card. I was playing with a different set of cards. The only argument that she could put forward was that her family was more important than her employer's family. She saw that I had figured that before she got there. She knew I was waiting, expecting.

She screamed. It was probably the only reasonable thing she could do. Rational argument hadn't worked, wouldn't work, couldn't work, and so she had to resort to childlike tantrums.

The screams became tears, and that's when the wailing began—rising to a crescendo then falling to a diminuendo before rising again in a repeating cycle, interrupted only by her stuttering intake of oxygen.

She fell to her knees, the wailing continuing. Every now and then, at a diminuendo, she looked up: "Please." My failure to bend was the signal to begin a new crescendo, and the wailing increased, with hands banging to exaggerate her distress. The next time I looked up, she was lying flat on the floor—the noise was somewhere between a wail and a screech as she slapped her arms on the tiles.

"Please, please, please." She was on her knees in front of me, holding her hands together, imploring. Then I felt her hands on me, unbuttoning my jeans. "I give good suck." I rebuttoned my fly. "Please," she wailed, throwing her head into my lap as if trying to perform some sex act through denim.

I stood and moved out of the way of the begging woman.

She hesitated. Enough for me to suspect that she was working out which card to play next—go for indignity that I had spurned her or continue with her pleading. She stayed with consistency and began to wail again. "Please, Mister Leathan, I need this job. My family."

I hadn't actually told her that her employment was terminated. I was pretty sure that I didn't have the authority to make such a decision, but I certainly wanted her to think—to believe—that she was fired. I definitely couldn't trust her and I figured that I could argue that I threw her out of the apartment with the sole purpose of keeping Clementina protected from someone who was earning money from two sources. I'd leave it to McElroy—he was a lawyer, after all—to figure whether she was fired or was to be assigned new duties elsewhere and away from the family.

"You're leaving," I said, over the wailing. "If there's anything in here that belongs to you, then get it now."

The noise calmed. There was a sniff. She looked at me.

"Now," I said sharply.

The wailing began again.

"Now," I said, raising my voice.

Silence. She wiped her cheeks and stood.

"Have you got keys to this apartment?" I asked, holding out my hand.

She opened a cabinet in the kitchen and pulled out a small handbag that she searched through before holding a ring of keys. I snapped my fingers to indicate my open hand. "My things," she said.

"Your apartment?"

She nodded.

"We'll go there," I said. "Are all your keys on that ring?"

Another nod.

I kept my hand out, twitching my fingers. Reluctantly, she gave up possession of the keys.

"These are the only keys you've got?" I asked.

A nod.

"If I go through your bag or search your room, I'm not going to find any keys, am I?"

"No." There was offense in her voice.

"Apart from your bag, is there anything of yours in this apartment?"

"In the closet," she said, pointing toward the main door. I waited for her to start moving and followed. At the closet that I had explored for the first time while Angeline was escorting Clementina, I watched as she retrieved a cardigan and a raincoat. She didn't open the key safe.

"Is that all?" I asked. "Nothing more of yours in this apartment?"

A single shake of her head.

She led us down to her apartment, where she stood by the door. "Go in," I said.

"You've got the key."

With two people in the room, it seemed far more crowded than it had when I was there earlier. As I closed the door behind us, the pleading started again. "Please, please, please." The tears flowed, and she dropped to her knees, wrapping her arms around my legs. "Please, Mister Leathan, please."

Her hands were around my waistband, unbuttoning my fly again.

"Please, please, Mister Leathan. I make you very happy."

My jeans dropped to my knees, and I tried to step backward.

One arm grabbed my legs, holding them tight with her face pushed into my crotch and her free hand scrabbling to drop my underwear.

I reached down, gently placing a hand to either side of her skull before increasing the pressure and levering her head away from my crotch. "No."

Without her head held tightly against me, she was able to pull my underwear down. I released her head to try to stop the hand that was grabbing at my cock.

She gripped, pulling me toward her mouth.

"No!" I shouted, grabbing at her hair and yanking it back. "No."

She released me and ran for the bathroom, slamming the door behind her. I redressed myself and sat on the small sofa, watching the bathroom door. There was sniveling, a toilet flushing, running water, and talking. I guessed she was on the phone, but I couldn't make out who she was talking with—through the piece of wood I wasn't even sure of the language.

After about ten minutes she emerged and without glancing at me headed toward the bedroom, breaking the direct route to pick up a roll of black trash bags in the small kitchenette at the end of the room. I cast a quick glance around the bathroom.

It had been tidy when I saw it without Angeline, but there were signs that there was an occupant—a toothbrush, a hairbrush, some makeup, and a few other pieces. Now the room was spotless and empty. The only hint that there may have been an occupant was a damp hand towel hanging over a rail.

In her bedroom, Angeline was moving around. I stepped to the door, peering in. She was either engrossed or ignoring me. The suitcase was open on the bed, and next to it two black trash bags sat open-mouthed. Angeline was gathering her clothes, carefully folding them into the suitcase. Her other possessions—photos, trinkets—were stacked in the black bags, layered between sweaters. The contents of the bathroom joined the other items in the trash bags.

I returned to the small sofa and sat waiting.

Three minutes later Angeline stood at her bedroom door. "You can't throw me out on the streets." Her tone was angry, defiant.

"Have you finished packing?" I asked.

"Did you hear me? You can't throw me out."

"And yet."

She snorted and returned to her room. I followed and found her sitting on her bed, her hand supporting her head like a petulant teenager.

"Have you finished packing?" I asked again.

She shrugged, looking at the suitcase and the two black trash bags beside the door.

I counted out four €50 bills. "Here's two hundred. That'll get you a cheap place for a couple of nights. McElroy will pay whatever is owed."

I held the cash toward her. She snatched it.

"Are you sure you haven't got any more keys?"

"I'm sure," she barked, holding open the handbag strung diagonally across her chest so I could see inside.

"If you want a cab," I said, "now is the time to call it."

I left her as she pulled out her phone and I moved her bags to the front door of the apartment she was about to vacate permanently.

When I turned, she was standing in the doorway to her bedroom, a look of defiance across her face—or was it petulance? I was never quite sure exactly what people were trying to communicate when they gave me a hard look.

I escorted her down to the main reception, carrying her case through the main door. There was a cab performing a three-point— or more accurately, nine-point—turn. I loaded Angeline's case into the trunk; she added her two trash bags. Without a further word passing between us, she got into the cab and left.

I watched the vehicle leave, staring at where I had last seen it long after it had gone.

"Angeline," I said to the porter as I went back into the lobby. "Angeline Bautista—the housekeeper for the Nordens."

The porter stared blankly. It was a different man from last night's sleepy guy.

"You are aware that the Norden family are staying in this block and that they have a housekeeper?" I asked.

The porter sighed, letting his head nod once.

"She is no longer the housekeeper. Do not let her back in. Ever."

The porter raised an eyebrow, questioning.

"Do you think you can let the other guys know?"

"Yeah," said the porter softly.

fifty-three

I sat at the kitchen counter. "Clemmy, it's Leathan. Yes, again. Can you give me a call?" I was about to hang up. "I hope you're having fun shopping." I thought about calling Reece and decided against—I wasn't happy with Clementina being with the driver, but I didn't want him to think that I didn't trust him.

There was a rap on the front door. Solid. Businesslike.

I was surprised at how accustomed I had become in forty-eight hours to ignoring the door, safe in the knowledge that someone else was paid to answer. That someone who I had just thrown out of the apartment.

I eased myself off the high stool, walked to the door, and opened it.

I wasn't sure who I expected to see—all I knew was that I was opening a door in an apartment where I didn't live, in a city I had only been in for two days. I hoped it might be Clementina and Reece; I suspected it might be Angeline, although the knock didn't sound right for her; and I wondered whether it might be Zack Norden, having dragged himself away from his deal for long enough to actually care about his daughter.

I was wrong, and the guy on the other side of the door seemed not to have been expecting me to answer.

We both had the same reaction. There was a moment of confusion, a flash of recognition—I saw the brown leather coat, he saw something that reminded him of Hoffman's hotel bathroom—and then we moved. I went to close the door, not moving quickly enough before he jammed himself into the gap.

He swung his arm wildly, bending it back on himself as he tried to reach me. I kept my weight on the wood, keeping him jammed in place, as I looked for something to push against. He had the advantage—the floor was tiled. A horizontal surface where my feet could slip. He got a foot against the doorjamb—the vertical, unshifting doorjamb—and pushed. I didn't have the friction to hold him.

The door catapulted open as I fell.

It seemed like a single movement for Mister Brown Coat to lever the door and jump on top of me. He made sure I felt his weight drop onto me, winding me before a blade appeared. Long. Straight. Designed for a specific purpose.

He let me see the sharp steel before he tugged at a tuft of my hair. The blade disappeared from my view, and the tuft of hair pulled gently and then released. He brought the now-cut tuft of hair in front of my eyes, then flicked away the cutting and let the blade come across my view before bringing it to rest with the point pressing on my cheek.

He held the blade in place, staring at me and slowing his breathing.

Not speaking.

I remained silent, meeting and holding his gaze.

When he spoke, he said one word: "Laptop." He spoke English, but with a French accent.

I felt a stupid grin spread across my face, pushing the blade's tip harder against my cheek. "I've spent the last twenty-four hours looking for it. It's not here."

He moved the knife, placing the tip of the blade at the top of my nose, level with my eyes. With the tips of his fingers he slowly rotated the blade, letting the sharp point twist and drag the thin layer of flesh covering the narrow protrusion of bone between my eyes.

I became aware that he was inhaling deeply and sighing as he exhaled, his warm breath rushing across my face. He didn't smell any better than he had last night, but his breath was, if not minty-fresh, not repellent.

With one hand he continued to slowly spin the blade. He flexed his other hand like an athlete readying. He concentrated, moving his focus from my eyes to the base of the hilt of the knife. He stretched his hand, splaying his fingers, his eyes not moving from the base of the knife.

Slowly he moved his splayed hand toward the knife, lining up the center of his palm with the knife's handle. Raising and lowering his hand through a few inches as if readying himself to hammer the knife with the butt of his hand.

At least that was what he wanted me to think. If he was asking for the laptop, then he didn't have it and neither did McElroy. If he'd gone to the effort of coming here, then clearly he felt I might have the laptop, and while he thought I had the laptop, he wouldn't kill me. This was just for show. This was intended to scare me, and while I wasn't terrified, I was definitely hugely discomforted.

"Laptop," he repeated, letting the weight of his hand rest on the knife and push the tip of the blade against my bone.

"Do you think I would have come looking for it if I had it?" I asked.

I felt the pressure increase on the blade.

"Why do you think I was in the hotel room last night?"

He lifted the knife, taking the handle firmly in his grip, holding it with the point in my line of vision.

"Your silence suggests there was something else in the hotel room that I missed."

"Laptop," he said, letting the blade find its way to my throat and rest its sharp tip on the side of my windpipe.

"Seriously—I don't have it," I said. "And if my searching for it at the hotel is not enough, then why did I look for it in McElroy's apartment?"

He snorted, twisting the blade in the flesh at the side of my windpipe.

"I was there last night...when McElroy went out and then came back five minutes later with you."

Something flicked across his face. He saw that I had noticed.

"Want proof I was there?" I asked. "Hoffman's messenger bag—I saw it there."

He sighed before standing and landing a kick in my ribs. I rolled into the fetal position as another kick landed and then pulled myself tighter, preparing for the third impact.

When it didn't come I looked up and found myself alone.

fifty-four

I found a cab and reached Norden's office within ten minutes.

"Shit," said Norden opening the door to the apartment that had been pressed into service as a makeshift office. "You look bad."

"Thanks for the vote of confidence," I mumbled as he led me through, offering me the sofa across from his desk. He took the other sofa in the butterscotch-hued room.

"Have you seen the guy in the brown coat—a brown leather coat?"

"The guy...the specific guy with a specific brown coat that he always wears, even in the bath?" Norden answered my question with a question.

"He's got a bit of a hygiene problem."

"Sometimes when I leave here, I think I can smell something in the stairwell—it lingers."

"That's him," I said.

"Still haven't seen him," said Norden. "If there was something a bit more tangible I might have seen—so far you've given me nothing that couldn't be fixed with a bar of soap and a change of clothes."

I was about to say something sarcastic, then figured that sarcasm wouldn't move us forward, so changed my approach. "I don't know him, and each time I've seen him, he's been wearing a brown coat and leaves a smell like a snail leaves a trail."

Norden noticed the change in my approach and sat back in his sofa, waiting.

"I first saw him last night when I broke into McElroy's apartment."

"How *did* you get in? I've been meaning to ask," said my employer. I waited. He noticed I was holding back. "Tell me later—this is more important."

"At the garden where Hoffman's body was dumped, someone said they saw a guy in a brown coat. Then at Hoffman's hotel—I was having a look around, and my friend in the brown coat turned up and let me feel the force of his fists."

"Why didn't you...?" Norden stopped himself. "Focus. Sorry, Leathan—I'm new to this." He smiled weakly. "Please." He indicated for me to carry on.

"The guy might have met Hoffman in a café in the Latin Quarter a few days ago."

"You've been busy," said Norden under his breath, more as an indication that he was paying attention than as a comment.

"This guy—whoever he is—is a creature of McElroy," I said, letting the assertion hang.

"You're sure?" asked my employer. I sniffed and blinked twice, opening my eyes wide. "You are sure—you've seen him, you've smelled him...you've seen him in McElroy's apartment."

"And I've fought him. Last night and then this morning," I said. "He turned up at the apartment, pulled a knife, and demanded the laptop."

"A knife?" said Norden, unable to keep the shock out of his voice.

I paused and kept my voice soft. "You're not listening—McElroy's creature came looking for the laptop."

Norden's mouth went to move as he tried to reply, clearly not used to being put in his place except when the instruction was prefaced with "Daddy bear."

Slowly, hesitantly, he started to speak. "You're saying that this guy isn't with McElroy?"

I sighed. "No. I'm saying that McElroy doesn't have the laptop. He knows it's missing, but he doesn't have it."

"But..."

I cut across him. "Like you've never bluffed when you're doing a deal."

He deflated.

"McElroy knew the laptop was missing—without you telling him—and made a guess as to what was on it. Your reaction told him there was something worth worrying about, so he's sent his man to find it, but in the meantime he's playing you."

The room went quiet.

Norden looked up, questioning, looking for direction.

"Don't tell him anything—don't agree anything with him," I said. "But be ready for him to react—once he knows that you know he's bluffing, then he's going to need to pull another stunt."

My employer muttered under his breath.

"You can try one thing," I said.

"Try?"

"I found an iPad in Hoffman's hotel room," I said, withholding his daughter's part in unearthing the device. "I reckon he will have got that from McElroy."

"What's on it?"

I shrugged. "Could be his holiday snaps, but I'm guessing it's something more."

"You didn't look?"

"There was a lack of time, and I wanted to put it somewhere safe," I said. "He's bluffing you—you bluff him back. It might give us a bit more time."

He nodded with little confidence.

"But once you tell McElroy about the iPad, then you're calling out his façade. He's either got to admit that he's on maneuvers or deny his involvement. And denying is much harder when you tell him we've got the iPad."

"I understand," he said weakly.

"In other news," I began with more confidence. "I've fired Angeline. At least, I've thrown her out."

Norden seemed to take the news like the baron of a multinational company being told that in one of the far-flung offices the mailroom boy had been let go for looking at pornography on the company computer. There seemed no regret and no question that I had the authority to terminate a member of staff.

"She's been receiving money—cash—in addition to her salary. Disproportionate sums. There's not enough to provide a full audit trail, but it was fairly obvious her loyalty is not to you."

"You did what was necessary," said Norden with little emotion, standing and returning to his desk.

I took the hint. "Have you heard from Clementina in the last hour or so?" I asked.

Norden shook his head as he sat, showing as much concern as he had shown over Angeline's exit.

"I'm going to have a chat with Clementina," I said, standing, ready to show myself out. "Are you sure you know how you're going to handle McElroy?"

"I've got a fair idea."

fifty-five

"Rue de la Paix," I said to the cab driver.

There was a slight hesitation on the driver's part. A judgment was being formed: Was I worthy of Rue de la Paix, or was I just someone who wanted to look and dream? He tilted his head toward the back of the cab, and I got in.

As we drove, I checked every social media outlet I had installed on my phone. Clementina had gone dark. There had been a lot of discussion about the clothes she had tried on yesterday and much deliberation over the merits or otherwise of bobo, with a few comments about the bobo lifestyle, but the last few comments had withered around the time Clementina had been distracting Angeline and Reece for me.

Any shopping that was happening was not interactive shopping. She wasn't broadcasting a live stream from wherever she was.

The cab pulled up at the north edge of Place Vendôme, near where it met Rue de la Paix, but not exactly at the junction. The driver was challenging me to ask to be dropped outside a specific store. I offered him a €50 bill, letting him get a glance at the small stack of bills before waiting for him to give me the full change. I got out without passing him a tip.

At its most basic, Place Vendôme is a square with a column in the middle. A column erected by Napoleon to commemorate the battle of Austerlitz, which also gave its name to the train station where Clementina and I had begun our search for Hoffman's hotel.

Getting more complicated, with the corners shaved off the square, the space has the feel of an octagon. An octagon where there was no sight of a seventeen-year-old who could easily spend more money in a few days in Paris than I might earn in a year.

Taking the first few steps away from the square and onto Rue de la Paix, anyone could quickly understand how so much money could be so quickly spent. Every store was a brand that screamed expensive and exclusive: Louis Vuitton, Bulgari, Boucheron—one of the original residents of the street—Cartier, Tiffany, Rolex, Breitling.

I walked up the left side of the street, checking each store. Most I could see into from the outside, but occasionally I had to fake interest and enter, wasting the next several minutes speaking with assistants who had a hope of commission but weren't smart enough to clock that I was the help and not the money.

Vianney recognized me on sight and greeted me warmly. "Have you seen Clementina today?" I asked.

He hung his head—the long, slow shake telling me she had not been past.

"Any action from the paparazzi today...anywhere on the street?" I asked.

"Not that I've seen," said Clementina's fastidious young helper.

I turned to leave. "If I find her, I'll bring her here," I said, watching the other man's face bloom with anticipation.

I went as far as Palais Garnier before turning and walking down the other side of the street. No Clementina. No Maybach. No paparazzi.

I was nearing Place Vendôme when my phone rang. "Leathan, we need to meet." It was Norden. There was an urgency in his voice that hadn't been there when we spoke earlier. He gave me the address of a café in the 7th arrondissement.

"Left Bank," I said. "I don't know it, but I'm sure a cab can find it."

Norden muttered something about it being more of a business area. Then the urgency returned. "Thirty minutes?"

"Yeah," I said, but something made me hesitate. "Let's make it an hour. I'm on the Right Bank—it'll take me some time to get there."

"One hour—twelve, midday," said Norden confirming the appointment.

fifty-six

I was there in less than ten minutes.

When I say there, I mean a short distance away from the café where I had agreed to meet my employer—that meeting now scheduled to occur in fifty minutes.

The street was another broad boulevard—a central road flanked on either side by a lane whose purpose was to provide parking. The separation between driving and parking was reinforced by the trees lining either edge of the main highway. It was a street that was more defined by where it wasn't than by where it was—heading north the boulevard would cross la Seine at Pont de l'Alma, and to the west stood that most recognizable Paris landmark, la Tour Eiffel. But here, there was very little to distinguish the locality.

The café was on a corner. The regular awning had been replaced by a more permanent structure on the sidewalk, and beyond that were two rows of tables on the sidewalk, but without any protection from the weather.

A quick search on my phone gave me the café's number. "Monsieur Norden," I said in perfect French when a female voice answered. "He said he was going to get some lunch. He left his phone with me. Could you let him know, please?"

"Certainly, monsieur. Hold on one moment." There was the sound of the receiver being placed down. A moment or so later, she returned. "I'm sorry, monsieur, Monsieur Norden hasn't arrived yet."

"Did I say Norden?" I asked, knowing exactly what I had said. "I meant McElroy. Monsieur McElroy left his phone with me. I'm so sorry for the confusion."

"No problem, monsieur. One moment." She returned shortly. "I'm sorry, monsieur, Monsieur McElroy has not arrived yet." With her French accent, she struggled to pronounce McElroy correctly.

"I'll drop by in about ten minutes," I said. "If you see a man without a phone, tell him his friend is on the way."

I hung up and called up the street map, trying to figure which direction my host—whether Norden or someone else—would approach from, and more significantly, where the man with the brown coat would watch and wait.

My guess was a cab from the south. I stayed to the north of the café, and across the street ducked into a row of parked cars to give me some cover if I had guessed wrong.

In forty minutes—ten minutes before the agreed meeting time—I watched a cab draw up. A man I recognized in a business suit got out. He muttered something into a phone clamped to his ear before ringing off and dropping his hand to his side. He passed a bill to the driver and, without waiting for his change, entered the café, sitting at a table just inside the permanent awning on the sidewalk. The customers sitting on the sidewalk outside the awning provided perfect cover him.

McElroy.

No Norden.

No brown coat, although like the bad smell he was, I was sure I'd get a hint of him soon enough.

I returned my focus to McElroy. He looked at the screen of his phone, then returned it to the table. A waitress came up to him. He said something—she smiled and made a note before disappearing. The lawyer returned to gazing out of the window, sitting casually— as far as anyone was concerned, he was just a guy in a suit getting a cup of coffee. A guy in a suit who periodically checked his phone and who took an interest in what was going on in the street.

I raised myself cautiously, looking for brown coat. I turned slowly through 360 degrees and took several deep breaths through my nose. I detected no sign, so I dropped down again, returning my focus to McElroy, who now had a cup of coffee.

Five minutes shy of the agreed meeting time, I pulled out my phone and called Norden.

I didn't like initiating calls to my employer and avoided doing so if I could. I could never be sure who was listening or whether he was being influenced to say something: If a guy's got a gun to his head, then he'll say anything. Face to face, I can see the reaction. That's not to say I'm a body language expert—simply that I find people are more honest when I look them in the eye.

Norden answered.

"Zack, it's Leathan. Something's come up, and I'm running late. I'll be there in an hour."

I hung up.

Something attracted McElroy's attention, drawing his gaze from the street to his table. He looked down and picked up his phone, frowning at the screen before clamping it to his ear. A few words were said, and the phone was returned to the table.

McElroy turned his attention to his coffee and didn't look out the window.

I stood slowly, feeling my muscles repay me for staying crouched for too long. A quick spin and deep inhalation—no sign of brown coat. I headed north, hailing a cab when the café had become a small enough dot that I couldn't make out the features of the individual customers sitting on the sidewalk.

fifty-seven

"Surprise!" My voice was bright, my tone sarcastic.

Norden, apparently rendered immobile by my appearance, held the door to his temporary office. His face started to move—first showing what I indeed took to be surprise and then softening. "Shit, Leathan. I'm sorry."

Something in his tone and the way he couldn't look me in the eye suggested he was contrite. He released the door as if accepting whatever fate would befall him and started toward the butterscotch room where his desk lived. I closed the door and followed, assuming my regular place on his sofa.

"What's going on?" I asked.

Norden sighed as he dropped into the seat behind his desk. "I got a call from Mallet—he's in London now. The press have been on to him."

He stopped talking as if he had given sufficient explanation.

I waited.

My employer noticed that I was waiting. There was a movement as if he was having a conversation inside his own head—a discussion about how he could release the smallest amount of detail and yet satisfy my need for more information. There was a move to make and he knew that whatever his last move had been, I had outplayed that move. My presence in his line of sight confirmed that.

"They've got a story about a missing laptop and a deal," he said.

"That's hardly a story," I said.

"It's weak—I agree. At least, it sounds weak. But you don't call for comment if you've got nothing. They must have more—they're trying to flush something out."

I let the room fall quiet. I'd like to say it was a strategy to force my employer to spit out further details—let the social awkwardness perform what a tough line of questioning might achieve—but in reality, I had nothing to say on this topic. As Norden said, it sounded like a weak threat and the sort of thing Orville Michael Mallet could handle easily. Doubtless, Awful—as Clementina called him—had called Norden only out of a combination of courtesy and a desire to prove how invaluable he was. You don't get gold stars for fixing a problem no one knows about.

"I spoke to McElroy," said Norden in a matter-of-fact tone. "He says it's not him."

"Did you tell him about the iPad?" I asked.

Norden bobbed his head once in affirmation.

"How did he react?"

My employer looked down, a slight heat coming to his cheeks. "He said he'd give me twenty-four hours if I sent you." His voice was weak, shameful, and he seemed incapable of looking up from his lap.

"Twenty-four hours to do what?" I asked.

He looked up, his mouth tight, pensive.

"And if you didn't send me?"

"Then I had an hour."

"How was my meeting with him meant to end?" I asked.

A ripple crossed his shoulders. "Don't know," he said quietly. "I didn't think that far ahead."

fifty-eight

"Hello, you two. We thought we might find you both here."

My employer and I had ground our conversation into tiny details, each of which we understood individually, but we couldn't figure how the details fit together or how McElroy—or whoever was trying to sell a story to the press—would act.

McElroy demonstrated his next move in person. There was the sound of key in the door, footsteps—two sets—on the exposed wooden floorboards, and the lawyer appeared. He dropped himself into the second sofa without introducing his brown-coated companion, who stood in the doorway, letting his odor slowly fill the room.

The lawyer faced me. "Mister Wilkey, so good to see you. Has our friend Mister Norden been telling you about his assets?"

I looked to the lawyer but said nothing.

"Hmm." The lawyer looked to Norden, raising his eyebrows. He turned back to me. "As you know, Zackary has been divorcing himself from the current Missus Zackary, mother of that little bitch Clementina."

He saw me flinch.

"Ahhh. How cute. You think she's a sweet kid." He snorted. "I don't wish to be rude in front of her father..." He slowed, looking to Norden. "Who am I kidding—he doesn't care, so why should I care? She's a spoiled little bitch." His face took on a look of faked compassion. "But not half the bitch that her mother is being through the divorce. Right, Zackary?"

Norden shifted uneasily in his chair. The junior man was throwing insults at the senior—insults of a personal nature—and the senior man seemed incapable of responding or even defending himself or his daughter.

The lawyer leaned forward, staring straight at me, and dropped his voice. "Let me explain it to you, Leathan. Mister and Missus Norden are in the process of divorcing. Most things are settled—they both agree that neither wants the child—but the big problem is money. I say problem: Missus Norden wants what is hers. She wants half. Zackary here doesn't think the mother of his child, the woman he married when he was poor, is worth half."

He sat back in his sofa, looking around the room, a storyteller keen to know that his audience was paying attention.

"I can see the motivation," said McElroy. "I have no love for that woman. But she is due half of the marital assets." He turned to face Norden, but spoke for me. "Zackary is quite a financial whizz. He couldn't argue against the principle that she was due half, but he could do something with the question of what. He's a financial guy—his job description involves making assets disappear and reappear—so he moved a few assets and didn't tell his former wife's lawyers."

The lawyer stood and moved to the corner of the room overlooking the red awning below. He rested against the butterscotch wall and locked eyes with me before he continued. "He thought he was protecting himself in his divorce, but there's another term for what he did. Financial fraud." The lawyer paused, letting the thought hang in the room like the bad smell coming from the guy in the brown coat. "The managing partner of a financial firm involved in financial fraud. Think about it, Leathan. What do you think the regulators will say? What do you think Missus Norden will say?"

"You're bullshitting," I said.

"Maybe I am," said the lawyer, appearing to be genuinely considering my insult. "Maybe I've got some of the details wrong. We all make mistakes."

He paused, letting his gaze move to my employer.

"But here's the thing, Leathan. Do you hear Zackary denying anything? Do you hear him saying that I'm lying or that I've misunderstood?"

"You don't have any proof," I said, looking toward McElroy, who was still focused on the man whose job he wanted.

"You want to take that risk?" asked the lawyer, who let his eyes move to the man filling the door with his body and the room with his aroma. "But you do raise an interesting technology problem."

"Laptop, iPad," grunted the man in the brown leather coat, standing straight and flexing his shoulders.

fifty-nine

I stood and tried to flex without looking as if I was flexing or limbering up. My shoulders were tight and my muscles sluggish.

A window and the red awning below might provide one exit, but I preferred the door and the stairs. I figured I could probably deliver one blow before Mister Brown Coat realized my intent. In reality the chance of being able to deliver a decisive blow with that first punch was small. But if I could do enough to surprise him—to take him while he wasn't suspecting my play—then I had an opportunity. If I followed up quickly with a second and a third blow—maybe if he went down and I could get in a kick or two—then I'd have the advantage and might be able to leave without further conversation.

McElroy, Norden, and Mister Brown Coat all looked toward me with varying degrees of interest. McElroy's look was haughty, dismissive, and yet still showed some anger that he had failed to bend me to his will. Norden was ashamed and still couldn't look me in the eye but compromised by gazing at my navel. He was the little boy who had been caught and cried. He cried not because he was sorry for what he had done, but because he was sorry for himself that he had been caught and humiliated. Brown Coat looked and saw lunch.

I took a step toward the door, then a second, becoming aware of the exponential increase in his pungency.

Brown Coat shifted slightly. It was the body-language equivalent of a mumble.

Another step on my part. Another movement by him, still no clearer than a mumble.

Another step. He made a clear movement, half stepping away from the door so that he was only half filling the frame. It was a clear communication, but it was an inconsistent communication. Half a step away said: "Please pass." Staying half in the door said: "I'm making a point." And saying "please pass" was another way of saying "please come within range so I can do you damage."

Another step. I scanned the room. All eyes were on me—there was no silent communication between the other three. Another step. Mister Brown Coat went to move.

His body shifted across my field of vision, moving away from the door. He stretched his right arm—his arm farther from the door—and flexed his hand. He had my attention. I fixed my gaze on the weapon at the end of his right arm being readied for action.

His left fist landed. I'm guessing he misplaced his punch, hitting the bottom of my rib cage. It hurt, but it wasn't enough to floor me.

He dropped his right hand—the lure that had attracted my attention and offered some balance as he swung his left. The right fist that now came toward me.

I already had forward momentum and kept moving forward, but turned to face my left side into the path of his right fist. His fist hit me weakly—making contact too soon—as I reached him, slamming my body into his and forcing him against the doorframe. I rammed the butt of my palm into his forehead, driving his head back and only stopping when his head hit the wooden frame.

He threw another weak punch, making contact but not bringing any pain.

I responded with a blow squarely in his gut, feeling the rush of spit-infused wind exit from his mouth as my knuckles made contact.

He doubled forward. I grabbed his lapels and spun him out of the doorway, pulling him fully into the room. Before he could find his balance again, I pushed him, taking two steps forward to bring my whole weight behind the thrust. I released, and he involuntarily took half a step backward before hitting Norden's desk and falling backward over the white surface.

"Good day, gentlemen," I muttered and left the room.

I closed the front door behind me and headed for the stairs winding around the elevator shaft, stepping gently as I wasn't yet sure what injuries I had sustained. Two flights down, and I hadn't heard the front door open.

The courtyard was quiet and maintained its consistent gray pallor, which can only be achieved by a deep well that is open to the sky but never sees direct sunlight. On the far wall there was a faucet; it was probably used for watering the few flowerpots that stood around the cobblestones.

I squatted in front of it and let the water run, scooping a few sips with my hand and refreshing my face.

As I closed off the flow of water and returned to a standing position, I heard the sound of the main gate onto the road open. I relaxed—if I could hear the gate, then while I might not have heard the front door to the apartment cum office, I would have heard the footsteps descending or the elevator.

Whoever had come through the gate was not walking quietly, and as I turned, I heard the footsteps getting faster. His body slammed into mine, taking us both into the wall—me acting as a buffer for him.

I now had the answer to whether my plan B exit—through the window and down the awning—would work. It would. Mister Brown Coat had seemingly used that route and returned through the front gate.

He stepped back from me and kicked my ankle—the first kick was aimed at the bone, the second was a sweeping kick behind the Achilles tendon to knock out my feet. I had the momentary sensation of weightlessness, and then I hit the cobbles. It felt like every bone in my body—apart from my skull—made direct contact with the hard stones.

As I lay groaning, he jumped on me, bouncing and letting his weigh crush my body into the unyielding rock underneath me, before grabbing my hair. "Technology," he said in a thick French accent, knocking my head against the cobbles and presenting his narrow blade in his other hand.

He had made his point. My lack of reaction seemed to have communicated sufficiently to him that I understood his point. We both remained silent and still—as still as two people panting can be—staring at each other.

There were footsteps and a shuffling of feet as the footsteps moved toward us. Two men stood beside us.

"Get off him," said one man. I recognized Norden's voice, but with the position of my head being controlled by the man on top of me who still had hold of my hair, I was unable to meet his view and instead maintained my staring competition with my captor.

"I've told you once and now I'll tell you for a second time," I said to the man with the brown coat, "I don't have the laptop and I don't know where it is."

The grip on my hair tightened. Norden mumbled something—he may have been negotiating with McElroy, assuming the other viewer was McElroy.

"I know where the iPad is, and it's safe. But as it's the only bargaining chip I've got, I'm not giving it up." The blade found its way to the side of my windpipe. "Kill me and the iPad's out there. While I'm alive, whatever is on it remains hidden."

He stared at me, more in pity than in anger.

I became aware of the conversation between Norden and McElroy—it was becoming more of an argument. Then there was a deep slapping sound, and my captor toppled away from me, losing his balance and falling to my side. Replacing the view of his face above me was a foot—a foot attached to Norden's leg.

I moved. I moved quickly, standing without thinking, and ran to the gate without another word to any of the three men.

sixty

I had been in Paris for too long.

I wanted to trust Norden, but I couldn't. People with problems tend to have more than one problem and fail to see their biggest problem. They only reach for help when they get close to desperate, and once they're desperate, then they're willing to throw anything— or in Norden's case anyone, as in me—at the problem.

Norden had lied to me: He had lied by what he said and lied by what he withheld. While I trusted McElroy less, I figured that he was probably telling something closer to the truth when he laid the accusation of hiding assets against Norden. But it wasn't my employer's lie that got me—it was the unreliability. When he decided to send me to meet with McElroy without giving me a hint that there was a problem, then I stopped trusting.

Not that there was much trust before.

The realization of what he had done also brought with it the realization that it was time to leave Paris, which was unfortunate because I'd come to remember how much I liked the city I had visited with my parents as a kid. I was getting bored with moving around Europe and wanted to stay in one place, and the notion of being unfindable within one city, rather than constantly getting on trains and changing country, was beginning to appeal more.

If I stayed in one city, then I could work, I could develop some contacts I could trust, I could see some friendly faces, rather than having to always be the new guy. Staying in one city would bring other problems—I'd have to fall off the grid completely so I couldn't be tracked. If the Bulgarians paid someone in a phone company who let on that my phone was always used in Paris, then it wouldn't take too long for the people who would prefer that my body was lying dead in a ditch to guess where I was.

But that was a thought for another day. For the moment, I wanted to sit down, have a coffee, have a shower, pack, and, if possible before I left, find Clementina. But if she wasn't around, I'm sure she wouldn't spill too many tears on account of my not saying *au revoir*.

The porter in reception was the same guy who had been on duty last night, the guy who had fallen asleep as I checked out the storeroom. We grunted our acknowledgements as I passed before taking the elevator to the top floor.

As I shut the front door, I took a few moments with my back to the closed piece of wood, knowing I was alone again and savoring the feeling of comparative security and relaxation that came with my own company. The odor of the guy in the brown coat had dissipated, and I was left with the fresh scent that had always trailed behind Angeline as she constantly buffed and scrubbed and polished, keeping the apartment clean.

At the kitchen, I put on the coffee and slumped onto one of the stools next to the counter as I waited for the pot to brew.

There was a noise.

Nothing big. Nothing serious. But a noise. Rustling. Rubbing. Moving. "Clemmy?" I called out. "Clementina, is that you?"

She didn't respond.

I headed for Clementina's room, hearing the loud slap of my feet on the leather floor.

As I opened the door, there was movement: a ghost hiding. You're sure you've seen it, but your rational mind tells you it was an illusion. What you saw disappear was a mirage, not a real person. Not to mention, that Clementina's hair was blond, and the apparition's hair was black.

"Clemmy?" I stepped into the room. "Clemmy, is that you?"

There was a sound from Clementina's dressing room. The thing about apparitions is that they don't make any noise—this one knocked something as she backed into a closet.

The dressing room had the look that Clementina had been there but that Angeline hadn't. This made sense—Clementina had finished getting ready this morning, and then she and Angeline had left together with Reece. Angeline had returned, but before she could complete her morning chores I had taken it on myself to fire her and throw her out.

The clothes that Clementina had auditioned and rejected were liberally distributed around the room—some were thrown on the floor, a few on her dressing table seat, and others hung over closet doors and closet handles. One closet stood out—there was nothing hanging in it, and the door was properly closed without the contents spilling out.

I opened the door, and the apparition pushed her way backward as if she might be able to find a way out. "Have you been trying to sell stories to the newspapers in London?" I asked.

The look of shock and surprise that preceded the look of indignation told me I had guessed right. The former housekeeper went to remonstrate with me.

"Don't bother," I said. "If you want to say anything, you can tell me where the laptop is."

"I don't know what you mean," said Angeline with a swish of her head—indignant, and yet somehow managing to ignore the fact that she was crammed into a closet.

"Play it your way. It's time for you to leave."

She came out of the closet without argument. I led her to the elevator, through the lobby, and to the front door. "There are better ways to make money from that laptop—you could have earned a lot more money."

She gave me a look, questioning, nearly begging for an explanation of how she could be earning more. I closed the front door on her without feeling the need to know where she was going.

The porter looked bemused. "She was fired this morning," I said. "Why did you let her in?"

"No one told me," muttered the other man, looking ready for a sleep.

sixty-one

By the time I had thrown out Angeline—for the second time that day—the coffee was ready.

I slumped at the counter with a fresh brew in front of me. First, I tried Clementina. I hung up when it kicked through to voicemail—she already had enough messages from me. Second, I tried Reece. As the phone clicked through to his voicemail, I composed myself, readying to leave a message in a light, cheerful tone. "Hiya matey, Leathan here. Give me a call when you've got a moment."

I hung up and exhaled, ejecting every last element of fake bonhomie from my body.

Half an hour ago, my mind was made up. I would come back here, have a coffee, wash, pack, and leave, getting the heck out of Paris before anyone could figure I was in the city. In particular, before anyone connected with the Bulgarians who were now in jail because of me could figure where I was. I had achieved the first aim—I was back here—and with the coffee in front of me I was achieving the second aim.

But something had changed over those thirty minutes. Clementina's lack of response was starting to make me twitch. It wasn't in her nature to be that quiet for that long—there was a neediness that required human interaction on her part. While I was sure she would be getting great pleasure from shopping, there was the flip side—the talking about it—that was missing here. It didn't matter who she talked to—it could be her friends and followers online; it could be people who understood and cared about fashion; heck, it could even be me. The point was, she needed to talk about her most recent acquisition, and so far I could see no evidence of acquisition or of discussion about potential acquisitions.

And that radio silence was starting to make me scratch.

Maybe this was how parents felt when their kids were home late. Maybe this was the explanation they give themselves. Maybe this was the bargain they made with themselves. I was starting to set deadlines and expectations for a kid who wasn't even mine, and for whom I had no right to set expectations.

But then, Reece wasn't responding either. I would have expected him to try to make it back as early as possible so he could slink away in order to singlehandedly kill heavily armed forces on his games console. But maybe the opportunity to spend all morning staring at Clementina's boobs was sufficient reward for the combat medals he was missing out on.

And Angeline's return was grating at the back of my mind. She must have had a reason to return. She didn't come just to look at the view over Jardins du Ranelagh or to do a last-minute bit of tidying and maybe to clean Clementina's bath.

Of everyone I had met since I arrived in Paris, with the exception of Awful Michael Mallet, who was now in London, Angeline was the one whose story I had the most tenuous grip on. But the picture I had painted—painted for myself, and I could be wrong—was that she was all about the money. There was a family back in the Philippines, and her sole concern was to earn money—in any way and as much as possible—to send back to the family.

If I was right with my assessment of Angeline, that meant there was something here that she thought could help her earn money. Or maybe she hid the laptop here and was happy to leave it because she knew she could get back. Even without keys, my guess was access to the apartment was only a blowjob away, and on that front she didn't seem to have any concerns about doing what she needed to do to get what she needed to get.

I finished my coffee. My departure was going to be delayed—maybe by minutes, maybe by hours, but it was going to be delayed. If I was being followed, I had to hope that the work I had done in an internet café in Brussels would pay off.

There had been a two-hour wait before I could get on the train in Brussels. During that time, I had posted a few photos to Facebook. I didn't care about social media, and I knew none of my friends cared about the photos I was posting—they were literally nothing to write home about. But they did have GPS data embedded. Real GPS data that was embedded when I had shot the photos in Northern Italy last month.

The only fakery was in the date of the photo. With a quick bit of editing, I had changed the shoot date from last month to three days ago—I had learned something while working with journalists. I didn't know how hard the Bulgarians were tracking me, but if they found my Facebook page and looked at the last post I made three days ago, then they would have confidently been able to work out that I had been in Italy—and if they had looked harder, they would have been able to determine the street in Turin where I had been staying.

The trouble for them was that I was posting from Brussels, just before I had left for Paris. I had to hope that was enough to keep them off the scent and that they had no reason to follow me to Paris and that neither McElroy nor his brown-coated friend knew any Bulgarians.

Those two were my concern, but now I also had to worry about Norden, the man who had brought me to Paris.

Norden was a man with secrets. I had no problem with anyone wanting privacy, and business secrets made sense to me—I understood and believed his argument that if people knew the deal he was working on, then that would tip the price. The secrecy about his assets—especially if he had lied about his holdings—also made sense to me, even if he was breaking the law. And if he wanted to keep his love life secret, that was fine with me.

But he also seemed to have leaks. Clementina, without realizing it, leaked information. The new girlfriend—the former secretary whose name I didn't know, even though I knew a lot about her breasts—seemed to have little concern about revealing intimate details to Clementina and who knows who else. The housekeeper appeared to have been well rewarded for leaking. The corporate lawyer seemed to want to gather Norden's secrets and use them against him.

But Norden didn't seem to have been concerned about these leaks, except in one area: Clementina, and he had seemingly addressed that problem by hiring me. But now that I didn't trust him, I began to wonder why he wasn't concerned about these leaks. Was he unconcerned because, in truth, he had a bigger concerns?

I didn't want to, but something deep inside was screaming that I needed to look around the apartment and look where I hadn't looked before. Reluctantly, I shuffled into the largest bedroom, which I figured had to be Norden's suite.

The bed was against the far wall and centered. It seemed to be making a statement. I wasn't quite sure exactly what that statement was, who that statement was aimed at, or who had decided to make the statement—the room likely having been created by an interior designer who would never have returned here after her work was complete.

On one hand, the room said "power." It told me, "I am a powerful person." But who needs to be told that in a bedroom? Is the master or mistress inviting guests and giving them the subliminal message that they should prepared to be dominated, to be overwhelmed if they stay in the room? Or was the intention that a couple would take the room and feel powerful together? I wondered if that improved the sex life.

But the room also exuded ostentatious luxury. The kind of luxury that was expensive, pointless, and just plain uncomfortable. And again I wondered—who is meant to be impressed by the pretentious and gaudy show of flamboyance?

For me, bedrooms have two key functions: They're the place to sleep and the place to have sex. I wanted to do neither in this mini aircraft hangar, which felt like more of a hotel lobby where someone had left a bed.

I wandered into the dressing room. Unlike Clementina's dressing room, this was tidy, which wasn't surprising given Norden's lack of presence in the apartment. The bathroom was equally tidy.

I stepped back from the marble floor of the bathroom into the windowless dressing room, feeling the thick carpet under my feet, and pondered where a man with secrets would hide his secrets. And would he hide his secrets here? There was only one way to find out—I started opening closets.

sixty-two

I had undertaken a quick scan of Norden's suite to get some sort of idea of what I had to search through—I opened the closet doors, opened the drawers, checked the nightstand, and looked under the bed. Ten minutes, and I found nothing.

That was when I got a screwdriver I had found in the kitchen when I was searching out a balloon whisk, and I began searching in earnest.

Something told me this place was all about show. As I levered off the decorative fascia covering the narrow gap where the wall and the closet met, I saw this to be true. Looking through I could see where the surface decoration had ended, leaving rough walls and particleboard flooring exposed underneath.

It had taken a while to figure out how to remove the plinth under the closets, and when I got there, I felt a sense of disappointment. All I found in the narrow gap between the base of the closet and the particleboard flooring was sawdust.

And I found a new conundrum—how the hell to get the plinth back into place. As I stared at the long, thin piece of wood, my phone rang. "Hi."

"Leathan, Zack." He said that as if he was unaware of caller display. "I thought you should know that McElroy and his pet Rottweiler have just left." He hesitated. "I think they might be considering taking you off their Christmas card list."

I snorted. "You've got to be on the list to be taken off, or maybe I was more popular with them than I thought."

He hesitated again. When he continued his voice was softer, almost pleading. "I'm sorry, Leathan. I'm sorry I got you into this shit. I'm sorry I lied. I'm sorry I ran you into an ambush. I'm sorry about it all."

I rolled over on the thick pile and sat up straight, resting against the closet without a plinth.

"I've fucked up, and it's all my fault. I'm sorry, Leathan."

I half mumbled a platitude, but it still felt like he was apologizing because my actions had made it necessary for him to kill me. Sure, he might be sorry, but he was sorry for himself, and I was still dead. And if I wasn't actually dead, then I suspected a visit to the hospital might be in my future if I met McElroy's brown-coated knife carrier.

"What do I do?" he asked, his voice tight, trembling.

"You mean how do you get out from under the self-imposed fuck-up that is your life at the moment?" The soft surfaces of the room made my overly harsh retort seem even colder than I intended.

"Yeah, that," said Norden. His voice had softened; my retort had amused him.

"McElroy wants you to quit," I said, stating the obvious. "You quit, and he can take the reins, and when he's in control, then he can shift things to his advantage. That's your basic notion, right?"

"Right."

"Under that scenario, he sees gain for himself only if you walk away. But if we flip the situation—so he needs you to stay—then that keeps you in place and removes any incentive he might have to blab about any bad behavior on your part—real or imagined."

From his tone, Norden was ahead of me and had ruled out the options. "How, Leathan? How do we do that?"

"We need to engineer a situation such that, one, he physically can't accept the role, and two, he needs money, so he needs you to stay as managing partner," I said.

Norden's tone became harder. "He may have done many things, but we're not going to hospitalize the man. I do have my..."

I cut across him. "Jail. If he's in a French jail, then McElroy can't accept the role of managing partner, and he's going to want you to keep earning money for the partnership so that he can pay his legal fees, not to mention to provide him with some sort of a nest egg on the other side."

"As far as I'm aware, Leathan, it's not a criminal offense to hurt my feelings."

I snorted for the second time in the conversation. "As far as I'm aware, the French take murder seriously."

"Murder?"

"Murder," I repeated. "McElroy and the guy in the brown coat murdered Hoffman."

Norden stopped talking, but I could hear him thinking—the small movements of his mouth, scratches, itches, irregular breathing. Eventually he spoke. "How do we...?"

"You need to find a lawyer—a French lawyer—fast. Your connections found me; call them and find a French lawyer. You need someone who understands the French legal system—you need someone with connections. You need someone who can work around the problem that McElroy seems to already be buddies with the detective leading the investigation into Hoffman's death."

I could hear him thinking again.

"And you need to find yourself a new lawyer to act for the partnership if the present incumbent is going to be indisposed."

He was still thinking, but he was able to mumble: "Yes, yes, you're right, I wonder if..."

"One other thing you should know," I said. "The source of the story that Mallet is trying to stop was Angeline. McElroy told you the truth on that one."

"Huh," said Norden. "A lawyer telling the truth."

"I'm at the apartment now," I said. "Angeline managed to find her way back in, so I'm going to hang around here for a while and make sure she doesn't return. Call me if you need anything more."

He grunted his thanks and hung up.

sixty-three

I rested the plinth back in place. The first person to touch it would find it wasn't fixed. But that wasn't my main concern: Now that Zackary knew my location—since I had just told him—my priority was to get out of the apartment.

I had figured the route through the service passages, which avoided the main lobby, and passing through the parking garage I opened the security grill to exit. There was no man in a brown coat or lawyer looking to improve his status. I saw no one, and the street seemed empty. As far as I could tell, my exit had been unnoticed by anyone.

Turning right, I headed into les Jardins du Ranelagh.

I had been through the open space several times since I had met the Norden family, and while I appreciated that the place did bring a certain amount of greenery to the city, the garden was still a place I looked at with contempt. The straight lines of straight trees, lining the sides of the road, seemed so antithetical to the nature of, well, nature.

Straight trees. Their trunks vertical with all side shoots removed to a height of about twelve feet. I let my eyes drift across the foreground. There were two trees out of place—not in rows and not grown to the uniform style. One was an oak, the other something equally big. Both trees were much larger than those that had been planted to line the avenues crossing the green space.

I suspected that both trees had been here long before someone conjured the notion of public gardens. Indeed, the oak had likely been here when the French royal family still had their heads and their title, and while this plot of land was miles outside the city of Paris.

The trees—the oak included—had lost their leaves in the chill that came with the change of season. The brown leaves still swirling along the ground and the last few brave leaves still clinging to the branches told a story of a recent change.

People look down—they don't look up. I had just looked down—I hadn't looked up. I gambled and did something I hadn't done since I was a kid—I climbed the oak tree. The knurled bark gave me enough grip to lift myself to reach the spreading branches and pull myself up. I had only raised myself through eight or ten feet, but my body felt like I had just completed a good session of weight lifting at the gym.

I felt like a child. If anyone looked up or had seen my climb, they would have thought I looked like a child. But my elevated position gave me a clear view over the front and side of the apartment block. All I had to do was wait. Norden knew where I was, and this was our own personal trust exercise. If someone—someone in a brown coat—arrived at the apartment, then I knew exactly where I stood with him.

But if no one arrived, then maybe—just maybe—he was trying to find a lawyer while I tried to find some comfort in the branches of the oak.

There was, of course, a third possibility. McElroy and friends might turn up at the apartment with the same intent I had—to find what could be found. If they did, then it wouldn't be a fast job—they'd tear everything out and still not find the iPad.

My phone rang, distracting me. Reece. I answered. "Hi."

"How do I control her shopping, Leathan? She's driving me fucking crazy. I need your help. Need, man. Need your help." There was an urgency, an immediacy.

"Slow down. Where are you?"

"Don't fucking ask where I am—I'm totally fucking lost. We've been everywhere this morning. Go here. Go there. No, not there... there. Honestly man, if she wasn't blond I would have strangled her by now." He paused. "Seriously, man. When can you get here? I need you, man."

I kept the phone pressed to my ear and stared back at the apartment block. "I'm going to be a while."

"Where are you?" asked the driver.

"Hospital," I lied. "I got beaten by McElroy's man."

"Hospital?" asked Reece. "You sound like you're in a street."

"It feels like I'm in a street," I said. "The emergency department is busy."

"Where are you? I'll come and get you."

It was an interesting offer from a man who had called me because his charge was driving him crazy.

"I'm not sure which hospital I'm at," I said, continuing my lie. "The cab brought me here. I had bigger concerns than asking for GPS coordinates."

"Of course, of course," said Reece. "Do you know how long you're going to be? I could come and get you then."

"I reckon I'll be at least ninety minutes," I said. "Why don't I meet you somewhere after that?"

"Yeah, do that." I couldn't see him, but I knew Reece was smiling.

"Where are you—where should we meet?"

There was a hesitation in Reece's voice—a slight panic as I pushed him to think on his feet. "We're fucking all over the place, man," he said. "Er, er...why don't you meet us outside Bercy Arena on Boulevard de Bercy?" He made his suggestion with all the subtlety of a man reading a script.

"Is that where you are?"

"Er...it's near where we are. You know how the girl finds all those really out-of-the-way stores... And there's a wide road here with good parking."

"Okay," I said, "Boulevard de Bercy—say at three-thirty. I'll look for the Maybach."

I hung up and continued to stare at the apartment. Over the next fifteen minutes I became increasingly uncomfortable, but the lack of visitors was enough to let me know that Norden probably was calling a lawyer.

That was enough to get me out of the tree.

sixty-four

I walked through les Jardins du Ranelagh, followed past the café angled on the corner, passed the Metro station, and found Rue de Passy, the road I'd last traveled with Reece when we were looking for Clementina. On that occasion she was meeting Hoffman at Gare du Nord.

I didn't think I'd find her here today. My reason for walking this way now was twofold. First, I had spent too long in the tree and I wanted to loosen up. Second, I wanted to get the Metro at Passy and pick up line 6, which would take me directly, albeit slowly, across the southern flank of Paris before turning north and crossing la Seine.

A quick review of the map around Bercy Arena showed that, after crossing la Seine, line 6 directly passed the arena. Line 6, which for much of its route was elevated. Line 6, which when it crossed la Seine was still elevated—there was a road bridge, and the Metro line was on a raised viaduct with cars below.

Having crossed the bridge, the Metro line then followed the length of Boulevard de Bercy, the road marking the eastern boundary of the arena. As far as I could see from the map and looking at street-view images, as line 6 passed along the Boulevard, the elevation lowered, with the line finally going underground a short distance past the arena to avoid the tracks coming out of a mainline station.

It took forty minutes for the Metro to find its way around the lower flank of Paris, but I was still half an hour early. I alighted at Quai de la Gare, the last stop before line 6 crossed la Seine. Walking to the end of the elevated platform, I looked out over la Seine. Bercy Arena—a center for concerts and conferences—loomed in the distance. An ugly modern construction that would have upset Baron Haussmann's sensibilities.

It wasn't much of a plan—it didn't get far and it didn't resolve— but it was a plan: I would be on the Metro as it traveled along Boulevard de Bercy. I could keep traveling between Quai de la Gare, where I was, and Bercy, the next Metro station, and with each pass, I could look out and view Reece's arrival.

There were no prizes for sophistication here.

I checked the time again—twenty-eight minutes until the agreed meeting time. A train came; I got on. The doors closed; we moved off, and within a minute we had crossed la Seine. As we reached the right bank, the road below met an intersection joining Boulevard de Bercy. The elevated train crossed the junction, letting me look down on the traffic.

If I'd been at street level, I probably would have missed it, but from my elevated position the Maybach caught my attention. Reece was out of the car, standing. He looked like he had looked when McElroy took me to identify Hoffman's body. Before the lawyer and I got out of the vehicle, McElroy had ordered Reece out, giving me and the lawyer a few moments of privacy.

Reece was used to this, although clearly from his present body language, he resented being evicted from his own domain, and the lack of status stung.

But if he hadn't been standing out of the car—looking uncomfortable, looking unhappy at the eviction—I wouldn't have seen where he was looking. I followed his gaze, looking down as the Metro moved along, shifting onto the downward slope along the length of Boulevard de Bercy.

If I'd been at street level, I would have thought Reece was just been staring somewhere else, uncomfortably. The pedestrians on the sidewalk would have obscured my view of the man who had become too familiar in my life—the man with the brown coat.

I was early for the meeting. Reece was even earlier and had brought with him someone who was good with his fists and carried a blade. Someone who was clearly expecting another to arrive and was keenly looking out for him. That someone was arriving, but that someone—now that I had seen what awaited me—wasn't going to walk into this trap.

The Metro moved on, gradually lowering itself, the reflection of the carriage's glass windows offering me some form of camouflage as I lost sight of the men.

sixty-five

As I rose, I became aware that there was no shadow cast over our exit. No shadow—no buildings casting shadow.

The up escalator from the Metro pushed us out onto the street level—dribbling us onto a small plaza like a weak garden hose.

The plaza was open, exposed, visible to people expecting and looking for a specific person. That specific person? Me.

I dropped my head, slumped my whole body, and tried to mingle, staying within the group of people being expelled from the station. Moving, but not moving too quickly or too slowly. Doing nothing that would draw the attention of anyone looking. I continued forward, letting the small cluster of people and then the momentum of my movement take me away from Reece.

Around a corner I stopped and pulled out my phone, scrabbling at the screen to bring up the street map. I wanted to go back and look at Reece—I wanted to observe him, but not be observed myself.

While I had stood on the platform at Quai de la Gare on the other side of the river, I had suspected that Reece might be involved with McElroy. He was too close, too friendly, calling him Johnnie, talking about him with a slight sense of awe. But I was happy to entertain the notion that this could be a slightly naïve guy being wowed by someone more intelligent than him who seemed to have stacks of money to throw around.

As the Metro crossed the river and drew level with the Maybach, I had seen Reece and the guy with the brown coat. That one look, where Reece glanced at the other man, was enough to tell me where Reece's loyalties lay. But it wasn't enough to tell me where Clementina was or to tell me what was going to happen next.

I turned back toward the Metro and leaving the cover of the café, I tried to get a view down Boulevard de Bercy. The angle was wrong—I was past the end of the street and needed to move around, and even then I reckoned I would have trouble getting a clear view. The Maybach was toward the far end—closer to la Seine than to me.

I crossed to the far side of the road and headed away. I figured Mister Brown Coat and Reece were looking for someone coming toward them—they weren't focused on someone walking across their line of view, if they could even see me at this distance.

Reckoning I was out of sight, I began to jog, taking the road that ran parallel to the road on which the Maybach was parked and that, after a minute's jog, led to Quai de la Rapée—the highway running parallel to la Seine. I crossed to get close to the river—eight lanes of traffic would give me some level of cover—and turned left again to complete a third side of a square, heading toward the foot of Boulevard de Bercy where it met the bridge.

The bridge had two separate tracks for traffic—three lanes heading in each direction. Running along the center of the bridge was a colonnade: two rows of columns with arches joining the columns along the length of the bridge. Between the columns was a cycle track, and on top of the columns was balanced the elevated Metro lines I had traveled over a few minutes ago. It was the sort of construction that would never be designed but had probably occurred with additions to the bridge over the years.

At least I hoped no one had designed it this way.

The broad stone columns gave me cover—at an angle, two rows of columns gave narrow slits through which I could see Reece and, with a few steps to the left, Mister Brown Coat. I stepped to the right; somehow it felt safer not seeing him.

Reece was still standing beside the Maybach, looking increasingly bored. He jerked as his phone rang and looked around furtively.

"Leathan?"

"Reece, man. I'm sorry. I'm going to be delayed. They say I need stitches and they're talking about an x-ray...head injury and all that."

Reece didn't offer any words of sympathy. Instead he looked around guiltily, as if he were embarrassed to be on the phone—he was like the guy in the office whose mother called him every day.

"Is Clementina there?" I asked. "Can I talk to her? Let her know what's going on."

There was a hesitation. A moment of silent panic at his end. He looked to the guy in the brown coat, he looked into the car, and he didn't respond to me. When he spoke there was a stiffness in his voice. "She's...er...she's in the changing room, Leathan. It's best I don't, you know..."

"Okay," I said. "Tell her I called. I'll ring when I know what's going on here."

I hung up and watched.

Reece looked through the windshield as if trying to attract the attention of the passenger who was shielded by the reflections on the glass. A figured stepped out. As he stood, the guy in the brown coat moved closer, joining a conversation that had already started—Reece was holding up his hands, metaphorically surrendering. Always the driver, never the responsible adult.

There was some pointing and looking. A debrief of the plan and reconfiguration of a new plan. The passenger turned, pointing, to indicate something to the other men. The passenger—McElroy. That was enough for me: I turned south, heading over the bridge toward the Left Bank.

Within a minute my phone rang. "Where are you?"

"Mister McElroy," I said, not offering an answer to his question.

"Where?"

"Hospital."

"Noisy hospital," he said.

I ignored the comment and waited.

After a few moments he exhaled wearily. "You know what boys are like. They like to brag," he said. I waited again—I saw no need to encourage him. "Shortly before Mister Hoffman's unfortunate— well, you saw him—he was kind enough to share some photos. Photos of a young lady with fewer clothes than she would normally choose to wear."

Above me a train began to rumble.

"Very noisy hospital—sounds like there's a train going through," he said. "It would be such a shame if those photos found their way onto the internet because you didn't stop them from being posted."

The train passed—I could hear it more clearly through the phone as it reached McElroy. "As I said, I'm in hospital after the last beating you arranged for me. Give me an hour." I hung up and kept walking.

sixty-six

I continued walking over the bridge toward the Left Bank, and at Quai de la Gare I took the stairs up to the platform. The third stop was Place d'Italie, where I got out and headed north on Avenue des Gobelins.

I paused to look at the red awning—looking for any indication of damage. The construction was sturdier than I had appreciated. I had thought it was, in essence, a large piece of fabric that pulled out from the wall. Looking closely, I realized I was wrong. On the top, there was a fixed roof. The sides were also fixed—there was fabric, but it seemed to be covering something far more solid and structural. The only piece of unsupported fabric was the tongue of red cloth, drawn down and held between the fixed sides.

Looking at it, it did seem to be strong enough to hold the weight of a man. Maybe if I'd paid more attention to the awning and spent less time looking for people, I could have avoided a beating in the courtyard.

The thought of the courtyard reminded me why I had come here.

Norden didn't seem surprised to see me as he opened the door. "Found a lawyer?" I asked.

"Maybe."

We took our customary places in the butterscotch-walled makeshift office, but I remained standing, looking for any signs of disturbance after my last visit. Norden's cheap but functional white desk had moved. Only a few inches, but it was definitely in a different position, and the papers on the desk had been rearranged too.

"I've told Mallet that the source of the story is Angeline and that she doesn't have the laptop."

"Huh?" I said, trying to draw my attention back to Norden.

"He's got it covered," said my employer, his tone crisp but slightly hesitant. "He thinks he can make the story go away."

"That good, that's good," I mumbled absentmindedly. "Still doesn't stop McElroy spilling anything, but it keeps us out of jail today."

I met his stare. There was shock, maybe fear. He was a man who didn't want to go to jail—not that I had ever met anyone who sought out or looked forward to the experience. I had just given voice to his fear—I had reached into the darkest, most secret part of his mind and pulled out the one thing that truly scared him. It wasn't just the notion of going to jail, although I'm sure that terrified him, but it was his understanding of what the process would entail to get there. The steps through arrest and trial as his life would be exposed and each little lie unpicked, before finally, once his money had gone and his business had been broken, he would be tossed in behind steel and concrete.

It wasn't helpful to have him thinking this way—I needed him to have certainty that there was another different future.

"How did the guy with the brown coat get out?" I asked, changing the subject.

Norden headed to the window. I followed. He slid up the pane and indicated for me to look down. I looked over the top of the awning, which I could see from this angle was a solid wood platform.

"The guy moved quickly," said Norden, returning to his desk and leaving me to survey the alternate exit route. I closed the window and went to the sofa. Norden had the look of someone tasked with delivering a message, but knowing that he wouldn't enjoy seeing the reaction. "They know you're around."

I tightened my mouth to acknowledge.

"McElroy said something about you bullshitting him about being in hospital." His voice was weak.

I gave a single nod to affirm that I had heard. He still had something to say, so I waited.

"They've got Clemmy." The hesitation, the fear, the anguish, the awkwardness—they all made sense. "The deal's simple—you for Clemmy."

I sat silently.

"Did you hear, Leathan? They want me to give you up, and they'll let Clemmy go."

I kept my voice soft. "You understand that what McElroy is trying to do is to split us—he wants to isolate you, and he's asking you to take the action to isolate yourself."

It was his turn to give a single nod in acknowledgement.

"You understand that once I'm gone, you've spent your bargaining chip."

When he spoke, there was a rasp of raw emotion I'd not heard before. "I need Clemmy safe."

I waited. I didn't need to tell him that this was a weak deal with too much risk—he was a man who spent his life doing deals. He knew that you didn't always get what you paid for.

"Is there a plan B?" I asked. "If he doesn't send Clemmy home."

He half shrugged and mumbled something that sounded like "give him what he wants."

"I'll go," I said. "But we're hoping this time the liar is telling the truth."

He nodded in a way that said, "What other option do I have?"

I nodded back in the way that said, "None, unless you want to escalate this thing like crazy, and that's a whole heap of other risks." We both knew, but neither was saying it.

He picked up the receiver and dialed a number. "He's here."

sixty–seven

I saw the nose of the Maybach pushing out from the corner.

I got into the backseat without making eye contact or saying anything to Reece. As the door closed he rolled the car forward and slipped into the afternoon traffic, which was starting to build in anticipation of the rush hour.

In the sound-deadened cabin, we both sat without exchanging any form of communication. The only sound was the touch of Reece's hands on the wheel, the occasional click of the indicator stalk, and the smallest of groans emitted by the leather of his seat as he moved when he turned the wheel.

I broke the near silence. "Where do you fit in, Reece?"

At first it was as if he hadn't heard me. Then he inhaled heavily through his nose. "In my business, you go up with your boss and die with your boss."

He stopped talking, concentrating on the junction. I looked to the mirror—his eyes and his head were in constant motion, keeping him aware of his surroundings as he gently drifted the large lump of metal forward.

"Johnnie is about to replace Zack," he continued as he pulled the car straight. "For once I get a second life. I don't have to become a minicab driver...not that they exist anymore with these call-a-car-on-your-phone things."

I waited. Hoping for more explanation, some elaboration. He offered nothing.

"When Zack wanted to hire me," I began, "why didn't Johnnie stop it? Why did he let Zack bring someone else in?"

I could see a small grin in the rearview mirror. "Johnnie thought you'd be compliant. He figured you'd do what he said, but Zack would pay you, and you'd keep Zack occupied."

"I guess he won't make the same mistake twice," I mumbled.

"I guess," echoed Reece.

"What's Johnnie's links to the cops?" I asked. "He seemed to be pretty friendly with them the other night."

"Don't know," said the driver. "He's a lawyer—there's no difference between the two, is there? It's all about dodgy handshakes and who you know." He seemed to contemplate what he had just said before he continued. "I told you, Leathan—I'm the driver. Johnnie's not hiring me for my knowledge of corporate finance."

That seemed to be all Reece or I had to say before we let the cabin fall back to near silence.

We reached a bridge over la Seine. It took a few moments to recognize we were on Pont de Bercy with the elevated Metro line over the cycle lane and the cars passing on either side. There was a click over the speakers and then the sound of a phone ringing. Someone answered: "Mmmm."

"On the bridge," said Reece. There was a click, and the call ended.

The Maybach headed off the bridge, continuing straight along Boulevard de Bercy, passing the spot where I had seen it parked with Reece and the guy in the brown coat standing near. We followed the road past the small plaza and the station exit, where Reece took the road forty-five degrees to the right—the road I had followed out of the Metro.

We passed the point where I had turned back and continued heading toward the bridge under the railway lines from Gare de Lyon. Just shy of the bridge, Reece took a right, up a narrow lane that seemed more of a historic legacy than a planned road. It threaded through the back of some tatty modernist blocks and older apartments. Baron Haussmann might have dictated how the frontages of Paris should look—he never specified how the hidden parts should look.

Reece pulled the Maybach to a halt next to a low white ironwork gate. On the other side was a path and a door to the back of an apartment block. The door opened, and McElroy stepped out.

sixty-eight

McElroy didn't offer a greeting before he turned and led me through the door.

There were two flights of stairs with no elevator alternate, which led onto a narrow landing—exposed boards that had been stained a dark color sometime around when the Nazis were drinking coffee in Paris, and rendered walls that had probably been painted white at a similar time.

The front doors had been painted more recently—probably in the sixties—and were now faded and chipped, and didn't stop the smell of damp, flowery air fresheners and fried food from seeping into the hallway.

The lawyer led to the last entrance on the left and entered, pushing the door and walking through. I followed, stepping into a dingy room, albeit a room that unlike the corridor did have natural light.

There was a creak behind me—a groan of a floorboard. The door moved to shut without me touching it, and then I felt the pain at the top of my shoulders and across the back of my neck.

When I came around, I tried to take stock.

I was in a dingy room—probably the same room I had walked into following the lawyer, but since I hadn't got a good look, I couldn't be sure. I was on the floor—exposed floorboards, stained like those in the hallway.

My legs were bound. My wrists were bound behind my back. There was tape over my mouth. I tried to move and felt the ache at the back of my head. The last thing I was sure I saw before I passed out again was Reece sitting on an old fabric-covered armchair, looking down at me.

The next time I woke, I woke fast, shocked. Someone tipped a bucket of water over my head. At least I assumed it was a bucket, I hadn't seen anything—I was dealing with the shock of being awake, the rush of water, the involuntary spasm of all my muscles, and fighting against whatever was tying my wrists and ankles.

I tried to lay my head on the hard boards, feeling the renewed pain at the back of my head as I closed my eyes.

Someone lazily kicked my thigh—a soft kick that comes from someone sitting down when they kick out, putting their boot to your flesh.

"The iPad," said someone.

I opened my eyes, trying to find the source of the voice without moving my head, but it hurt even to move my eyeballs.

There were two seats—a single armchair and a sofa. At a guess, both were more than fifty years old. Their old and faded fabric showed a pattern of swirls that would have looked kitsch even in the sixties, and the wear marks didn't enhance the charm. The sofa and armchair were detailed with gold fringing, picked thin where hands had customarily lain. Reece sat in the armchair, picking at the gold fringing, and McElroy sat on the sofa, his attention focused on me.

"iPad," he said.

I tried to meet his stare. "I haven't got it."

There was the sound of leather, a groan of a floorboard as the weight it held shifted, and a boot made contact just under my ribs. I tried to wince, but found every movement caused me more pain.

"I haven't got it," I said again, weakly.

The floorboards groaned again.

"Please." I heard the panic in my voice. "Please."

"Where is the iPad?" asked the lawyer, his tone one of exasperation as he spat each word out.

"I left it at the apartment," I said.

A glance passed from McElroy to whoever was using his boot on me. I guessed from the odor penetrating my nose that the person applying his boot to my body wore a brown coat.

"Angeline took it," I said.

McElroy frowned but couldn't stop his eyes being drawn to the man behind me—he looked, questioning, his eyebrows suggesting he wanted affirmation.

"Angeline who also has the laptop," I added. "Angeline who you paid..."

I moved my head, felt the spasm in my neck, and decided to give in and let the darkness wash over me.

sixty-nine

The next bucket of water woke me as sharply as the last.

There was no pain from the water—just shock as I rapidly went from unconscious to very conscious—but still I contorted, and the contortions tugged on my painful muscles, which pulled against my bruises, hurting me more.

When I finished twisting and pulling, I saw there was a new chair in the room, placed between the single seat, which was now vacant but where Reece had been sitting, and the sofa. New, as in it hadn't been there when I passed out. In truth, it was old—twentieth century, probably 1930s-type old—and made from wood. I suspected the wood was oak, although clearly while I was tied up I couldn't get a closer look. Whatever wood it was, however old it was, it certainly looked sturdy.

And it was definitely sturdy enough to restrain Clementina, who had been tied to the chair.

The chair was an upright chair—maybe intended as a dining chair. Clementina's legs had been taped to the chair, and several wraps of tape crossed her stomach, holding her arms, which were pulled back to the chair. To complete the picture, there was a wrap of tape around her wrists, and a length of tape had been slapped over her mouth but had also caught a handful of hair, which in turn fell in a fixed position across her right eye.

I noticed the hair over her eye first. There was something about this inconvenience that annoyed her more than any of the other indignities forced upon her.

"Hi. How are you?" I said.

She mumbled something unintelligible from behind the piece of tape over her mouth. Her eyes looked to her right, indicating the trapped hair, and she lifted her hand—flexing at the elbows, which were held in place. She could only raise her two hands taped together as far as her throat, but that didn't stop her flicking in the direction of the trapped hair.

"Now, Leathan," said McElroy. "You can see the dynamic has changed. We don't need to hurt you." The lawyer let his gaze drift slowly to Clementina. He didn't need to finish the sentence—I understood exactly what his look was saying: "We don't need to hurt you, because we can hurt her and it will be much more painful for you to watch that happening."

The thumping pain in the back of my head made my calculation harder. Should I say, "Please don't hurt her," or should I go with, "I don't care, do what you want"? The calculation was which response by me would cause least pain for Clementina.

If I went with "please don't hurt her," I could acquiesce and tell them everything—or at least, tell them I had told them everything I knew. If I went with "do what you want," that could sow a seed of doubt—maybe there was no point in tormenting Clementina, at least if they wanted me to tell them where the laptop and the iPad were.

"I tell you, Johnson, over the last few days there have been times I've wanted to tie her up and make her feel pain, and I can't lie—I really am tempted to dick you about just to see her scream—but the thing is, you've already had the truth out of me. Angeline took the laptop and the iPad. She's the one you want."

I watched Clementina's eyes change.

I suspected that I was the first friendly face that she had seen for a while. She noticed that I had noticed her hair trapped across her eye. She saw that I understood how utterly annoying she found having the hair trapped. I understood her—she appreciated that.

But now I was being dismissive. Now I was being openly hurtful and talking about her like I was a bitchy teen. A range of emotions raged from her eyes: hurt, upset, anger. She wanted to beg me, to shout at me, to tell me she never liked me.

McElroy stood, walked over to her, and pulled the tape over her mouth. Gently he eased the adhesive away from her skin to reveal her lips, but left the tape hanging—still attached to her hair and ready to be slapped back in place at any time.

"Leathan," said Clementina, the hurt in her voice washing over me like acid.

"Shh," the lawyer said to her, returning to the sofa with the gold fringing.

She went to speak again. He held up a finger and silenced her, then pulled out a phone and started flicking at the screen. He held the phone toward me to show me something. The angle was wrong—it looked like I was looking at a matte gray piece of glass.

He stood, walked behind Clementina's chair, and reached around to hold the phone in front of her. He reached his free hand around Clementina on her other side and manipulated the screen. With his arms encircling the teen—but not touching—he whispered something in her ear.

"Leathan," said Clementina. There was panic in her voice. "Just tell him, Leathan. Where's the computer? Where's the iPad? Give them to him."

The focus on Clementina gave me time to try to catalog where I hurt. Lying on the hard boards, everything hurt and I soon lost track of each individual ache. I looked up and behind me; the man with the brown coat was standing, waiting for an opportunity to unleash more pain. "Is this your place?" I asked. "I like what you've done with it—you've really captured the *I don't give a shit and I've got no standards* vibe."

He shifted his weight, getting ready to kick.

"Please don't," I said.

He snorted as if he were doing me a big favor by choosing not to let his boot find my ribs.

"Do you have any painkillers?" I asked. "Because I think I'm going to have quite a headache when I stand up."

He mumbled something.

"Leathan!" Tears were starting to roll down Clementina's cheeks. "Leathan."

"McElroy," I said, trying to infuse my tone with a sense of disappointment. "Stop."

He looked at me with that childlike look that's usually followed by the line: "Are you going to make me?"

"Sit," I said.

He hesitated and returned to the sofa. He settled himself, then expectantly waited for me to continue.

"Honestly? Kiddie porn," I said. I hadn't seen what was on the screen, but from his earlier threat and Clementina's reaction, I put the pieces together.

McElroy's brow narrowed.

"She's seventeen. That makes those images kiddie porn." I tried to shrug nonchalantly, but found it impossible while lying on my hands, which were tied behind my back. I looked up to Mister Brown Coat. "How are we doing on those painkillers?"

He mumbled something. I suspected his primary method of communication might be smell, and if I had taken aromatherapists seriously, then I might stand a chance of understanding exactly what he was trying to convey. As it was, I felt able to make a reasonable guess—and it involved me and more pain for me, not less.

I eased myself onto my side and returned my focus to the lawyer. "You might be great with legal matters, but this whole getting out of the office and doing things notion isn't working out too well for you."

The lawyer said nothing.

I continued. "You're trying to persuade her father to take a certain course of action. Have I said that in appropriately legal terms?"

He stared at me. I doubted they taught him to stare like that in law school.

"But kidnapping his daughter makes Norden's life easier." There was a flick across the lawyer's eyes, but he didn't stop me. "She was a pain in the ass, so he hired me. But now you've taken her out of the game. Sure, you can make her suffer—but that only hurts her. It doesn't persuade her father."

The lawyer didn't meet my gaze. Instead, he looked to the man standing behind me, who stepped toward his boss. The lawyer leaned forward, took something, and then slumped back in the sofa. When he started talking, he had something long, thin, and metallic in his hands. "I hear you, Leathan. But you don't want to see Clementina hurt, do you?"

Without waiting for my reply, he stood and walked behind Clementina's chair. In a single motion, he slapped his hand around the side of her face, bringing the tape that was still hanging from her hair back over her mouth.

Clementina tried to let out a small scream, but it was muffled by the broad black strip across her mouth.

"I hear you. I hear you." The lawyer stood straight, holding the long, thin metallic object above Clementina's head and out of her eye line. I recognized it now as the knife that had been held to me more than once.

He lifted a lock of her hair. Clementina flinched at his touch. Theatrically, he cut the lock. Clementina showed some discomfort as her hair was pulled, but was unaware of what was happening—this was show for me.

The lawyer held the cut lock of blond hair in front of Clementina. Her face twisted as she processed the new information offered by seeing her hair removed outside of a salon. As the realization hit, she screamed—the scream muffled by her lips being held with the tape—and shot me a look of panic.

McElroy dropped the hair onto Clementina's lap and turned the point of the blade into her cheek. "I could cut her. Even with the best surgeons, she would still know that she had been scarred."

Clementina froze.

I sighed. "Cut away."

The fear radiating from Clementina's eyes turned up another notch.

"Cut," I said. "If you cut her, then the value of your kiddie porn goes down."

McElroy applied more pressure to the tip of the blade pushing into Clementina's cheek.

"Your kiddie porn is only useful for getting information out of her. She's the only one who worries about it—her father won't care; it's never going to make the press...it being child pornography." I smiled—half forced, half real. "You can use the kiddie porn to get information out of her, but I'll save you some time."

I stopped and waited for McElroy to notice. He made a slight movement of his head—a near involuntary tilt. The kind of movement one makes when encouraging the other person to elaborate.

"Big secret time," I said. "She knows fuck all. I mean, yeah, she knows a lot—a lot—about fashion. Seriously, if you want to know anything about clothes, jewelry, and accessories, then she's your gal. But if you want to know where the laptop is or where the iPad went, who Angeline is with, or about her father's business, then she's totally clueless."

The lawyer seemed to be thinking.

"I'll let you into another secret," I said. "As soon as you cut her, then you can't use the kiddie porn against her."

McElroy frowned.

"Think about it. She's worried about that stuff getting out—but as soon as you cut her, that will be all she cares about. She won't mind about the pictures then." I laughed. "This is your first time and you're not good at this stuff, are you?"

McElroy pushed the knife's point deeper into Clementina's cheek, making sure I saw the flesh move on the knife's command.

"You see—that's why you need her dad. He understands how to make a deal. You don't, and it shows. You might be great at collecting all the pieces of paper, but you're not good at coming up with a package, are you?" The blade remained fixed in Clementina's cheek. "When you threaten someone, you're meant to stack up the tension; each new torment should be worse than the previous and should build on the previous."

I had the lawyer's attention.

"But you've given us an either/or dilemma. You haven't ratcheted up the need for us to tell you what we know—remembering, of course, that I've already told you everything I know, and she knows fuck all." I looked to Clementina. "I'm sorry, but you do know fuck all."

The lawyer released the pressure on the blade, leaving the tip touching Clementina's cheek.

"You need to do better next time," I said. "You've overplayed this one and got it wrong. You've got no one who can tell you anything, the laptop's still missing, and the press aren't interested in a story about Zackary Norden being a financial fraudster."

McElroy dropped my gaze and looked over my head toward the other man.

I tried to make myself comfortable on the boards. "There's nothing more for me to say here," I said. "I'm going back to sleep—wake me in the morning."

seventy

There was a ripping sound behind me. The sound of heavy-duty adhesive being pulled as a length of industrial-strength tape was drawn from a roll.

The feet moved closer—one to either side of my head, coming together like a vice clamping my skull—and then Mister Brown Coat leaned down, slapping tape across my mouth.

"Reece!" shouted McElroy.

The driver appeared from a door at the far end of the room.

"Keys," said the lawyer, holding out his hand. "You stay here. Watch them."

The driver hesitated. When he spoke, he stammered. "S...sss... stay?"

McElroy looked pained. "Stay." He clicked his fingers. "Keys."

"B...b...but..."

The lawyer sighed heavily and held out his hand in expectation of the keys.

"You're not insured," said the driver weakly.

"For fuck's sake," mumbled the man in the brown coat, his French accent making the English expletive amusing. He moved toward Reece.

The driver put his hand in his pocket and retrieved the keys. "How long?"

"Long enough to find out whether Mister Wilkey is shitting us. And if he is, then she'll be the first to scream," said the lawyer. The man in the brown coat led, followed by McElroy, who paused at the front door, laying the knife he had used to torment Clementina on a small dresser. "Any problems," he said to Reece, pointing to the blade.

The lawyer closed the door behind them, but the sound of the footsteps was still audible as the two men walked along the passageway and began their descent of the stairs.

I became aware that some of the intensity of the odor—the odor I had been trying to ignore, which wasn't that difficult given how much I was focusing on the pain in my head—had gone as the room fell quiet, apart from the creak of floorboards as Reece shifted uncomfortably.

I waited as the driver took in his new situation. He had the look of a child who had been left outside a pub while his father went inside drinking. He was trying to be brave—he knew daddy was only a few feet away, and he knew there were familiar faces around, but still he was scared about being on his own.

His eyes scanned—as they did when he drove—a constant motion letting him build a picture of his surroundings. As he built the picture, he let his eyes flick to the new potential hazards in his view. His eyes dropped to Clementina—just a flick, then back to his scan of the room. Then to me—a glance at my bound ankles—and back to scanning the room, taking in the dulled white paint, the dark boards, and the worn furniture with its thinning gold fringing.

I fixed my gaze on him, waiting for his scan to cross my stare. When it finally did, I was ready.

He wasn't.

His gaze crossed mine. For the slightest moment our eyes locked. I kept my gaze fixed—his moved on, jumping with the sudden fright of meeting my stare. I waited—not that I had any other option. Slowly, timidly Reece's gaze came back to me.

Our eyes met.

We broke eye contact as Reece looked down, shamefully dropping his head as he silently acknowledged his part in my present predicament.

I grunted.

He looked up.

I puckered my lips, rippling the tape over my mouth, and grunted again.

Reece hesitated. He knew his gut reaction was to remove the tape, but somewhere in the back of his mind he was trying to remember the precise instructions he had been given by McElroy. He leaned forward as if to step, then paused, moving his weight back.

I frowned. "Hmmm." He looked up. I made my eyes as pleading as I could. "Hmmm," I repeated.

Reece sighed and moved to remove the tape, gently lifting the corner and slowly pulling the adhesive as it gripped my flesh. He placed the strip of tape on the dresser where McElroy had left the blade and then returned, dropping into the sofa where the lawyer had been sitting.

"Thank you," I said.

Clementina look at me, frowning a question and puckering her lips. I gave a single shake of my head.

"Do you understand what has just happened?" I asked the driver.

"They've gone to find Angeline."

"No. You've just been set up for murder. Or if not murder, then kidnap."

I watched the emotions show across Reece's face as he took in my words. There was fear, dread, and then panic. The panic gave way to disbelief—he could not connect his situation in this room with the proposition I had put to him. Clearly I was wrong in his mind, and that led to a certain amount of bravado and a feeling of superiority at finding a lie.

A smile spread across his face. I waited. Reece was human—Reece would be plagued by the same self-doubt that plagues every other human, sociopaths excepted. Slowly the second wave came, and the certainty of the smile faded. He frowned and leaned his head and shoulders toward me—he was now waiting for me to explain his predicament.

"They're not going to find Angeline," I said, understanding the ambiguity of my statement. Reece was processing—did I mean they were never going to find the housekeeper or did I mean that their intent was not to search for the woman? I answered his question—and the next question that would come. "I put her on a train."

This statement triggered many thoughts in Reece's head—why, which one, where was she going, how will McElroy find out she's gone—but clearly the most pressing question was what the implications of this action were for him. And this question rendered him mute.

"And by the way," I added. "The laptop? The iPad? La Seine."

I caught a glance from Clementina. She narrowed her eyes and twisted her head as if to say: "Really?" But it was easier for Clementina—unlike Reece, she didn't have to understand how sitting in a room could end with her in jail.

I sighed, pulling Reece's attention back to me. "Do you want me to explain the situation?"

Reece nodded. His eyes were pointed at me, but he wasn't looking at me.

"McElroy is trying to manipulate Norden into quitting as managing partner. Are we agreed?"

Reece nodded, still not focusing.

"All the basic tools to influence Norden have gone. Angeline is on a train and the laptop is in la Seine. That leaves one point of leverage."

I waited. Watching as Reece took in and processed the information. He continued nodding as he thought, and then he focused. "One point of leverage?"

"One," I said, shifting my gaze from him to the teenager. "Clementina."

Reece followed my gaze; as his head turned in profile, I could see his jaw hanging, the muscles twitching as he thought.

"If Johnnie becomes managing partner tomorrow—the new broom cleaning out the cess pit—then he's going to need to make sure that his hands are clean. He can't come in and say: 'That guy was a financial crook, but you can trust me...my only crimes are kidnapping and murder,' can he?"

Reece was still staring at Clementina. His hanging jaw moved left to right, as if to acknowledge what I was saying.

"So if there are any problems—if Clementina and I don't get out... If our dead bodies are found or if someone calls the cops... Tell me, Reece, who do you think is in line to take the blame, because it's certainly not Johnnie?"

I let the room fall quiet and watched as Reece slumped back into the sofa as he tried to assess the situation in which he found himself. I was fairly sure that until this point he had been able to justify what was going on by telling himself that he wasn't really involved—he just happened to be close when unfortunate events occurred.

Clementina furiously tried to get my attention, as much as she could while she was taped to the chair and trying to communicate without the driver noticing.

I mouthed "Shhh" at her.

"What?" said her reaction. "You want me to shush?" She had a point—as well as hearing a lot about her father and his business affairs and being taken hostage, I had just implied that she and I might die. Or if not die, we might suffer any number of unpleasant outcomes—the full range of which were clearly being auditioned inside Clementina's head.

"I know," I mouthed.

The frown became a scowl.

"I'm sorry," I mouthed.

She nodded downward, as if indicating herself. I frowned—she nodded down again, as if trying to indicate she had a question about herself.

"You?" I mouthed, confused.

She hung her head to the side, eyes crossed, and jaw twisted as far as it would given the tape over her mouth.

"Dead?" I mouthed.

She nodded.

I shook my head. "No," I mouthed and let my eyes lead her gaze to the driver.

She gave a quizzical look.

I smirked at her and then let my face fall before talking. "I don't wish to interrupt your thoughts, but there's something else you need to know, Reece."

"I'm sorry, what was that, Leathan?" The driver seemed distracted—he certainly hadn't been paying attention to the silent communication between Clementina and me.

"There's something else you need to think about," I said. "There's always the chance that Johnnie's plan falls apart." I waited a beat for dramatic effect. "Murderers usually don't get away with it."

Reece was a drowning man who thought he'd seen someone who could throw him a lifeline.

"If Johnnie fails, then Zack will still be managing partner."

I watched as Reece put together the pieces. "You're saying that I..." He relaxed, with a smile spreading across his face.

"Unfortunately, I'm not. I went through your room this morning."

Reece seemed about to remonstrate for the invasion of his privacy, but held back at the last moment.

"I've seen them. All of them." Reece froze. Clemmy frowned, questioning. I turned to her. "You know you think he looks at your boobs?"

She nodded.

"You were probably right—he's been taking pictures of you. Lots of pictures of you."

Clementina pushed herself back on the chair, like a small child recoiling when told to eat her vegetables.

"Don't worry, you're clothed." She relaxed. "But I know more about your underwear than I wanted to know."

Her eyes narrowed; her face said: "Really? Really, really, really?"

Reece bowed his head and said nothing.

"You'll get a reference," I said to the driver. "As long as I—as long as *we*—get out of here, I personally guarantee to you that you'll get a reference. But you understand you can't remain employed and working with the family."

Clementina shot me a glower. I wasn't quite sure what it said, but it definitely started with Reece's testicles and heavy machinery. I tried not to laugh as I turned back to Reece. When he lifted his head, his eyes were moist and his bottom lip trembling.

"And without wishing to heap further..." I began, "you do understand that those photos will be item one for the prosecution if anything happens to us. You won't be able to argue circumstances—any court will see this as planned...premeditation on your part."

Reluctantly, Reece nodded, wiping a tear.

"You see that you're in a lose/lose situation?"

Reece exhaled. A long exhalation, trembling as if he were sobbing. His head fell again. Clementina threw her eyes to the dull ceiling dismissively.

"There's a way out of this, Reece," I said, trying to be comforting, not sure if the pain I was feeling would let me.

"No there isn't," he mumbled sulkily.

"For fuck's sake, Reece. The way out is simple." It was easier to be dominant than sympathetic.

He looked up, his eyes still moist. "What? Let both of you go. I suppose that's your answer." He snorted and shook his head. "No. Not going to happen."

I counted to five before I continued. When I spoke, my voice was calm. "Did you drive the white van?"

"What white van? I'm a chauffeur—just because there's a vehicle, it doesn't mean I drove it."

"The white van that carried Hoffman after he was beaten," I said, answering his question that preceded his indignant outburst. "If you didn't drive the van, then you've got a chance of getting out from the murder charge."

"Don't be stupid, Leathan. I didn't murder anyone—you know that!"

"I might know that—but that counts for nothing if I'm dead. And more to the point, we're not talking about what I know, we're talking about what charges a very smart lawyer can pin on you."

The chauffeur stared at me; his breathing was heavy.

"The truth and what a jury believes are different," I said.

"I know," he mouthed.

"There's a third option," I said. "And it doesn't involve you letting us go."

I kept my gaze focused on the driver. On the side of my field of vision, I could see Clementina desperate for my attention, and I knew what she wanted to know: "Why? Why would he not let us go? This—what's happening now—is illegal. We should be freed."

Reece looked at me, slumping as if conceding that I could speak.

"McElroy told you to watch us. He didn't say you couldn't go out and get a bite or have a beer."

Reece acknowledged.

"So go. Leave us. But go somewhere safe—like London—and when you're on the train, then call the cops." Reece frowned. "If they come back—which they're not going to—then I'll say you went to get a bite ten minutes ago. They might be annoyed, but they won't chase you because they'll think you've just gone to get something to eat."

Reece cocked his head, readying himself to speak.

"Don't say anything—just go now," I said. "You'll have to put the tape back over my mouth, but leave the knife."

Reece's look questioned.

"How are you going to explain carrying a knife if you're stopped? Added to which, they're pretty sniffy about blades on the Eurostar, and the metal detector will pick it up."

"I suppose," said Reece under his breath.

"Now," I said. "You need to go now—it's your only chance. Put the tape over my mouth, then leave."

The driver went to the dresser and returned with the tape. "You're sure about this?"

"Certain. Now get that thing over my mouth."

Reece placed the tape over my mouth and stood. "I would shake your hand, but..." he half smiled in the shared joke. He turned to Clementina. "I'm..." His voice stopped, strangled into silence. His head dropped, and his eyes misted.

The door slammed behind him, leaving the sound of his footsteps walking away.

seventy-one

I stared at Clementina.

Clementina stared at me.

I was in pain—physical pain.

Clementina didn't appear to be in physical pain, although I would have been shocked if the last few hours did not cause, at the very least, a certain degree of anguish.

She tried to talk. To question. To remonstrate. The talk came fast, and her face was highly expressive as she spoke. However, the tape over her mouth rendered her words as a series of muffled sounds. This didn't seem to concern her, but it did make it tough for me to get a handle on precisely what was upsetting her most.

I pretended to pay attention, but it was like watching a foreign film on the TV when there are no subtitles—you can follow to a certain point, but eventually you have to give in and admit you don't have a clue what's going on. But you do know the guy with the thick eyebrows is the crook.

I admitted it—I didn't have a clue what was going on in Clementina's mind. So I shifted my focus to more practical matters, like how to get out.

Clementina was taped to her chair. There was tape around her shins, holding each of her legs to a chair leg. Her torso had been taped to the back of the chair—when her torso was taped, her arms were by her side, so her upper arms were taped. This gave her the freedom to move her forearms from the elbow; however, her wrists had been taped together, meaning that the movement she was afforded was highly limited.

I suspected that if Clementina tried to stand up—or at least transferred her weight from the seat onto her feet—there would be enough play in the bindings around her legs that she could take tiny steps forward. However, I wasn't sure how I could communicate this to her since my legs were bound, my hands were bound behind my back, and my mouth was also taped.

More significantly, even if she could move, given the limited mobility of her hands, I wasn't sure how she would be able to pick up the knife that was on the dresser by the door and use it to free either herself or me.

She was still talking, but I had resigned myself that it was me who would have to move and get the knife. That wasn't the hard decision—the hard decision was about how much pain I was going to cause myself by rolling and twisting on the hard floor, applying weight and pressure to each spot where I had been kicked, punched, and bruised.

I needed to concentrate.

Clementina's noise was distracting me.

I stared at her. She met my stare and continued talking. I shook my head, feeling my eyeballs move as they kept their lock on Clementina while the rest of my skull moved around them.

Clementina went quiet, but quiet in the way that a teacher goes quiet when she has asked an unruly child a rhetorical question. Sure, there was no noise, but she was letting me know that she had the floor—it wasn't my turn to speak. Slowly her forehead began to crinkle, her head tilted. She was giving way; she was questioning. It was my turn to offer something.

I rolled, feeling the spasm of agony when my weight transferred directly through my elbow joint as I passed over, before the release, where the agony was replaced by the simple pain of resting on my shoulder, which had been bruised, although I couldn't remember when it had sustained that injury.

That roll alone felt like a day's work.

I lifted up my knees, bringing myself to the fetal position, and tried to roll from there. My intent was to use my head and knees as a fulcrum and to push myself with my elbow—as much as I could use my elbow for leverage given that my hands were bound—and roll myself up to a kneeling position.

I lifted with my elbow—something in my knee as it rested against the floorboard told me I had received a blow there. My skull was free from pain where my forehead pressed against the cool board, but my neck reminded me that someone had hit me there. My neck further pointed out to me that it was not designed to hold the entire weight of my body—it was designed to balance my head on top of my shoulders. Its muscles were for turning my head left and right, up and down, not for lifting weight.

I acceded to my neck's request and stopped trying to lift my body before rolling back onto the floor, trapping my arm under me.

There was a sound behind me. Clementina. It took me a few moments to realize that this was Clementina laughing—laughing at me. I fixed my glare on her. She looked back, her eyes smiling, and shrugged.

I rolled over onto my stomach. It hurt. It hurt in places I didn't know it could hurt, but I wanted to stop cataloging my pain and focus on getting out. Lying flat, I tried to lift my ass and pull my knees under me.

As I pushed my ass higher, the laughter behind me started again.

I pushed higher and tried using a combination of shoulder, neck, skull, and elbow to lift my body far enough to create some space to get my knees under me. I pulled, I pushed, I felt my muscle spasm, I felt the fulcrums resting on the floorboards yell, my neck shouted, and then I toppled and fell back on the floor.

Clementina was silent. When I looked at her, I'm sure she tried to say: "Nearly."

I wiggled on the floor, moving closer to the old sofa—but not too close. Pulling up my knees, I tried to estimate the distance from them to the sofa. I wiggled again, until there was a gap about as wide as my ass, then flopped back onto my back, drawing breath.

On my back, I pulled up my knees and began to rock—left to right to left to right—feeling the pain on my wrists taped behind my back. As the arcs grew longer, I counted: one and back, two and back, three.

I rolled, throwing my whole weight into the momentum of the turn. My knees and my skull slammed into the boards, and my elbow pushed. Slowly, I felt myself turn through 180 degrees, coming to the vertical on my knees.

As I reached the top of my travel, I felt the momentum carry me over. At the point that momentum was about to turn my triumph into a disaster, my ass made contact with the sofa, stopping my movement in the vertical position.

I wobbled.

I swayed.

Then I found myself in the vertical position—on my knees, with my hands behind me, and my head resting on the boards in front of me.

The room was quiet. The still was broken by Clementina cheering. Again, that's what I guessed she was doing, her mouth still being taped. Then she started chanting. I couldn't be certain of the words, but the rhythm was: "Go Leathan! Go Leathan! Go Leathan!"

It was harder to straighten myself than I expected. As I tried to stand, I was reminded of the binding around my ankles, preventing me from doing as I would normally do and lifting one leg. Instead I flopped onto the sofa and wiggled myself into a sitting position.

The friction from the wiggling gave me inspiration. I leaned against the back of the sofa, gold fringe tickling my cheek, and rubbed the side of my face against the old fabric.

Clementina made a sound—inquisitive, asking what I was doing.

I turned. "Hold on," I mumbled under my taped mouth and returned to rubbing against the back of the sofa while contorting my mouth, trying to get some purchase to start to lift the edge of the tape.

Clementina made another sound—urgent, insistent. I turned. She pointed her head sharply in front of her, as if she wanted me there, then looked down at her fingers, which she wiggled.

I frowned.

She repeated the action, looking to me, to the floor in front of her, and then to her fingers, which she wiggled.

I got it.

I stood, sort of. I half jumped, half shuffled in front of her, then cautiously squatted before letting my weight fall forward with my mouth coming into contact with her hands. She got a nail under the tape and in one yank pulled off the gag.

"Thank you," I said, slowly standing and feeling the slight burn around my lips that I'm sure everyone who subjects herself to cosmetic waxing feels.

There was some quid pro quo due. I looked at her gag. The tape covered her mouth and held it tight, but like mine, the tape had been removed and refixed. Clementina saw where I was looking. "I've only got teeth," I said. "It's not going to be pleasant...but it'll be something you can tell your grandkids."

She scowled at the suggestion of her as a grandmother.

"Do you want me to try?"

She nodded vigorously.

"You don't want to wait until I've got my hands free? That would be much easier."

She shook her head with equal vigor.

I leaned close—close enough to kiss her, but standing awkwardly with my legs and wrists tied. She flinched. "Hold still," I said, leaning forward until my front teeth made contact with her cheek. I raked my teeth over her skin, pulling until I felt them bump over the edge of the tape.

Clementina giggled and twisted away.

I stood to relieve some of the tension in my back and ease the crick out of my neck. "You're going to have to work with me."

She nodded apologetically and tilted her head back, giving me clearer access. I leaned forward and again began raking my teeth across her cheek and onto the tape, feeling as the edge became more pronounced. I kept raking, feeling the edge lifting.

"We're about to move into weird territory," I said.

Clementina muttered something, and I ran my top lip over her cheek, following the path my teeth had taken, feeling for how much tape I had pulled. I reckoned there was enough to grip between my teeth so pushed my jaws to either side of the tape, clamping it between my teeth, and pulled. Slowly and gently, feeling as the adhesive tugged against Clementina's skin and then yielded.

I repositioned my bite and pulled more firmly. "It's like being rescued by a chipmunk in slow motion," said Clementina. I dropped the end of the tape and stood up. Her mouth was half covered, but that didn't stop her. "Is there some bizarre competition that you guys have? Who can rescue a woman in the most unusual manner?"

"Conventionally, thank you," I said and shuffled away from her.

She paused, nodding a silent apology to acknowledge the broader point. "Thank you, Leathan." Then she sighed. "But you did take your time to ride in on your white horse. I've been with these people all day...and that guy in the brown coat stinks. That's what I smelt in Hoffman's room."

"I was busy," I mumbled, "and I didn't know they had you." I paused—there was something I couldn't figure. "How did they get you here?"

Clementina looked down.

"Clemmy?"

Her cheeks flushed, and she wouldn't look at me, but slowly she started to talk. "Reece told me I was being interviewed—they wanted me to talk about fashion. He said the interview was in a rundown old place..." She looked around as if indicating that was the only reason she had let herself be led there. "He said something about shabby-chic..."

"So you came here to discuss whether this piece of fabric or this twist of metal is more beautiful than another turned piece of a different metal attached to a piece of leather?"

"What can I say?" asked Clementina. "I'm a leader, not a follower."

"And if there's a dark cave?" I asked.

"Oh, then you're going first. No question," she said. She looked around the room, then stared straight at me. "Why didn't you ask pervy the driver to untie us?" A second wave of thought hit her before I could answer. "What was that about photos? Of me?"

"He's been taking photos of you. You're dressed...but it's still not pleasant." I started shuffling toward the front door, talking with my back to her. "And I didn't ask him to untie us because he said he wouldn't."

"You could have asked," said Clementina.

"I could, but I wanted him gone, and that discussion would have been another dilemma for him. I figured if I asked for that, then he might think about what I was wanting him to do."

"And what did you want him to do?"

"Run. Get the hell away from here."

"Why?"

"Because he's too easily influenced, and if he's not here, then he can't cause any problems for us."

"Oh," said Clementina.

I reached the dresser by the front door. The knife was lying on the top. The object that had tormented me was now about to free me. I turned and reached behind me, feeling for the knife with my fingers. Slowly I began waddling back to Clementina, the blade behind me.

"And what's all that stuff you were saying about Angeline?"

"What stuff?" I asked. "I made up half of it."

"So where is Angeline?"

"I don't know. Paris, I guess. I threw her out because she's been sending more money home than she was paid, but I didn't take her to any station."

Clementina paused. "Does she have the laptop?"

"I don't know that either, but my guess is no."

"The iPad?"

"Nope. I've stored that."

"Oh," said Clementina, falling quiet and watching as I completed my waddled journey to her.

"If I kneel in front of you," I said. "Do you think you could take the knife and cut my hands free?"

"I could," she said. "Whether I want to, that's another matter. I still think you need to suffer more for being so slow in getting here. Is that how you lost your last woman to the Bulgarians?"

The question stung, but not enough to stop me kneeling in front of her. She took the knife and clumsily cut at the tape. "There."

I stretched my hands and arms, feeling the stiffness that had built in my shoulders.

"Ahem," said Clementina. "Some of us are waiting, and I'm not taking no for an answer. I've got a knife."

I took the blade and rolled onto the floor, cutting my ankles free before leaning toward Clementina and cutting the binding around her wrists. Her hands immediately went to her mouth to remove the tape that was half stuck to her face and half stuck to her hair.

While she delicately removed the tape, wincing as the adhesive tugged at her, I set to work to free her legs and her torso.

"I need to pee," said Clementina as she stood, pulling the last few pieces of tape still stuck to her.

"There's a café round the corner," I said. "Our first priority is to get out of here."

I had the front door open before she could argue.

seventy-two

Clementina pushed a piece of chocolate cake around her plate. It was her third slice since we had arrived, so I wasn't surprised to see her slowing down.

"I sent your dad a text," I said. Clemmy looked up from her chocolate cake, then returned her gaze to the only food she had eaten that day. "He knows you're safe."

"So why are we having coffee?" Clementina used the term coffee to encompass my coffee, her soda, and our accompanying food.

I wasn't sure how Clementina would feel or react to the experience she had been through. It would be easy to use words and minimize what had happened. It would be easy to say *only* this happened or *only* that occurred or, my favorite, *it would have been much worse if...* I was very aware that if I looked at the fundamentals of what had happened, there were several facts. Fact one: Clementina had been kidnapped—she was taken and forcibly held against her will. During this kidnapping, Clementina had been physically assaulted. And further, during the kidnapping, Clementina had been mentally tormented.

This seemed significant to me, and I wasn't about to tell a teenager how she should react to a situation. For that matter, I doubted that she knew how she wanted to react.

When we got out from the apartment—which Clementina thought was where the guy in the brown coat lived—Clementina had been desperate to pee. She had been desperate to pee before we left, but I had insisted on leaving. A short distance away there were three cafés close together—we took the third.

While Clementina was in the bathroom, I sent a text to her father, and then I used the payphone in the café to call the cops. I spoke quickly—and I spoke in an accent to try to hide my voice, which given that I had little ear for regional French dialects was a challenge. I gave a few details—Hoffman's murder, Hoffman's body dump, Hoffman's hotel. I named McElroy; described the guy in the brown coat; mentioned the office that McElroy shared with Zack; identified the place Clementina and I had been held; and gave them the location of the penthouse that Zack had rented in the 16th near les Jardins du Ranelagh. I was fast and gave them facts—I figured they could make the connections. They had officers; they could get out and look for the two men.

As I hung up, Clementina was coming out of the bathroom. She wanted food. She wanted drink. I got her a bottle of water and we left—there was always the chance that McElroy and his brown-coated friend would return, so I wanted to be as far away as possible.

Clementina grumbled but understood as we descended to the Metro. She understood the anonymity. She understood the constant movement away from the place where bad things had happened. When we got off the Metro near the apartment where she was staying, I led her to the café on the corner. The café where she and I had last seen Hoffman. I was hesitant as to whether it would have resonance for her, but she didn't seem to notice.

"We're having coffee," I said, answering the question she had posed, "because you—well, we both—need to eat. Why here? Because it's as safe as anywhere. No one knows we're here."

Clementina pushed the remnant of her chocolate cake to the side of her plate and laid down her fork. "I got why we ran—it wasn't safe near the smelly man's apartment. The Metro made sense, and no one will ever argue with chocolate cake, but what do we do next? We can't live here until the arrival of the grandchildren you seem so convinced I'm going to have."

She picked up her fork, looked at her cake, and put the fork down, returning her attention to me.

"I told your dad we'd meet him at the apartment." I yanked out my phone and checked the time. "It's been more than two hours since we got free. That's long enough for the cops to start looking for McElroy if they're going to take this stuff seriously. Whenever you're ready, we'll go."

seventy-three

We walked slowly through les Jardins du Ranelagh.

It had been dark for about two hours, and the evening chill was becoming noticeable—for me at least. Clementina, fueled on adrenalin and chocolate cake, seemed unconcerned by the falling temperature.

As we stepped from the gardens, there was a level of activity in the street that I hadn't seen before. There were two marked police cars and two other cars that none of the residents would ever own—they wouldn't even keep them for their staff. There was a uniformed officer standing at the door to the apartment block and other officers on the street—all talking urgently, pointing, arguing, suggesting—and the occasional person without uniform and clearly not dressed as a resident or member of staff entering or leaving the block.

One person stood out.

One person obviously wasn't a cop.

One person who was arguing with the officer at the door.

"Hey!" I shouted, and the two of us jogged the few steps to the door.

"Go," I said to the woman.

"Oh, Miss Clementina," said Angeline, tears suddenly gushing. Clementina recoiled.

"She was fired this morning," I said to the officer.

"Get off me," said Clementina, as the former housekeeper went to throw her arms around Clementina. "You're a…" She stopped as I laid a hand on Angeline's shoulder.

"Go now," I said and leaned forward to whisper in her ear. "And go forever unless you want to spend the next twenty years in a French jail."

The tears stopped. Angeline wiped her cheeks, turned, and walked away.

"I'm sorry, you can't come in," said the officer.

"I live here," said Clementina sharply.

The officer seemed to be rendered mute and stepped back, allowing us both to pass.

The porter's desk was empty, but somehow the absence didn't feel like a loss to the safety and security of the building and its residents. Clementina stepped into the elevator—I followed. "Interesting," I said as the doors closed.

"Hmm?"

"Why did Angeline come back again?"

Clementina pushed out her bottom lip and made that strange sound that teenagers make—two syllables of sound in place of three syllables of words, to say: "I don't know."

"Last throw of the dice?" I asked myself under my breath. "Sent by McElroy? A last throw of the dice by him. Maybe the laptop's still here?"

"You did look under the mattresses?" asked Clementina.

It was my turn to make a sound: "Huh?"

"For the laptop—you did look under the mattresses? Between the mattress and the base?"

"No," I said quietly.

"Why not?" Clementina sighed. "It's the place where house-keepers put things—remember where I found the iPad?"

I cursed under my breath. "I looked under the mattress in her room. I looked under the mattress in Reece's room. But I didn't look under the mattresses in the apartment."

"My word," said Clementina. "You were a busy little bunny this morning, but you need to work smarter, not harder."

The elevator doors opened and she stepped out, leaving me mentally kicking myself.

seventy-four

"Daddy bear!"

I was still closing the door, but I could hear Clementina reaching the kitchen area. I walked through the hallway and into the large open space of the apartment to find the daughter with her arms wrapped tightly around her father, and tears flowing.

Zack seemed slightly embarrassed by his daughter's show of affection, but he still mouthed, "Thank you."

Clementina squeezed him tighter. "I'm home, daddy bear."

"I know, baby bear. I know." He looked to me, questioning. It was a look that said: "Tell me everything." The follow-up line would be: "Who do I have to kill?"

I nodded, affirming that I understood the weight and the magnitude of what he wanted to understand, and mouthed, "Later."

He squeezed his daughter tighter, turning his head into hers as she sobbed.

I wandered back to my room and dropped to my knees in front of my bed before reaching between the mattress and the base. I ran my hands from end to end, then changed sides and repeated the process. When I was satisfied that the laptop wasn't under my mattress, I headed to Clementina's room.

There were a few scrunched-up tissues under Clementina's mattress, some underwear, and an empty condom packet—which I pocketed for later disposal—but no laptop.

I stepped silently toward the kitchen. Father and daughter had moved to the sofa—they were still locked together, but Clementina was talking.

I turned back and headed to Zack's suite and thrust my arms under his mattress. My fingers hit metal—I gripped and pulled out a laptop. I looked at the brushed-aluminum case and snorted. I couldn't fault Angeline's logic in hiding the computer in the place it would never be noticed because Zack never slept in his own bed.

In the dressing room, I placed the laptop on a chest of drawers and contemplated the loose kicker board—made loose by my hand. This was job done, right?

seventy-five

"Was it where I said it would be?"

"Exactly where you said."

Clementina smiled broadly. "See. Told you. It was the obvious place."

"Obvious..." I began, then stopped. It hadn't been and still wasn't obvious to me.

The intensity of the father/daughter reunion had passed. The memory was still there, but even sitting next to each other on the long sofa, the moment was gone. Both were now like drug addicts looking for their next fix—him looking to move the deal forward, her looking for a connection on social media.

"I'm going to have a shower," said Clementina. This was code I could readily translate. In English it meant: "I'm going to have a shower, then get changed, and before, during, and after this process, I'm going to engage with friends and followers in any number of ways on social media through my phone."

I wasn't going to argue. She had had a tough day, and it had been a long time since she had interacted with any of her friends—real or virtual.

I sat across from Zack Norden, turning back to watch Clementina leave. The laptop balanced on my knee. She disappeared from sight, leaving the gentle sound of her feet walking toward her room. I listened as her bedroom door opened and closed before I turned to my employer, holding the lump of engineered aluminum toward him.

He took the laptop. "Thank you." He looked to where Clementina had disappeared, "thank you," and then looked at me directly, "thank you. Leathan, thank you." He laid the laptop beside him, where Clementina had been sitting.

"None of my business and all that," I began, "but now that you've got it, I'd remove the hard drive and smash it to pieces. Destroy it before it destroys you. Act before it becomes evidence."

Norden looked at the lump of metal.

"It's maybe not the sort of advice a lawyer would give you, but I'm not a lawyer, which I guess is a good thing."

"Definitely a good thing," said Norden, his gaze still fixed on the machine.

"And just so we're clear—whatever misunderstandings there may have been around your assets, I'm not suggesting that doesn't need sorting. But that sort of sorting needs people with years of experience. I'm just suggesting that if there is material that could be interpreted unfavorably, maybe you get rid of it in a permanent way."

"I understand, and my lawyer is on it." He snorted. "My lawyer in London is on it. My lawyer in Paris is occupied with other matters."

I waited.

A smiled pushed its way across Norden's face. "McElroy has been arrested. The Paris lawyer called just before you two got back. There's no sign of Reece or the guy in the brown coat."

"What's the charge?" I asked.

"Murder. Murder of Clemmy's friend." He paused. "Why did McElroy...? I always thought the kid was a plant by McElroy."

"And yet," I mumbled before meeting his gaze. "I suspect Mister Hoffman might have found his loyalties shifting. Maybe he was taking an insurance policy, maybe he was unwilling to do their bidding, or maybe he fought back and they beat him harder than they intended."

He cocked his head, questioning but not putting words to his question.

"I don't think the plan was to kill Hoffman—at least, not then. I think it happened, and...with the eggs broken, they decided to make omelets."

We fell quiet.

Norden broke the still. "The iPad?"

"Let's leave it where it is," I said. "It's not hurting anyone."

He shrugged.

I pulled out my phone and took out the SIM card, dropping it on the table. "I've been in one place for too long—I'd rather not have people track me. I'll get a new SIM. If you need to get in touch, for the iPad or anything, then call our friends in London—they'll be able to find me."

"You're leaving..." he began.

I nodded, standing. "I'll say goodbye to Clementina, then I'm off."

Norden stood, holding out his hand to shake. "Thank you again, Leathan."

seventy-six

"It's Leathan the rescue chipmunk."

Clementina hadn't made any effort to shower or change. She was sitting on her bed, the tension in her wrists as she looked up when I entered suggesting she had been focused intently on her phone.

I closed the door behind me and sat at the end of her bed. "I've come to say goodbye."

She dropped her phone. "No." Her mouth was open, her eyes misting.

I nodded, silently affirming that I was leaving.

"No," said Clementina, lunging forward and throwing her arms around my neck. "No, Leathan. You can't leave. You..." She stopped talking and began to sob, gripping me tighter and tighter.

Eventually she released me, held me—one hand on each shoulder—and stared at me through her wet eyes. "Leathan, you can't leave me."

"And yet," I said, pausing before I continued. "I'm done. You're safe, the laptop's back, and McElroy has been arrested."

She dropped her hands and sat back against her pillows, exaggerating her pout. "That stuff you said to Reece." Her tone was hesitant, questioning, disbelieving. "You're not going to..."

"What? Give him a reference?"

She nodded.

"No."

Her face twisted as if asking a question.

"He needed to see a way out, so I showed him the way out, and I'm not going to apologize for telling him a lie." Clementina seemed to be weighing the moral conundrum. "I couldn't tell him the truth—that there's no way in hell that your father will ever give him a reference and that he'll be lucky to ever work again."

Clementina seemed shocked. "But he didn't..."

"Maybe not. But say the next girl is fifteen, or fourteen, or younger. Say she isn't as smart as you. Say he goes beyond taking photos at a distance. Do you want to be the one who said, 'He's great—you can trust him'?"

Clementina weighed the proposition.

"And let's not forget that he was pivotal in taking you and holding you against your will. I'm not saying there will be a trial, but there's a word for what happened."

Clementina seemed uncomfortable having her memories laid in front of her. "So what about Hoffman?"

"McElroy's been arrested, but I'm not sure whether he killed Hoffman or was responsible for his death. I'm pretty sure he was—but I can't prove anything. I want to see McElroy in jail, and I'm leaving it with your father's lawyer to handle that one."

"Oh," mouthed Clementina. "So where are you going?"

"I'll travel for a few days. I like the idea of the Adriatic—Northern Italy, Venice maybe, perhaps onto Slovenia—but I'll go wherever I can get a train to."

"And then?"

"Then... Then, I might come back to Paris. I've been moving for too long, and I want to stay in one city. Paris is crowded but I can hide in that crowd."

Her face brightened. "If you're going to come back, then why not stay?"

"I need to be gone for a few days. If anyone has figured where I am, then I'd rather not be here if they come looking."

Note from the author

If you enjoyed this book, please join my readers' group.

When you join my readers' group I'll send you my introductory library for free. The introductory library is a collection of books to introduce you to some of the characters and the worlds of my books. And of course, as a member of my readers' group, I'll let you know about my new releases.

Join my readers' group and get your free books here: simoncann.com/readers.

Other books by the author

Be sure to check out Simon's latest books at simoncann.com/books.

Leathan Wilkey series

Diplomatic Baggage

Leathan Wilkey thinks he has been framed for murder by the victim's father.

The Camera

The only way for Leathan Wilkey to bring about justice for his murdered friend, is to track down the cause and ensure it is eliminated, permanently.

Boniface series

The Murder of Henry VIII

When the author he is representing is murdered, Boniface realizes the job demands more than he expected. And when the man he is talking with is shot, Boniface runs.

Pollute the Poor

The first Boniface knows about the dead body in the next room is when he is arrested for murder.

Tattoo Your Name on My Heart

When his client's wife disappears, Boniface uncovers the secret she has been keeping from her husband.

About the Author

Simon Cann is the author of the Boniface, Montbretia Armstrong, and Leathan Wilkey books.

In addition to his fiction, Simon has written a range of music-related and business-related books, including the *How to Make a Noise* series, the most widely ready series about synthesizer sound programming, and *Made it in China*, about entrepreneurs building businesses in China. He has also worked as a ghostwriter on a number of books.

Before turning full-time to writing, Simon worked as a management consultant, where his clients included aeronautical, pharmaceutical, defense, financial services, chemical, entertainment, and broadcasting companies.

He lives in London.

You can find more about Simon at his website: simoncann.com.

You can also find him at:

- Facebook: simoncann.com/facebook
- Twitter: simoncann.com/twitter
- Google+: simoncann.com/gplus
- YouTube: simoncann.com/youtube